ANOTHER MAN'S GOLD

THE SETTLERS
BOOK THREE

REG QUIST

Another Man's Gold
Paperback Edition
Copyright © 2023 Reg Quist

CKN Christian Publishing
An Imprint of Wolfpack Publishing
9850 S. Maryland Parkway, Suite A-5 #323
Las Vegas, Nevada 89183

cknchristianpublishing.com

This book is a work of fiction. Any references to historical events, real people or real places are used fictitiously. Other names, characters, places and events are products of the author's imagination, and any resemblance to actual events, places or persons, living or dead, is entirely coincidental.

All rights reserved. No part of this book may be reproduced by any means without the prior written consent of the publisher, other than brief quotes for reviews.

Paperback ISBN 978-1-63977-129-5
eBook ISBN 978-1-63977-128-8
LCCN 2023930628

ALSO BY REG QUIST

ANOTHER MAN'S GOLD

NEWLY ELECTED COUNTY SHERIFF RORY JAMISON HAD been slowly riding, and then crawling, through the eastern Colorado grasslands, onto a rising edge, alongside a swale that, at the present time, was dry, but would be a drainage run during one of the infrequent rains. It seemed as if he had been on his knees and elbows for hours. In point of actual fact, he had been dodging prickly pear and beehive cholla for little more than a few minutes. His .44-40 Winchester, which he had hoped to balance across his arms as he crawled, had caught on the taller growth so often that he had finally taken it in his left hand, leaving his right hand free to grasp one of his belted .44s if the situation deteriorated to that point. However, he had securely buttoned his canvas jacket, top to bottom, to protect his belted weapons. The move slowed his progress even more.

TWO DAYS BEFORE, about midmorning, a frantic twelve-year-old boy had ridden a lathered and done-up bay gelding recklessly down the single main street of the old fort, pulling to a dust-gathering stop in front of the recently constructed county jail and sheriff's office. His actions startled a couple of slow-walking wagon teams and caused one buggy horse to break from its half-asleep stance and charge, in fright, down the street. The buggy was carrying a farmer's daughter, who was taking a rest in the shade of the fringed top, while she secretly admired a young cowboy busy with toting sacks of provisions from the general supply store to a buckboard tied off not far from her.

The girl didn't scream or bother crying for help. She simply plucked up the reins, brought the animal under control, and turned the rig around on the street toward where the boy had drawn to a stop, hollering for the sheriff. She was busy gathering up the words she would use on the kid when the sheriff stepped out of the door, asking what all the noise was about.

"Rustlers, Sheriff. Pa sent me in, hoping for some help. He's alone on the place, with just Ma and me and a couple of kid sisters, for help. If Pa goes after the rustlers, it would be just me and Ma on the place. The kid girls ain't no help. Likely never will be, being girls and all. We can't no way do the work that needs doing, and anyway, Pa's mighty cautious about leaving his family alone."

The girl in the buggy, who had pulled to a stop close by, said, "Where's your hired man, Jody?"

"Pa says it looks as if he's one of the rustlers. Anyway, he's gone, and all his stuff and truck gone with him."

Sheriff Rory said, "I take it your name's Jody, young fella. Where's your ranch at?"

"We're a bit north and maybe fifteen miles east."

The girl in the buggy, who seemed to have invited herself into the conversation, said, "That would work out good for you, Sheriff. The Trader's Triple T Ranch is right close to the Gridley spread. Not more than a few miles. You could probably get a dinner, and maybe a look-see with Julia. If you play your cards right, that is."

Rory turned to the girl with a grin on his face.

"And who exactly are you, young lady, and shouldn't you be in school?"

Jody spoke up. "That's Trish Hampton, Sheriff. I'm not so sure even the teacher would want her in class. That's suppos'n we ever get a school. Never stops talk'n. Thinks she knows everyth'n. She lives out our way too. Thankfully, not too close. With Trish, the more miles away, the better."

A man walking up behind the buggy said, "Unfortunately, there's some truth in all of that, Sheriff. I'm Buzz Hampton. Trish is my oldest. Oldest of four. She does talk some, and that's a fact. Doesn't appear to be any solution for it. None I've found yet anyhow."

Trish remained silent while the two men shook hands.

Perhaps giving some indication where Trish might have learned her habit of speaking out of turn, Buzz questioned Jody, taking over the sheriff's normal role, and asked, "What's this about rustlers, Jody?"

"As I just was telling the sheriff before Trish butted in with her two cents' worth, Pa's missing about fifty head. Tracks are plain. East, about two days old."

The young girl couldn't seem to hold back her every thought and question. "How do you know they were rustled? They might just have grazed further away.

There are no fences out that way. They could be anywhere."

Jody, with a disgusted look on his face, said, "A girl wouldn't be expected to know, but cattle on the loose don't bunch up and drive themselves off in one direction, walk'n a straight line like."

Rory's patience was being tested, but he found the whole matter somewhat humorous too. The boy was right in everything he said except, perhaps, in his opinion of girls. Rory figured that had a good chance of changing before long.

When all the talk had been done, and Rory had more exact information on the location of the Triple T Ranch, he suggested Jody take his gelding to the stable and stall him in trade for a livery rental animal for the ride home. The bay gelding didn't have another fifteen rushed miles left in him.

Finally, Rory found himself standing alone, with Buzz Hampton climbing into the buggy while Trish tongue-clicked the horse into action.

RORY AND JODY rode side by side on the long trail to the Triple T. At the ranch, a discussion with Logan Trader had Rory convinced that a theft had indeed taken place and that the guess of a two-day start might be accurate. Mrs. Trader cranked things up in the kitchen and put an early dinner on the table. Rory set out well before dark, following the wide trail the driven animals had left in their wake. Always admitting to himself that he knew too little about tracking, he couldn't tell if he was gaining on the herd, but there was a good chance he was. His big Double J Ranch bred and raised blood-red bay riding animal still had some travel left in him. A blind man could have followed the trail, allowing Rory to ride well into the late evening. He stopped to rest the gelding at the first trickle of water he came to. With a few hours of sleep, he was back in the saddle. He had never really enjoyed his own camp fare. After several long-distance rides in his job as sheriff, he had developed the habit of riding early and making his coffee and the first meal of the day when the sun was noon high. That bit of self-discipline had become the pattern of his life on the trail.

His gelding had stepped right out, and now the signs of travel were much fresher, judging from the still sloppy, wet droppings, if nothing else. Then he saw dust on the far horizon. It was too far away to identify its source, but given the sparseness of the settlement in the area, it was a safe bet to lay the gray mass to the rustled cattle. That there were still substantial numbers of buffalo running on the plains entered his mind, but he pushed that concern aside in the belief that he would have time and space to retreat to sheltering distance if needed. If the buffalo swept the cattle along with them, the game would be over, and the cattle probably lost. Thinking it through, Rory decided he could close the gap between the herd and himself considerably with no fear of being seen. If it was the rustled herd bunched up under the dust, the riders would be pretty busy pushing for their destination, with little time for studying their back trail.

Rory urged his gelding into a slow lope, knowing the animal could hold that pace for mile after mile. He knew that he, too, would be raising a dust cloud, although it would be much smaller than the one he was narrowing in on. And, he rationalized, if the riders were enveloped in the dust up-ahead, they would never see the small cloud on their back trail.

As he closed in on the herd, the objects beneath the dust became identifiable. He was able to brush the concern about buffalo out of his mind. He could not yet distinguish cattle from horse and rider, but that would soon come. He pushed the gelding a bit, thinking to close the gap by another mile or so. Reaching that vantage point, he could see there was a single drag rider. It was enough to satisfy the questions running through his mind. A light pull on the reins brought the gelding to a stop. Proceeding at a walk after a ten-minute rest in a bit of shade would keep him in contact with the stolen cattle. He would stay with them until nightfall, assess his situation at that time, and form a plan.

First, while there was little chance of the rustlers seeing what he was doing, he scouted around until he found a bit of sitting water that had gathered in a hollow at the base of a couple of stunted cotton-woods. The shovel marks around the hollow suggested that the hole was man-made. He stepped to the ground and bent to the water, carefully checking for snakes. He truly hated snakes. Scooping with his hands, he managed to enlarge the hole, letting another small bit of water seep in. He then slipped the bridle from the gelding and dropped the saddle to the ground, knowing the well-trained horse wouldn't wander. The small bit of water available was less than what the animal really needed, but it would have to do. He had adequate water for himself in the two canteens he habitually carried.

As the gelding pulled at the summer dry bunches of grass, Rory leaned against the cottonwood and tipped his hat down to shield his eyes from the glaring sun. He would catch a bit of rest while he trusted the horse to warn him of anyone approaching.

As EVENING slowly drifted over the land, Rory saddled the horse and made his way toward where he had last seen the dust cloud. The cattle couldn't have gone more than four or five miles in the time since he had last seen them. Wanting a look at the camp, if he could do it without exposing himself, he stepped the gelding's pace up a bit, watching carefully for an outpost guard. But the land was so flat and so barren there was little chance of avoiding exposure for the rustlers or for himself.

Rory heard the bawling of thirsty cattle before he saw them or the rustlers' camp. Ahead, just a half mile, was a slight rise in the land, leaving a small swale behind it that Rory intended to try to use to his advantage. In a bushed or forested area, he would have tied the animal off and walked the last half mile. But in this open country, it was clearly best to hold his ride close. He had no other means of escape.

Trusting the horse to stand, he dropped the reins and slowly, carefully crawled up the edge of the grade. He removed his hat as he neared the top and eased up until he could just glimpse the rustler camp on the other side. Three men were sitting around a small fire with their horses held close. He could see a fourth rider with the cattle. It was difficult to judge from the distance, but he didn't think he had ever seen any of the men before. One man, the one tending the fire, was clearly Logan Trader's former hired hand, judging by the description of man and horse Rory had been given. It was decision time. What to do? No matter how he sized up the situation, he could see no outcome that didn't involve gunfire and, probably death, quite possibly his own, given the four-to-one imbalance in manpower. He eased back down the slope and gathered up the reins. He would ride back, out of easy-sight distance, and think it over.

Stepping down from the saddle where he was reasonably sure the rustlers wouldn't see him, he settled in. He would wait for full dark, and possibly for the hour before dawn, depending on what the rustlers did. It was a long wait. He allowed his eyes to close a couple of times, but he dared not sleep soundly. It was no exaggeration to think that his life could be the price of carelessness. But finally, the time had come.

He tightened the cinch on the gelding and stepped into the leather. This time the slope-surrounded swale would be a nuisance, separating him from the rustlers. He made a wide sweep around the camp, heading for a small patch of brush he had spotted that afternoon. He was well past the time when there would have been a change of night guard. The man on duty would be there until breakfast was called. And Rory could see by his posture in the saddle that he was getting weary. Sunrise and coffee were still one hour away. The timing for Rory's plan was perfect.

He rode slowly, hoping not to be noticed by the night man until he reached the clump of brush with a few scattered rocks among it. He tied the horse off on the back side of the shrubs and crept forward, anticipating that the rider would come close enough on his next round. He held his carbine in his right hand. He had taken to carrying Lance Newley's Big Fifty in a second saddle scabbard. The weapon had been given to him by Newley himself when the Lance Newley Gang had been brought down. But that was a heavy weapon. Even though Rory was a strong man, he wasn't sure he could do with the fifty what he could do easily with the carbine.

Choosing the darkest place he could find, he waited, watching every move the cattle or their guard made. Here and there among the herd, an animal struggled to its feet. After a dry drive and a dry camp, they would be up and bawling for water before the sun was fully risen. The rider was still on the opposite side of the gather. Riding slowly, watching for worrying movement from the cattle, the man was ignoring the darkened space that concealed the sheriff. If nothing changed, the rider would pass Rory's location in just another minute. He would be close. Less than ten feet away when he passed. Now Rory needed silence and stillness. No movement from either him or his horse. Nothing to distract the rustler.

Crouching in the darkness, Rory waited. *Wait. A bit closer. Just a bit more. Three or four more steps from the rider's gelding. Now.*

As silently as possible, Rory burst from his crouch with the carbine in his right hand. His arm was fully extended to the side, his fingers wrapped firmly around the stock grip, his index finger nowhere near the trigger, but ready if it all went wrong. As he rose, he was already stepping forward. His arm was moving. If he missed, there would be a shooting situation. He didn't miss. Even the thick felt of the man's hat couldn't blunt the damage the barrel of the .44-40 Winchester delivered to the man's skull. Rory could see little more than an outline, but he could hear the *thunk* of steel against flesh and bone and feel the reverberation clear down to his shoulder. The man's horse made two quick, startled side steps, dumping the unconscious man to the turf. A few cattle raised their heads but soon settled down.

Rory had come prepared with tie-off strings in his saddlebags and a single pair of handcuffs. He pulled the cuffs from his pack and knelt to the unmoving man. He rolled him over and soon had him trussed in the steel with his wrists behind him. Rory then pulled a single, narrow piece of leather from a jacket pocket and trussed the man's feet. With a second strip of leather, he lashed the feet to the handcuffs, bending the rider's legs until his feet nearly touched his wrists. A gag formed from the rider's own neck scarf put the finishing touches to the task.

Not knowing, or much caring, if the man was alive or dead, Rory left the unconscious crook where he was and rode slowly back to the camp, carefully picking his route, hoping the hoofbeats of the gelding didn't awaken the other rustlers. When the small camp was in sight, he circled to his right and ground hitched the gelding. He dropped to a crawling posture and tackled the outside slope of the rise of land.

SUFFERING the effects of crawling over and around the cactus, with a quarter-hour of slow, almost silent, crawling behind him, and not knowing if the camp had come alive or the men were still in their bedrolls, Rory eased his head and the carbine over the grass-covered ridge. He was barely two feet above the camp. He wiggled and squirmed up the grade until he was on his knees with just his head showing over the lip.

With just a small wiggle to settle his knees, weapons at the ready, he could have gone right to shooting. Instead, he chose a less intrusive assault on the camp. And, hopefully, a safer one.

One half-asleep man was tending the fire, which had burned down to coals. He had a handful of twigs, laying them one by one on the coals. He would soon have a blazing fire, and that would not be to Rory's advantage. The wonderful aroma of coffee filled the small camp area and Rory's nostrils. He knew it would be the remnants of the last night's brew and barely drinkable—strong and bitter. He pushed his desire for caffeine aside and rose a bit higher, still holding to his knees.

Loving the law work but hating the shooting and killing, Rory had determined to use other methods as much as possible. But he had also learned that there was nothing that could grab and focus a man's attention more quickly than a half ounce of lead projected from his .44-40, carefully aimed, not to kill but to frighten into immobility. Lifting the Winchester to his shoulder, he put the first shot into the fire. He had noticed before that having flames and hot brands from the fire scattering in all directions was almost as effective as the shot. But it was not as effective as a multitude of shots. With all those beliefs stowed safely away in his mind, he commenced shooting.

His first shot into the fire caused the half-asleep rustler to come fully awake, leaping from his knees, then falling onto his back, and reaching for a gun he had not yet wrapped around his waist. Rory put two more shots at the man, one on each side of his head, scattering dried grass and dirt onto his face. Turning to the two sleepers, who were frantically throwing their blankets aside and scrambling for weapons, Rory put shot after shot beside them and over their heads. They both dove to the ground covering their heads with wrapped arms.

Just to make it interesting and, perhaps, to convince the rustlers that there was more than one man shooting, he pulled his .44 and drove four shots at the men, one at each man and one more for the fire.

Knowing he had only seconds before the rustlers managed to get their wits about them and grab weapons, he shouted, "Don't move, and you may live through this day."

Rory's heart was beating about as fast as he had ever felt it. His palms were suddenly sweaty, even in the coolness of the dawn. He had nearly pulled this off. He couldn't fail now.

The man beside the fire lifted his arms, even from his position on his back, and shouted back, "Don't shoot."

A man with his feet still tangled in his blanket hollered, "You coward." With that, he rolled to his side and grabbed his gun belt. Before he got a pistol free, Rory pulled the trigger again, putting lead through the man's bicep. He screamed and dropped the belt.

Rory hollered, "No more, or I'll simply shoot all of you. County Sheriff Jamison here, fellas. It's over. No need for anyone to die this day. Now turn on your stomachs and lie still. You turn back over or reach for a weapon, and I'll kill you dead.

"Now, you by the fire, stand up and turn your back to me. Hold your hands in the air. Do it now."

When the still terrified man had complied, Rory had the other two do the same, standing side by side, their hands extended upward. The man who had taken a bullet held up his one good arm, complaining all the time about bleeding to death. Rory ignored him while he tied the other two firmly, with their hands behind their backs. He then had them sit while he tied their ankles. Only then did he look at the injured man.

After cutting and tearing off the man's sleeve, Rory said,

"It's not bad. You may even be able to use the arm again. Use it for whatever they'll have you doing in prison." He tied the dirty sleeve around the wound to staunch the bleeding and, ignoring the screams of pain and humiliation coming from the man's mouth, tied his wrists behind him.

When all three men were tied and seated, Rory said, "You fellas sit tight for a few minutes. I have to go to gather up your friend."

Ignoring the shouted questions, he walked down the slope and stepped into his saddle. Fifteen minutes later, he arrived back in the hollow. The bound and unconscious man was draped over his saddle and firmly tied there. His legs had been allowed to drop to a more normal position.

"Stag dead?" asked one of the men.

"Stag, that his name? No, he's not dead. Not yet, at least. Could be he'll die before we get you boys back to some settlement. I had to thunk him pretty good to take him off his horse. Don't much matter. A man that would steal from the brand he was riding for isn't much of a man. I figure from the description I was given that I've named off the right crook. Or is one of you the man that took Logan Trader's wages and then double-crossed him?"

No one corrected Rory's assumption, so he let it go.

He kicked around the bedding, looking for weapons. Two handguns and one knife dropped onto the ground. With the side of his foot, he slid them into a pile with the other carbines and holster belts. He then dumped out their boots, looking for a hideout derringer or, possibly, a knife. When he was sure he had all the firepower in one stack, he took the cleanest blanket he could see, wrapped them all up, including the carbines from the men's saddle scabbards, and tied them behind his own bedroll.

"Alright, men. One by one, I'll loose you. You get dressed and saddle your animal. When you're all mounted and secured, we'll head back. We'll leave the cattle here. And listen up. I told you once already. I'm County Sheriff Jamison. You're under arrest for cattle rustling. We're going to ride as fast as ever we can. If you slow down or cause me trouble, I'll shoot you. You've managed to completely wear out my patience, what with chasing you halfway to nowhere and eating all that dust. All the while doing without sleep or coffee. You don't want to push me any further.

"We're going to be back where there are people while the sun is still lighting the way. Now stand still while I have a cup of this coffee, as bad as I know it is. Because of you fellas, I've missed some meals. Some sleep too. And I truly hate missing either one."

Rory used the hot coffee to rinse out a cup that was lying beside the fire pit and poured a cup for himself.

"What about us?"

Rory looked over the rim of the mug and said, "Yes, what about you?"

Rory gulped down three scalding tastes of the coffee and then dumped the remaining liquid onto the flames. Holding the men under the threat of the .44-40, he nudged them toward their horses. When they were mounted and tied, he said, "Fellas, when I took this job, I vowed to not kill any more men than necessary. But that doesn't mean I won't pull the trigger. For you, it's not worth the risk, so move ahead, straight west. And less you think you can get away with a quick nudge of the spur, you need to know that I don't even remember the last time I missed a shot."

With the well-trussed Stag lying across his saddle and tied firmly, the sheriff and his four captured rustlers rode west.

SHERIFF RORY JAMISON was just a couple of weeks shy of his twentieth birthday. Too young still to vote in the election that had put him into office.

With the well-trussed Slim lying across his saddle and
ted firmly the sheriff and his four men rode off rustlers
rode west

2

SHERIFF JAMISON ARRIVED IN THE CITY AFTER THE USUAL
hateful two-day ride on the bumpy, rattling stage. He
wasn't sure whose responsibility it was to build or repair
the road, but he hoped someone would sort it out soon.

His first stop was at the county sheriff's office, where
he turned his prisoners over to the jailer on duty, along
with copies of the court's findings. From there, they
would be transferred to the state lockup.

Newly appointed Judge Anders P. Yokam, presiding
over the county court at the old fort, in rented space
where the assay office had once been, had listened to the
sheriff's story. That telling of the theft, chase, and
capture of the rustlers, bolstered by the rehash of the
much-shared tale of the rustling and betrayal of the
Triple T Ranch, as repeated by rancher Logan Trader,
was enough for the judge. Rory had some thought that
the men would confess if given the opportunity, hoping
for mercy from the court, or present some argument.
But when they stood closemouthed after being asked for
their rebuttal, the judge banged his gavel, a delight that

16

all judges seemed to relish. With a firm glare he declared, "Yule Jasper. Pony and Clive Tribute, brothers. You are found guilty of the theft of cattle. Rustling, in other words. This court has to believe that when you undertook that venture, you were fully aware of the seriousness of rustling in cattle country. You are therefore sentenced to serve ten years each in the state penitentiary.

"This court finds it unfortunate that a fourth man, one Stag, no family name known, has escaped this county's justice. It is, however, a comfort to know that he will stand before a much higher court, a court that makes no mistakes and whose word is final. You three, on the other hand, if you think clearly, and act accordingly, will one day see freedom again. It is hoped you will use that privilege wisely.

"Court dismissed."

WANTING to clear his mind and stretch his legs after a long stage ride, Rory, relieved of the guard duty over the three prisoners, walked the several blocks to the downtown area with his carpetbag in his left hand and his carbine held firmly in his right. He would bathe, dine, and rest that afternoon and report to Oscar Cator at the state administrator's office the next morning.

Almost from his first visit, Rory had been amused as he tried to get ahead of the often cranky and always officious Bertha, who guarded the door to the state offices. After his first visit, where she did everything but hold him to ransom, he had walked right past her, allowing her admonishing words to fall unheeded behind him. On the last couple of visits, he had taken her small surprise gifts, discovering in that way that she was especially weakened where chocolate was involved. But wishing to vary his tributes, this time Rory had brought a small box of carefully wrapped fruit, grown locally at the fort, padded with shredded newspaper against the bumps and heaves of the only mode of transport from the fort to the city, since the railway had, for reasons of their own, bypassed that settlement.

"This is in appreciation for your community service from the good folks up at the fort. Lots of fruit trees planted up that way now. It's late in the season for cherries and early for peaches, but there's some of each here. The heat and the long stage ride probably didn't do them any good, but perhaps they'll still be edible."

With that, he left the bewildered Bertha struggling for words and trooped directly to Oscar Cator's office. A single wrap with his knuckles received the response, "open," and Sheriff Jamison entered the office of the man who, if one was to ignore the electors, was his boss.

Being familiar with the ways of the young man, Oscar just shook his head and quietly said, "You keep me guessing, I'll say that for you. Me and Bertha, both."

More loudly, he asked, "What have you got for me this time?"

The telling of the rustling case didn't take long. It didn't take long for Oscar to glance over Rory's report either. Oscar then pinned the newly elected sheriff to his chair with a studied look and said, "Something for you to consider. Block Handly was past this way a couple of days ago. He was asking for you. When I told him the results of the election, I got the feeling he was unhappy about it. He didn't say right out loud, but I had the feeling he intended to put pressure on you to join the federal force. He said something about a letter. And since you still don't have the enjoyment of instant communication with the telegraph, I assume the letter will arrive in its own good time."

Rory had no ready response. When he said nothing, Oscar filled the silence with a question.

"Have you given any thought to joining the federal marshals?"

Without waiting for an answer, Oscar continued, "Actually, I'm surprised Block didn't pin you down after the Lance Newley matter was wrapped up.

"I might add that if the marshal's report was even close to accurate, your actions would already have songwriters scratching their heads and scribbling ditties. Lonesome cowboys will be sitting around their campfires singing about Rory, the roaring sheriff, or some such drivel. Every eligible young lady, and a few who are not truly eligible, will be humming your songs and dreaming about heroes.

"And there'll be a brand-new penny dreadful coming out of New York or Chicago, written by someone who has never seen the West, or a gun fight, either one. Your name will be on the cover, and you'll have done so many exploits that by the time the third copy is written and finds its way out here, even you won't know what the truth is anymore.

"And here, in this new report you just laid on my desk, four rustlers taken by a single peace officer, who just happens to be the very same Sheriff Rory Jamison. That alone calls for another song and another penny dreadful.

"One rustler taken down and knocked off his horse, and three frightened into submission with a series of shots that were intended to terrify but not kill. The songs just keep coming. I could almost make one up myself."

Ignoring the administrator's question about federal service and his creative enjoyment of the situation, Rory got to his feet. He picked up his leather carrying case and said, "I believe I'll look around a bit today. Enjoy the sights of the big city and such. I'll catch the stage tomorrow morning. I'm not sure Bertha has plans to share those peaches, but you could ask. I'll see you next time."

Oscar laughed and said, "Think about it. Federal service, I mean."

Rory left the little office without offering an answer.

The county administrator allowed a few seconds to go by before he spoke. With the interior partitions of the offices being shy of the ceiling by a good two feet, his voice carried easily. "Bertha, don't let that man leave!"

3

RORY HADN'T SAID A WORD WHEN OSCAR'S VOICE FILLED the office. Bertha pointed a sympathetic look Rory's way and said, "You heard the man."

Whether it was his respect for the older man, his understanding of how the county hierarchy was designed to work, or possibly his desire for peace, something prompted him to stop and turn around. He didn't point any steps toward the interior office, but neither did he point any toward the outer door. He simply stopped and waited. Only a few seconds passed before he heard a chuckle coming from Oscar's direction. Turning his head just slightly, he locked eyes with Bertha. No words passed between them, but for the first time, Rory thought he might have seen just a hint of humor in the overly serious doorkeeper.

There was a sliding of chair legs across old oak flooring, and then enough foot falls to carry Oscar from his chair to the door of his office. He turned the knob, pushed the door open, and spoke to Bertha as he crossed the outer office.

"Bertha, the sheriff and I will be out for a while. Assuming he doesn't do me serious bodily harm over lunch, I should be returning in the early afternoon. I doubt if the world will fall apart in that time."

With a grin on Oscar's face, a mismatch for the serious countenance displayed by the sheriff, the two men walked outside. Oscar took the lead. Rory, having no idea where they were going, or why, kept pace with the older man, glancing, as he always did, at the people and events they were passing. There was nothing noteworthy except one finely constructed, older wooden building trimmed generously with gingerbread wooden scrollwork and painted with a clash of colors. The artistry and evident craftsmanship on the building made it look out of place between two newer but unimaginative brick structures. Oscar followed Rory's eyes and smiled.

"I've noticed you looking at structures before on our other walks around town. I'm going to guess that your father instilled the appreciation of quality and workmanship in you at a young age."

"That would be a good guess, Oscar, but an even more important guess would be what's going on in the alley on the north side of the brick building."

Oscar took a longer look. "You have a fine eye there, Sheriff. I totally missed that action."

With no words, Rory stepped onto the street and began weaving his way through the horse and wagon traffic. He had his determined eye on two men who were grappling with a young woman, laughing drunkenly all the while. Rory had no idea if the victim was an uptown lady on a shopping trip or a saloon girl fighting off patrons who had started their day's celebrations early enough to be inebriated before noon. Nor did he care. A woman was to be treated with respect. He didn't see any city police in the area, so, in his mind, it automatically became his responsibility. His decision had little to do with being the sheriff of a faraway county. It had much more to do with being a man of conscience.

Rory had left his carbine in the hotel room, but he had flipped his gun belt around his waist and tucked the two Colt .44s into their holsters before he left his room. He was in the habit of keeping his jacket carefully buttoned. Carrying weapons was frowned upon in the big city. As he approached the sidewalk, he undid the buttons, making the weapons accessible, but held the jacket together with his left hand.

Rory had managed to squeeze between two moving wagons, leaving Oscar well behind him. Several running steps brought the administrator huffing up beside him.

"What do you have in mind, Rory? This is well out of your jurisdiction. We should leave it to the city police."

"Fine. You show me where there is one."

Oscar had no response. Rory kept walking. There was just one more slow-moving mule-hauled wagon to ease around, and he would be on the sidewalk. Oscar stayed with him, having to almost run to keep up with the taller and longer-legged sheriff. A few quick steps on the sidewalk, and they both turned, facing into the alley. Several pedestrians and a steady flow of wagons and riders all somehow managed to not see the tussle right before their eyes.

Sheriff Rory had never seen any good results coming from delay. The two men had the woman pressed against the brick of the building. Rory had wondered why she hadn't screamed. But now he could see that one thug had his big hand pressed firmly over her mouth. Oscar stood stock-still on the sidewalk, somewhat frightened, but mostly curious. He had no idea at all what he would do if confronted with the necessity of rescuing the lady and was glad someone else was relieving him of that responsibility.

The two men's backs were toward the sidewalk, with one man half-turned, presenting his side to Rory. Their drunken laughter blocked out any noise of Rory's approach. With no warning or order to end what they were doing, Rory grabbed the man closest by the collar and, with a wrench that could have torn a small tree from the ground, pulled him off the woman. With a single movement, he yanked the man to the side and rammed his forehead, full force, into the brick wall. The bully dropped soundlessly to the filth of the alley and didn't move. The second man let go of the woman and turned toward the sheriff, holding both arms up in front of him, his hands curled into fists. He staggered just a bit, indicating his degree of intoxication. Rory reached right through the raised fists and grabbed the fellow by the shirt front.

He pulled the man further from the woman, twisted him sideways, and rammed the back of his head into the brick. He fell soundlessly on top of his companion. The two drunks lay in a huddle with blood flowing from both their heads. Judging from the closeness of the bits of hair stuck into drying blood on the jagged brick edges, the two men had met the bricks within a couple of inches of each other.

Knowing the men would not be causing more trouble, Rory quickly buttoned his jacket before he turned to the woman. After her time of fright and the abuse she had endured, she looked ready to collapse. She had her face buried in her hands. Tears were dripping down her cheeks, and great sobs were escaping from behind her hands.

Rory knew he was no judge of city women, but his first glance told him the victim was a lady. Her clothing alone attested to that fact. But her beautifully designed and sewn white dress was torn at the collar, with dirt marks marring both front and back in several places. Her shoes, so delicate and pretty, as they had been originally worn, were wet with filthy water, the residue of an overnight rain. Still, with all that had happened, the lady managed to retain a hint of dignity, if not composure.

Gently, Rory slipped his hand onto her elbow, turned her to the alley entrance, and quietly said. "Come, let's get you out of here."

With stumbling half steps, the lady followed the sheriff to the sidewalk. Several walkers made a point of not seeing what was happening. Once clear of the alley, Rory was unable to think of what to do next. He finally said, "Oscar, would you like to escort this lady to a safer place? Maybe get her a cup of tea somewhere off the street?"

He then said, very quietly, "Ma'am, this man is a gentleman. You can trust him."

It took a few moments for the lady to overcome her fear, but finally, after just the briefest glances at her rescuer, she walked away, allowing Oscar to lead her by the elbow. Rory watched them for a few feet and then turned and went the other way. He would walk for a while, looking at the sights, and then go to where he and Oscar had met for lunch on his last visit. Perhaps Oscar would think to do the same, and they could have their planned meeting.

25

OSCAR ESCORTED the frightened and abused lady along the sidewalk until they came to a small bakery that offered a few inside tables and advertised *Fresh Baking, Tea, and Coffee*. They turned in. When a middle-aged woman, dressed all in white with a full-length apron covering her from neck to knee, approached, Oscar said, "We'll have a cup of tea, please, and perhaps a sweet treat, but this lady has been through some unpleasantness. Is there some place she can wash up and pull herself together?"

The words in response were heavily accented. *German* thought Oscar.

"Come wit me, ya? Is goot. We fix."

In the quietness of the little shop, Oscar could hear water splashing, along with coughing and spitting and nose blowing, such as he might have heard in a cattle camp in the semi-light of an early morning. Wondering if he should simply leave the shop and disappear, Oscar waited alone for what might have been a full five minutes. Finally, the lady, led with care by the baker, re-entered the front space and was directed back to the table where Oscar waited. He nodded his thanks to the baker, and she hustled off to put the tea together.

The abused woman sat staring at Oscar as if she was trying to figure out who he was and what all had happened. He decided to open whatever conversation they were to have.

"My name is Oscar, ma'am. I am employed with the state government, in charge of county matters. I apologize on behalf of what is normally a beautiful and peaceful city for what you had to endure this morning. Is there someone I can call for you? Perhaps someone who could accompany you to your home?"

The woman stared across the table in silence, leaving

Oscar with the question of what to do next. He was momentarily distracted by activity at the entry of the alleyway they had recently vacated. Fortunately, he and the lady had chosen their seats at the little table in a way that put the outside activity where the lady couldn't see what was happening.

Oscar was about to repeat his question when the baker arrived at the little table with a tea service on a small silver tray.

"For you to feel better, ya? You sit. You rest. You drink the tea. I get nice thing to eat. You soon much better, ya?"

The baker walked away and returned in short order with a white porcelain plate with blue decorations along the edges. On the plate were four small pastries.

"Is goot. You eat. You stay. No hurry. Ya?"

Both Oscar and the lady nodded their thanks. It was the first display of thought or response Oscar had seen since Rory had freed her. Finally, answering Oscar's question, she said simply, "Hebert Tremblay, Rocky View Bank. My husband is the president."

Oscar replied, "That's not far from here. Excuse me for a moment, please."

He stepped outside and flagged down a passing carriage for hire. He was back inside in just a moment. "I've sent for him. I'll stay if you like, until he gets here."

"Yes, please."

She hadn't touched the pastry, but she took a small sip of tea. With pleading eyes, she said, "Thank you for being there and for your patience with me. I know I look a fright, and my actions have been most unladylike. I suspect you could hear that awful coughing and such when I was trying to clean myself. That dreadful man had his filthy hand over my mouth. I fear that no matter

27

how unladylike I am and how often I spit it out, I'll have that appalling taste in my mouth forever.

"But I almost forgot. Who was the young fellow who so easily manhandled those two?"

Oscar had known the question would be asked. He had thought of several answers. None were satisfactory. But now, with the question openly before him, he simply said, "He was just the right young man arriving at just the right time. Don't worry about it any further."

"In other words, it would be best for him if his name was kept out of the incident. I understand. If you happen to see him again," she said with her first small smile, knowing full well her two rescuers had been together, "please relay my sincere thanks."

Oscar had no time to respond before the door burst open, smashing back against a display case, and a frantic man rushed in. He was a tall, slim, dapper-looking fellow, clearly a gentleman, but one who could easily intimidate with a scowl and a look. Expensively dressed and well-coifed and put together, in spite of the frantic carriage ride, weaving through traffic on his rescue mission. The room was small. The space from door to table less than five feet. A single step put the man close enough for him to ask, "Frieda, what happened? Are you alright now? Who is this man?"

Oscar stood to his feet and introduced himself, with Hebert Tremblay looking at him with grave suspicion the whole time. No handshakes were offered. It wasn't until Frieda said, "Hebert, this is the man who rescued me. Him and some young man who did not hang around after. It would be more appropriate if you were to thank him rather than pointing your suspicions his way."

"I apologize, sir. But someone needs to tell me what happened and if the police have been involved."

Oscar remained standing while he said, "Your wife can tell you what happened and who was involved. I'll leave the two of you to sort that out. As to the police, just a few minutes ago, I saw them drag the perpetrators from the alley and carry them off in a wagon. I'm sure you can find out all you need to know, all in good time. Now I will get on with my day's work. I wish you well, Mrs. Tremblay."

Tremblay sputtered a bit and made motions as if to stop him from leaving, but Oscar turned his back, walked the few feet to where the baker stood watching, pressed a coin into her hand and stepped outside, gently closed the door behind him, and walked away. It was yet an hour before lunchtime when he hoped that Rory would think to go to their known lunch restaurant. He would like a few more private minutes with the young sheriff before he left town. In the meantime, he had something important to do.

WHEN RORY ENTERED THE RESTAURANT, Oscar had already claimed a corner table. He wasn't alone. Sitting beside him was Anthony Clare, the sheriff from the county closest to the big city. After the greetings and handshakes, the two men retook their seats.

Anthony grinned and said, "First, congratulations on your election. And second, it sounds like you had an exciting morning. Good for you."

When Rory waved off any discussion of the matter, Anthony caught on to the fact that his fellow officer didn't wish to discuss it. Changing the subject, he said, "Oscar has been telling me about his theory regarding campfire songs and penny dreadful stories. I was skeptical at first, but I'm beginning to lean his way. I don't know whether to be thankful no one notices me or jealous that they don't."

Completely ignoring the topic and the comment, Rory said, "I haven't seen you since that fiasco up north with the Slade Duhamel bunch. Have you recovered from your wounds as well as you look?"

"I'm doing fine. Thankfully. And thankful, too, that you came along at just the right time to wrap that mess up. Came along dragging half the county ranchers along with you. The ranchers and a very pretty young lady."

With a grin and a feigned faraway look, he continued, "Ah, yes. I can almost hear the songs and see the pictures on the covers of those magazines with the beautiful rancher's daughter looking spellbound at the very sight of you."

The conversation was interrupted when the waitress appeared. Rory ordered immediately, hoping to make the break in the talk permanent.

As they ate, Oscar briefed Rory on the events at the little bakeshop. Rory listened without comment.

Sensing that Rory had heard all he wished to hear about penny dreadful magazines, his table companions moved on to other small talk, most of which he let drift past his ears and mind without comment. Oscar finally got serious.

"Rory, the big city is not quite like the countryside. While I admire your actions this morning, and certainly Mrs. Tremblay was thankful, the city police might think you went a bit too far. This will all blow over, and no one will know who you are. I was careful to keep your name and position private, although Mrs. Tremblay clearly figured out that we had been together. She made no issue of it, only passing along her thanks, 'in case you and I ever happen to meet again'. The bottom line here is you need to ride out. I'm trusting that no one took particular notice of you or will remember what you look like the next time you visit. In a short time, it will all be forgotten.

"I've taken the liberty of gathering your things from the hotel. It's all tied to my personal horse out back of the restaurant, beside Anthony's animal. I'm suggesting that you two ride out immediately. Keep my horse until you're coming this way again. I have others. Let the story die out. I'll do my part here, which will mostly be pleading ignorance."

With little more said, Oscar shook hands with his two most favorite county sheriffs and watched as they swung onto their saddles.

4

RIDING INTO STEVENSVILLE JUST BEFORE THE DINNER hour two days later, Rory pulled his animal to a stop in front of the marshal's office. Ivan immediately walked out and took the reins, tying the horse off as he spoke his greetings.

"I don't recognize the animal. I'm guessing there's a story behind that."

"Short story, Ivan, and not worth the retelling. How are things in Stevensville?"

"Been awful quiet since you pulled out for the fort. Hardly any point in having a marshal."

"How would you like to come to the fort? There's a deputy sheriff position open. I'd like if you would fill it."

Ivan pointed a long study Rory's way but said nothing. After a time of foot shuffling and internal questioning, Ivan said, "I was just about to ride up the hill, visit the folks for the evening. Key Wardle has agreed to stand in for the afternoon and night. Ride along and you can tell me why I should move to the fort."

Three hours of poky riding later, they rode onto the

yard of the I-5. The Ivanov Ranch, Ivan's home. They both waved at Ivan's mother, who was watching from the kitchen porch. From there, they rode on to the barn. They dismounted outside the small building and led the animals inside, tying them in stalls.

When Rory stepped back outside the barn, the dog rescued from Kiril's place came rushing from somewhere behind the corral. A steady whine and bark announced his approach. The dog completely ignored Ivan, preferring instead to charge at Rory with a happy bark and a frantically wagging tail, attempting, at the same time, to leap into Rory's arms. Rory laughed and ruffled the dog's neck hair while saying, "Well, hello there, old fellow. What's this all about? You're acting like we're old buddies when, actually, we hardly know each another." He was laughing and scratching the dog's head the whole time. The excited animal refused to settle down, making circles around Rory and again trying to leap into his arms.

"That's your dog, Sheriff. You may not even know it, but that's the truth. He whines around here day after day, looking through the whole ranch yard, searching for something. Then he runs back up to the cabin in the bush and I have to get him before he starves himself to death. I never knew what he was looking for, but now it's obvious. He's looking for his rescuer. That would be you. That's sure enough your dog. You'd best take him with you when you leave," Ivan said.

Rory was taken aback by the suggestion, but finally, he said, "He's a sure enough good dog. I've got to give Kiril that much. No idea where the old man came up with him. Probably some ranch dog back in the hills produced more pups than the situation called for. Sure. I'll take him. We'll be good pards."

The family and Rory ate, drank coffee, and visited the evening away. There was no extra room in the little cabin, but when Rory picked up his bedroll from the floor beside the kitchen door with the intention of heading for the loft, Mrs. Ivanov wouldn't hear of it. Through a stream of gestures and broken English, enhanced by a laughing explanation from Ivan, Rory finally figured out that the family was offering Sonia's bed for the night. With all arguments brushed aside, Rory finally relented and followed Ivan's directions to the small sleeping room.

Ivan and Rory stayed one night and were set to leave early the next morning when Rory took a notion.

"Ride up to Kiril's with me, Ivan. I'm going to follow that downhill trail again. You can bring the horse down to town for me. The dog will come along on my walk. I still have some questions I can't seem to get my mind to leave alone."

"Want to give me a hint on those questions?"

"Well, the main one would be why go to all the trouble and work of coming to town along that long and steep trail. Your family would not have stopped him from riding across the I-5 and back with his purchases. Haven't found a way to understand that yet. Of course, it just could be that Kiril had notions of his own that we'll never understand. But I still want to take another look."

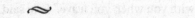

IVAN ARRIVED BACK to a town that was alive with traffic crowding the summer-dried and dusty streets. He stabled the horses and took up his position outside the marshal's office, waiting and watching for Rory and the dog to find their way down the wooded slope.

It was near enough noon before the barking of the dog announced their arrival. Rory came from around the livery barn and called the dog back. Tippet greeted the sheriff and said, "Water over here for the dog."

Rory led the dog that way and then walked to the marshal's office, taking up the second chair beside Ivan.

Ivan looked at his trail-weary friend and said, "Find anything new?"

"There's more than one trail through that wooded hillside. I missed that before. I'll need some time to sort it all out."

"Why bother?"

"I'm still troubled by some unanswered questions about Kiril. I'm thinking there's more to the story that we haven't figured out yet.

"Anyway, it has nothing to do with the trail, but there's been someone using the cabin. There's newly cut and split firewood laid up and fresh droppings in the corral. Looks like four or five horses."

Ivan stood and walked into the small office. He returned with an unopened envelope and passed it to Rory.

"Came in on the stage. Addressed to you."

Rory accepted the envelope, turning it every which way to see what subliminal message there might be on the outside. The only thing he could read into the folded and wrinkled paper was that the writer had big hands. And that the writer had been sweating when he addressed and sealed the envelope. The once-damp imprint of the writer's hand was much larger than the envelope could contain.

Ivan, watching this study of the envelope, laughed and said, "You're looking at that as if the writing should be on the outside. You ever get a letter before?"

"No. Can't say that I have."

"Well, I haven't either, my friend, but I'm just guessing here that you're going to have to open the thing to find out who sent it and why."

The sheriff grinned at his friend and continued studying the envelope. Finally, after examining every detail, he pulled his belt knife and slid the sharpened point under the corner of the flap. With studied care, he slit the top of the envelope open and replaced the knife in his belt sheath. Instead of simply reaching in with his fingers and extracting the slip of paper, he opened the cut edge by pushing the two outer corners together, causing a bulge in the center. Holding it up to his eye, he carefully examined the contents.

Running out of patience and ready to burst into laughter, Ivan grabbed the envelope out of Rory's hand and pulled the letter out. He dropped the envelope onto the boardwalk at his feet and flipped open the folded single page. Making a game of following his friend's lead, he turned the page every which way, backward and forward, upside down and right side up.

"Looks safe enough, Sheriff, but hold on just a minute while I pull my gun. I'll keep the weapon pointed on that paper while you read what it says. One unexpected move from that note, and I'll put a hole through it."

Rory could easily recognize the humor in the situation. He imitated Ivan's actions for just a few seconds and then spread the page on his knee. He looked first at the signature near the bottom—Block Handly, Deputy US Marshal. He then glanced at the top to confirm that the missive was meant for him. It was.

Although I am still hoping one day to entice you into the federal service, I wish to congratulate you on your election as county sheriff. Keep your eyes opened for more information on the gold coin matter. The federal people are very much interested. Let me know immediately if anything new turns up.

Ride carefully,
Block Handly, Deputy US Marshal

Rory passed the note to Ivan with, "It's safe enough. You can put your weapon away."

Ivan had read over Rory's arm, so he didn't bother to take up the paper.

"There's been talk before of the federal marshals. You interested?"

"Not right now. But who knows the future?"

Rory put the letter back into the envelope, folded it so it would fit in his shirt pocket, and leaned back in his chair.

EARLIER, around midmorning, as he sat waiting for Rory to work his way through the bush, Ivan had reconciled himself to the county deputy position. He had gone immediately to the ranch supply store and dragged Key Wardle off to the side where they could have a quiet talk. Almost as if he had been anticipating the invitation, Key had easily come to see the merits of moving away from retail clerking and into the entry levels of the law enforcement industry as the Stevensville town marshal.

5

BY THE TIME RORY AND THE DOG BURST FROM THE hillside forest, the talking and the small negotiations necessary for the swearing-in of a new town marshal were well underway. Life was bound to get much more complicated as the community grew, but for the moment, simplicity was the order of the day.

Hip Dawson, of Stevensville, left his small bakery in the care of his one helper, hung up his flour-saturated white apron, and made his way down the boardwalk to Browning's, where he would be joined by Ma Gamble in the back room of the mercantile store. There, the three town councilors would perform their solemn duties, that of assigning the peacekeeping responsibilities of their tiny village to Key Wardle, a man too young to legally hold the position if the full letter of the law were to be upheld. But with the precedent set by the state bureaucrats themselves, in their selection of the underaged Rory Jamison as deputy sheriff of the county, and with no one else stepping forward to offer their services, the trio of town administrators welcomed the young man and gave him the nondescript badge Ivan had so recently returned to them.

What with Browning taking time to wait on two customers and Ma Gamble wanting to know a bit more about the new marshal, who had ridden into town some months before without explanation, the solemn moments stretched considerably. And with the participants choosing the most comfortable sack of feed they could find to sit on while they waited for Browning, the time continued to stretch. That the young marshal was fidgeting and anxious was missed by the others.

ON THE STREET, a new byplay was fixing to insert itself upon the good folks of Stevensville. County Sheriff Rory and the newly deputized Ivan were drinking coffee in the shade of the marshal's office roof and passing the morning, waiting for the new marshal to walk across the street and take up his responsibilities. They were anxious to saddle up and head to the old fort, where the county sheriff's office had been established. It was a pleasantly warm fall day. The few gray clouds skirting the hills to the west held the promise of rain but no threat of early frost or snow. It was a good day to be alive in Stevensville.

Ivan glanced toward the north entrance to town, looking over Rory's shoulder. His eyes held a question for a short moment that Rory managed to pick up on. Seeing the question in his friend's eyes, Rory turned his head. He skittered his chair in a quarter circle, recrossed his legs, and leaned back to watch as a group of riders approached. With the excitement and promise of new gold strikes in the hills to the west of the village, there had been many riders coming through in recent days and weeks. Some stopped for a meal, to get a horse reshod, or to stock up on provisions. Most rode right on past the offerings of the merchants along the single street. But this group somehow called attention to itself.

A big man riding a beautiful bay with a black mane and tail and a liberal scattering of white leopard spots on his powerful hind quarters, was in the lead by a half-length. By sight alone, Rory estimated the Appaloosa to be a well-muscled and filled out sixteen hands, and he would have to be to carry this man along any length of trail. The man himself looked indestructible, sitting like a king on his throne. The fact he was wearing a fleece-lined, waist-length canvas coat with an upturned collar, a rigging much beyond the needs of the coolish morning, only added to the vision of size and strength.

The horses the other men rode stood in excess of fifteen hands, with big feet suitable for snow country. From each rider's hat hung a hurricane strap, lying loosely beneath their chins, holding their hats in place in the event of high wind. Taken together, the sight spoke of northern riders. To the leader's left, a scarce three feet away, rode the man's younger duplicate, less the fleece coat. To his right, an equal three feet distance, rode an even younger version, one that failed to show the size of his father but nonetheless looked to be much of a man.

A little further to the left and a half-length to the rear, rode an Indian, a man dressed totally in smoke-stained buckskin, with a feather worked into the single braid dangling from his uncovered head, hanging low over his collarless shirt.

Riding behind was a girl. She showed the family resemblance but nowhere near the size. Her horse was Appaloosa but smaller, dancing in the dust of the street on dainty feet. The hat on the girl's head had been chosen for style as much as effectiveness, as if at least one member of this traveling family should show some awareness of the niceties of coming to town. Rory suspected the horse had been selected for much the same reason. Going to town, after all, was not something most ranchers' daughters did every day.

As the group neared the marshal's office, the girl swung off to her left, crossed the road, trotted a further fifty feet, and dismounted directly in front of the millinery shop, leaving the reins crossed over the well-disciplined horse's neck.

Nancy Jamison had done the exact same thing just a minute before. Rising to the boardwalk, the two ranch girls nodded and passed each other, with Nancy moving on to the mercantile and the visitor entering the millinery shop. Rory gave a brief glance when the girl settled her reins and stepped up to the walk. Taking quick note of his cousin Nancy's appearance and sensing no threat from the newly arrived girl, he turned his head back to the approaching riders.

As the father and two brothers neared the marshal's office, the Indian dropped further back, rode behind the other three and along the road to a position about opposite the millinery shop. He then stepped to the ground at the edge of the road between the marshal's office and the livery. The horse made no motion to walk off, simply dropping its head to an untouched rim of grass along the boardwalk. The Indian ignored the goings-on at the small law office and concentrated his full attention to the other side of the street.

As if on an unspoken command, the trio turned to the marshal's office and the two men seated there. As he was proceeding down the street a couple of minutes before, the father had pulled his carbine. He held it now with the butt resting on his right thigh and the muzzle pointed to the sky. Foolishly, he had his hand on the action, his finger pressed lightly on the trigger.

As the man neared, Rory took note of the rider's thickness of neck, the piercing eyes, the block of a jaw, showing several day's growth of black whiskers. He and his sons might have been considered handsome, in a rough kind of way, if somehow a smile could have broken through the hard exteriors.

There was no greeting or preamble, "Looking to find my son."

The growling voice was the voice of a man used to unquestioned command, a voice that would either snap someone to attention or raise the hackles on the listener's back.

Rory glanced at Ivan and then back up at the speaker. He still sat with his left ankle resting comfortably on his right knee. The coffee mug was balanced on his boot with a single finger through the mug loop. Without making a show of his actions, Rory transferred his coffee mug from his right hand to his left. The movements were slight.

Rory, too, over the past couple of years, had learned how to lend considerable authority to his voice.

"You pouch that carbine and tell me who you are, and perhaps we can talk about it."

The response could be heard up and down the street. The words and actions were totally out of place on that peaceful morning.

"No man tells me what to do nor speaks to me in that manner. Nor do I take lip from young fools. You'll keep a civil tongue in your head or by all that's holy…"

The speaker's first glance, only a few seconds before,

had shown a coffee mug dangling slackly from Rory's fingers. Now, those same fingers held a Colt .44. There was nothing casual about how it was held or where it was pointed. He had neither uncrossed his legs nor made any attempt to rise to his feet. No one saw how the weapon got there, but the smaller of the two sons said, "Pa. For God's sake, man."

"Shut up, Junior. This is the time for you to listen and learn."

Both Rory and Ivan were immediately mystified by the aggressiveness of the visitor.

As if he could outstare this man who had flashed a weapon without spilling his coffee, like the bull of the woods he thought himself to be, the still-mounted man focused his ire on Rory while fingering the action of his carbine, sorely tempted. So sorely tempted, but just hesitant enough to hold to his last thread of judgment.

NONE of the men were to notice, but about that time Nancy emerged from the mercantile. Finding that Browning was busy with town business, and she was in no particular hurry, she sauntered back toward the millinery shop. At the shout of, "No man tells me what to do," her head snapped up, and in an instant, she took in the growing confrontation across the road. With very real urgency, she nearly broke the door off the millinery shop and grabbed the girl who had entered only moments before.

"Is that your pa who's about to get his tail feathers shot off, there across the road?"

The girl looked up, screamed "Pa," and with a single leap, she rose from the boardwalk, landing a bit offside on the saddle of her gelding, her feet missing the stirrups. In less than a flash, the horse was running with stirrups flapping. The girl was screaming, but no one but the Indian turned his head her way.

To take his eyes off a man holding a weapon could turn out to be the last thing a man might do. Neither Ivan nor Rory was distracted by the scream.

She crossed the street with her gelding digging in as if he knew what his rider wanted. She was frantically whapping the poor beast across the flank with her hat.

Just as it looked as if she might ride right up onto the boardwalk and into the marshal's office, she swung the gelding in a sharp right and suddenly pulled him to a halt, his rear hooves digging in and his belly only inches from the ground. They came to a stop right in front of the three men. As if her right arm was an extension of her innermost fears, she ceased whapping the horse and turned her energies to whapping each of the men, knocking one brother's hat off his head and distracting her father from his growing hatred and fear of the young man in the chair.

"Pa, sometimes you're dumber than a sack of hammers. You might get away with being stupid up in Wind River country, where everyone fights shy of you, but this is town. Give me that carbine and back off."

"I'll do no such a thing. This man has spoken in a manner I can't and won't abide and pulled iron on me. I'll have my satisfaction or know the reason why. Now move off. Move, I say."

The girl turned her eyes first to one brother and then the other.

"You two are just as stupid. I suspect this man you're facing is the sheriff. You might have noticed he's sitting in front of the jail. With another sheriff, you might already be dead, lying on the road. Now you two move off. Junior, take Pa's carbine. Take it and move back. Micah, take Pa's horse after he steps to the ground."

As if the news of Rory being the sheriff had suddenly brought some sense to an otherwise strange, long minute, the brothers did as they were told. Boon Wardle, never once taking his eyes off Rory, stepped to the ground. The other two followed suit.

Still not rising to his feet, Rory said, "Take off that coat and unbuckle your hardware. Let it all drop to the road. And you other two. Do the same thing. Drop your hardware. All of it. And Miss, I appreciate you calling your father off his path, but the same goes for you. All the hardware. Right there on the road. And turn those horses loose."

As angry eyes studied Rory, one gun belt after another fell into the dust. The carbines, rather than being dropped, were laid down with some care. Rory appreciated the care of the weapons, but he also watched every move. The girl was the last to comply. When she showed further hesitation, she sensed movement beside her. Turning her head just slightly, she looked into the warning eyes of Nancy. Nancy nodded her head toward the two chairs that held Rory and Ivan.

"Cousin Rory generally means what he says."

SEEMINGLY OUT OF NOWHERE, Tippet was standing there with a double twelve-gauge resting in the crook of his left arm. Glancing at the sheriff as if he could read his wishes, he made his own decision. He stepped first to the girl. Holding out his right hand, he nodded at the horse. Without more hesitation, she passed him her reins. As that was happening, Nancy was gathering up the reins of the other three mounts. With just a quick glance to assure themselves that all was well, they headed to Tippet's barn. Neither Tippet nor Nancy could ever see a horse in need of feed, water, or grooming and not step up to the task.

Acting as if they were working off a script, Ivan rose to his feet, tucking his Colt back into its holster. No one seemed to have noticed that he had pulled it to the ready. He stepped to the big man, now standing coatless in the morning sun, and took him by one elbow. The man resisted for a bit but finally allowed himself to be led into the small office and right to the back of the space, where an open door beckoned entry into the single cell. Just before closing and locking the iron-barred door, Ivan said, "Fella, if I should find you holding a hidey weapon, I'm going to be real unhappy."

When the man offered no further weapons, Ivan closed and locked the door. He then went outside and gathered up all the guns. He was just in time to hear Rory say, "You three are free to go. But don't be doing anything foolish."

"What about Pa?"

"We'll have to see about that."

As if the previous incidents were dealt with and behind them, Rory asked the girl, "What was that talk about, looking for another son?"

"Key. Key Wardle. He sent a letter that he was settled down around here. Pa came to fetch him."

Nancy exploded with, "Key Wardle? Is that what this is all about? Key Wardle? You couldn't ask like civilized folks? You had to make this big fuss and nearly get yourselves a small space in the ground behind the church, and all you had to do was act decently?"

She turned to the sister, grabbed her by the arm, and said, "Come with me. Fools. You're all fools. Deserve whatever happens to you."

With Nancy still grumbling, she half dragged the sister to the mercantile. Inside, without stopping or hesitating, she pushed open the door to the back room and shoved the sister inside.

Key Wardle did a quick double take and then shot from his seat on the grain sack.

"Tempest? That you, Tempest? What gets you all the way down here? And why?"

He was about to ask more when Tempest said, "It's Pa. He wanted the family back together, so we rode down."

"Pa's here? Where is he?"

"In jail."

6

LATER THAT SAME AFTERNOON, TOWN MARSHAL KEY
Wardle sat uncomfortably behind the office desk. Before
him lay the badge he had decided not to wear, taking the
experience of County Sheriff Rory Jamison as a pattern
to follow. Across the small room, seated quietly on an
office chair, and surrounded by the rest of his kin, sat
Boon Wardle, owner and chief war dog of the Mirrored
W Ranch, the original and still largest ranch in the
remote Roaring Creek wilderness area of Wyoming, a
holding he had won and held with the gun, first against
Indians and later against rustlers and land-grabbers.

Marshal Wardle had no real idea what to say or how
to proceed. He fidgeted with the cell keys and avoided
looking at his father. The old man sat there like a tree
stump, immovable, unrepentant, and in no mood or
frame of mind to discuss his life decisions. Key knew full
well, from a lifetime of experience, that his father was
not about to recognize him as a grown man, let alone
town marshal. But as the new marshal, he had to say and
do something or fail on his first test as a lawman.

Forcing his head and eyes up to where he could look his father full-on, was one of the most difficult things the young man had ever done, but he did it.

"Pa, the sheriff left you in my hands. What was to become of you was passed on to me. So, here's what I've decided to do. Exactly nothing. That's what I've decided to do. You're free to go. You and the others too. But before you go, I'm going to tell you what you're too stubborn to see for yourself. Making unnecessary demands and challenging the sheriff in a strange town is one of the stupidest things you have ever done. And that's saying something, Pa. You've been known to do more than just a few stupid things. Someday you may come to understand that Rory had every right to put you in your grave. I've thanked him from the family that he held off doing that."

After an uncomfortable silence, with Boon Wardle studying his youngest son, not at all seeing what the young man had become, he finally blurted out, "Get your stuff and saddle up. We're heading home, all of us."

Key burst right out laughing, an unforgivable sin in the father's eyes.

"You still don't get it, Pa. I've told you. I wrote and told you, and I told you a few minutes ago. I like it here. I'm not going back. You may want to live in the wilderness on the backside of nowhere, chasing low-grade, half-wild cull cattle out of one coulee, only to have them escape into another, and living with the gun, but I don't. You've made you a wasted ride if that's all you came for."

Tempest spoke into the strained silence.

"I'm not going back either, Pa. I've taken over the job Key left at the supply store. I'll be staying on."

Micah, the oldest son, said, "That means My Way will be staying too. He only came to look out for Tempest."

Boon Wardle was seething inside but still too stubborn in his ideas of rightness to bend. Uncrossing his legs and stomping his foot to the wooden floor, raising a small cloud of dust, he slapped both big hands on his knees and, without lifting his eyes from his youngest son, stood to his full height.

"Do as you like. Both of you. You no longer have any place or right on the Mirrored W. Don't look for an inheritance when the time comes. Micah. Junior. Saddle up, we're leaving. Leaving just as soon as we have our hardware back, that is."

Key was forced by circumstances to say, "You'll not be getting your hardware back until you go to the sheriff's office up at the fort. Then you'll be placed under personal bond for as long as you're still in the state."

"That half-growed sheriff expecting us to ride without protection? I'll break his neck the next time I see him."

"You'll do no such a thing, Pa. If there's a tougher or more determined man, I don't know where you'd find him. You think you're pretty much of a man but you ain't hardly seen one yet. Don't you be crossing Rory Jamison. You head home. Ride easy, thankful that you're still able to ride at all. You go to the sheriff's office and ask politely for your weapons. Then you head home. If you go to cause trouble, you're guaranteed to lose.

"As soon as things are settled here for me in this marshal's position, I plan to ride up to Laramie. I have a hankering to see Ma. If you see her when you ride through, you take her a greeting from me. Tell her I think of her often."

7

RORY AND IVAN MANAGED TO RELAX AS THEY WATCHED the remnants of the Wardle family pulling away from the fort, heading north and home. Boon, the father and self-imagined family patriarch, remained glum and wordless, sitting in his big Appaloosa as his sons, Micah and Junior, entered the sheriff's office. A few words, unheard outside the office, passed between Rory and the young men as they strapped on their gun belts and took up their carbines. Micah slung his father's rig over his shoulder and turned to leave.

Rory said, "All those weapons are empty, and I cleaned them for you. Don't load them until you're well out of town."

The glum young men had nothing to say, but Ivan had a question; "Where's your sister? And the Indian?"

Junior answered, "Staying in town with Key. Pa ain't happy about it, but that cut no ice with Sis. My Way stays wherever Sis stays."

Ivan prodded a bit. "Just to help us understand, what's the story there?"

"Tempest, Sis, that is, came across the Indian wounded, fly-infested, and dying up one of the box canyons on the Mirrored W. We never did find out how he came to be in that condition or in that canyon. Sis, she boiled up some water and gave My Way some jerky to chew on and a canteen to wash the dust down with while she soaked the scabs and the yellow puss out of the wounds. She lived through a good deal of cussing, I'm thinking, ignoring it all because she only knows a few words of Blackfoot."

Telling the story seemed to break a bit of ice between the lawmen and the two brothers.

"The way she tells it, she was doing alright until My Way started singing his death song. That come near to being her undoing. But she stuck with it, cleaning the wounds and then stripping the rags he was dressed in and washing his body. Not sure I could have done that, but she stayed with him till the end and won the old man's forever allegiance. Finally, she wrapped him in her blanket and walked the horse home, with My Way sitting on the saddle. By that time, he had stopped with the singing.

"We don't know his history, but he's been peaceful enough since he settled in at the Mirrored W. I fear what might happen, though, if anyone should make a threat toward Tempest. I think it's best to just leave him alone."

AN HOUR after the Wardles had left, Rory was bored. There was no logical reason for a lawman to hope for anything but peace, and peace is what he saw on every hand at the fort. But a man can only hold down a half-barrel chair so long before something has to give.

"It's time we took a walk around town, Ivan. You head out to the south. I'll go north."

"What are we looking for?"

"You know, widows in distress, outhouses that need attention for the sake of the community, bad guys skulking around, a pretty girl you could ask to the dance, supposing someone should organize one. All the normal stuff."

"If you say so, boss. Wouldn't want to miss any of that normal stuff."

The two men grinned at each other and set off on their walk around town. The walk was slow and thorough, with several folks wanting to meet the new sheriff and deputy and have a visit. On his return, Ivan was nonchalant about the whole matter, but Rory came away feeling like a politician out for votes. He was just walking from behind the three retail establishments that adjoined the new sheriff's office and jail when Ivan came rushing toward him.

"Got a note here, Sheriff. Tate just pulled the stage in from the south. Passed along a note for you. Said it came from Key Wardle."

The two lawmen stood in the shade of the overhang in front of the office as Rory tore the envelope open. He stood on no formalities as he had with the note from Block Handly. He read the note out loud.

"Sonia rode down the hill alone this morning. Came right along wishing to report that a group of unknown men had taken up living at Kiril's place. Pavel rode close and got warned off. He said it looks like trouble."

"That must be the same bunch you thought had stacked up firewood for themselves, Rory."

Silently, as Rory held the note by his side, the two men were studying the situation. Not at all sure what to do, Rory said, "You see, Ivan, here's just one of the things I don't yet understand about this sheriffing job. There are apparently some folks taking up residence at Kiril's old claim. But so far as we've been able to find, Kiril left no will, so, really, one person has as much right to the cabin as the next person unless it's you by reason of your long friendship with the old man. But so far, you've shown no real interest in claiming land or building, either one.

"And then, we don't have any evidence that this bunch has done anything wrong. Could be they're prospectors or loggers. There's a sight of timber up there that could be turned into valuable lumber and sold into a growing community. And then, there are more and more mines being opened in the area. So far, the mining operations are small and simple one or two-man operations. But just as soon as a bigger strike is brought in, you'll see the big boys with the deep pockets move up from the established holdings to the south, storming the area.

"Kiril's cabin was sitting empty and a temptation to anyone needing shelter. So, what do I do? I could be kept busy every day chasing maybes. On the other hand, I'd feel guilty if I did nothing and later found that these fellas were up to no good."

Ivan followed the thoughts that were behind the conversation, nodding when he found himself agreeing. But he had a few thoughts of his own too.

"Except for Kiril himself, there's no one knows that area like I do. I know trails and hidey-holes that none of these newcomers will know. You keep your eye on things here and I'll ride down to the homeplace. I'll leave my horse on the I-5 and scout around on foot. I guarantee no one will see me or be able to follow. Give me a few days up there and I'll know everything there is to know about that bunch."

~

LATE THAT AFTERNOON, Ivan tied off in front of the marshal's office and jail in Stevensville. Key Wardle noticed his actions through the recently cleaned office window. Stepping outside, he greeted the deputy sheriff.

"Evening, Ivan. What brings you to our little town? I thought maybe the bright lights up at the fort might have pulled you in and not let you loose again."

"A lantern's just a lantern, Key. Don't mean much no matter where it sets."

"Well, speaking of sett'n, step down, take a weight off your tailbone. Come tell me what's happening."

The two men stood for a few minutes talking of home and hopes before the subject turned to the happening in the hills above the town.

"No one knows those hills like I do, Key, now that Kiril's gone. Heard of some happenings up there. Might be good to take a look. And then the miners have been moving up this way for the past while. Might drop in to a few of the small ranchers up there. See what they can tell me about the goings-on in the hills."

Key walked along as Ivan led his horse to the livery.

"First planned to ride up to the ranch this evening. Spend some time with the folks. Might be best, though, to go in the morning. Let my horse take a rest before we face the hill trail."

Wondering where Ivan might be figuring to take his rest for the night, Key had to search for words. Sharing the two cots in the small room at the back of the marshal's office had been the normal practice, but that was before Key had become marshal and before the Wardle family had arrived from Wyoming, stirring up unnecessary dust. When they headed back north, Tempest, Key's sister, had stayed on. My Way, with no particular plans in life and not appearing to much care, had appointed himself guardian over the young woman. The past couple of nights, Key had talked the Indian into taking the second bunk. Fortunately, Ivan solved the question without really addressing it.

"Figure to see if the barber is still at his stand. Might get a clip and a bath, then take a hotel bed for the one night."

"Join us for dinner after you're settled down? Might have a thought for you to mull over."

"Sure enough. I'll get my bath and then whistle you up. What do My Way and Tempest do for living space?"

"Tempest has a room over where Sonia stays. My Way bunks in with me. My Way prefers the grub down at the cantina. I'll see if Tempest will join us for dinner. It might be good if the local law could see that some of the Wardle family are fit to trust in the town."

SITTING with a final cup of coffee after taking on Ma's finest dinner, Ivan asked, "Does My Way speak English?"

Tempest answered, "He does, when he speaks at all, which is rarely. He speaks in single words anyway. I think he understands far more than he speaks. Why do you ask?"

"I'm working over an idea. I'm heading up into the hills first thing in the morning. I know the trails and the hidey-holes, like I already said, so I can slink my way through the country pretty well. I have a need to know what's going on up there. Nothing particular to my suspicions. Just thoughts. But two men who know how to be quiet can see more than one. I'd take My Way along if he wanted to go and if he's able to communicate on some level."

Key studied his sister for a moment and then said, "I'll talk to him. He likes to keep his eye on Tempest, watching for threats and such, but I'm sure the town must appear pretty safe to him. I can't imagine he enjoys just sitting all day. I'm guessing he'll be ready when you're ready in the morning."

MORNING FOUND Ivan and the Indian riding up the hill to the I-5. The Ivanov family were a bit hesitant at first at the sight of a buckskin-clad Indian, but when he took a place at the breakfast table and ate with a fork, although he cut his meat with his belt knife, ignoring the table cutlery laid out by Mrs. Ivanov, the tension seemed to break.

The two men left their horses at the I-5 Ranch and proceeded on foot. My Way carried a Henry rifle. Ivan carried a .44-40 Winchester and a belted .44.

WHILE IVAN and My Way were exploring the hillside trails behind his home ranch and upward from Kiril's cabin, life for the sheriff was quiet at the fort. One thing was bothering Rory, though. He felt he could sense that the townsfolk were thinking of him as town marshal as well as county sheriff. Several small matters had been thrust his way. Matters that would drag him away from his elected position but were not, in truth, a part of his job.

He made his way for a talk with Grady Stiles.

"Morn'n, Sheriff. Everything quiet this fine day?"

"Just as fine as good weather and good folks can make it. I have a question, though."

"Fire away, Sheriff."

"It seems clear the townsfolks are accepting of me as the county sheriff, but some have mentioned being town marshal in the same conversation. I can't fill both posts. Being sheriff will often mean being away for some length of time. It's a big county. And with the mining claims working their way north into our area, there'll be more and more work for me up there. I'm thinking town council should put their heads together and find themselves a marshal. We could share the office and lockup if that would help."

Grady Stiles grinned and answered, "Way ahead of you, Sheriff. There was a young man in here a couple of days ago asking for the job. Town council will decide at our meeting tonight."

SATISFIED WITH THAT NEWS, Rory rode down to the ranch for a couple of days, hoping to get a bit of rest before Ivan returned with whatever trouble he managed to uncover up in the hills.

When he returned to the fort, as usual, he tied off on the shady side of the county office and strolled slowly around the corner, to the marshal's door. He found it unlocked. Immediate concern coursed through his mind, while vigilance caused him to grip one of his Colts, without actually lifting the .44 from its holster. He took a cautious step inside and stopped, staring. There, sitting in the office chair, looking as if he belonged, was a somehow familiar man. He couldn't immediately place the fella or pick a name out of the many names stored in his sometimes overpacked memory. The two men studied each other, Rory with a questioning look on his face, the other with a grin forming on his lips.

"I was told you were formally elected sheriff here now, Rory. Of course, there's been much talk of your actions freely circulating around Cheyenne for the past year and a half, near enough. But you don't remember me, do you?"

"I see something familiar, but you're going to have to help me out here. At the same time, you can explain why you're here in this office, looking as if you belong."

"That's because I do belong, Sheriff. Wiley Hamstead. We met on the train. I was doing a poor job of escorting your cousin Hannah home to your family ranch. You pulled Hannah, and me, too, out of a tight spot. I believe I thanked you at the time, but I'd be pleased to tell you again how frightened I was and how out of my depth I felt. I could have as easily protected the lady from a lightning storm as from that fella who was making such a nuisance of himself. So, thank you, Rory Jamison, county sheriff and, I hope, future friend."

Rory let his hand drop away from the Colt. Not quite returning the seated man's grin, he said, "I remember the incident, of course. But you've grown some since that time. Put some beef on your bones. Filled out some in the face too. The eastern softness is gone. I see a couple of scars on your hands. Almost as if you've been in a situation or two that demanded a physical solution. And the hat and boots, plus the belted Colt, say you have either become a westerner or a play actor. The one could bring you a welcome. The other could make you dead if you pretend to be something you're not set up for."

Wiley Hamstead stood and held out his hand. "The town fathers accepted my offer of taking up the marshaling duties. I've been deputy for the Cheyenne City sheriff since coming west. Learned some hard lessons fast. Found I like the West, and I like peace-keeping."

The two men shook hands, and each dropped into a chair, with Wiley holding to the seat behind the single desk. Neither man spoke for a long half minute, but finally, Rory said, "Last thing I would have expected, you taking up a sheriff's or marshal's duties, either one. You made mention of having studied for the law. I would have expected to find you wearing a suit and tie and appearing in court on some legal matter."

"And you may yet see that happen. I continue to read legal journals and keep up as best I can with the eastern press as they report on court cases. But in the meantime, I have to make a living, and wearing a badge has done that for me. And speaking of badges, I see you don't wear one."

Rory repeated the shortened version of his close call because of the tell-tale pinholes in his shirt. "Threw that shirt away. Never since wore a badge. Got it in my pocket in case of the need to identify myself."

The two men talked away for the next hour, with Rory wanting to know what experiences Wiley had seen in Cheyenne, and Wiley trying subtly to change the conversation to the Double J Ranch and Hannah. Both men were fully aware of what the other was doing. Finally, Rory stood, adjusted his gun belt, and replaced his hat.

"I'll buy you lunch, just this once, as a welcome to town."

They didn't think of it themselves, but they made a sight that called attention from several onlookers as they crossed the road to the hotel dining room; two tall, well-put-together young men, carrying the strength and hopes of their youth and the badges that announced that they were the law in the county and at the fort.

Sitting at lunch in a quiet corner of the dining room, Wiley eased into a matter that Rory would just as soon forget, wishing it had never happened.

"There was a story circulating around the Cheyenne area that got a lot of attention. Strange, though. There were no names in the story, yet everyone appeared to be sure it centered around this young deputy sheriff who was making a name for himself down this way. We'll call it gossip, because that's really what it was, though it got a lot of attention on the rougher side of the tracks. Wasn't long before the wild ones were daring each other to take a ride down this way. Get the truth of the tale, you might say. At least one would-be gunman, young fella named Sky Blue, rode out but never returned. That story got folks wondering."

When Rory didn't take up the story, one of the bitter memories he had of holding the badge, Wiley allowed it to drop.

AFTER LUNCH, back in the marshal's office, Rory said, "I'm heading down to Stevensville for a while. My deputy is up in the hills above town checking on a report that came in. Since we don't have the telegraph yet, if you need to get a hold of me, the best way is to write a note and pass it directly to the stage driver. It's not a fast system, but it's what we have. In the meantime, I'm sure you've noted all the travelers wending their way through town. Some will be men following up on the news of new mineral strikes, and some will be folks looking to find a new home and a place to settle. Some, and not just a few, I'm thinking, have come to find a way to profit from the work of others. You'll find you need to use discretion and judgment in sorting the builders from the potential troublemakers.

"And it's really none of my business, but to save you asking more questions that I have to find a way around, Hannah is teaching school in town and living on the ranch. The ranch is only about two miles from town, so it's not a long ride for her, morning and night. What you do with that information is your own concern."

Wiley found no need to comment, but he did wish Rory safe travels, smiling the whole while.

8

IVAN WAS ALONE, HUNCHED DOWN, UNDER A WIDE-LIMBED Engelmann spruce tree, where the ends of the bottom branches lay draped on the grass like the train on a lady's fancy dress. He had spent an uncomfortable night there, wishing every minute for a second blanket and a pot of coffee to ward off the uphill coolness. My Way had disappeared the evening before. He had simply said, "I look," as he pointed to a jumble of windblown trees laying every which way over the large gathering of moss and lichen-covered rocks at the base of a cliff. Ivan hadn't seen him since.

For the first three days of their vigil tracking and watching the men who were camped at Kiril's abandoned cabin, Ivan and My Way had been able to quietly make their way into the loft above the small barn, spending their nights half buried in hay. Ivan had been able to use his belt knife to split one roof shake, pushing the two halves apart far enough for him to keep a periodic watch on the happening in the cabin and yard. It would have taken a keen eye to notice the misplaced shingle from anywhere in the yard. The four men housing themselves in the cabin had shown no interest in barn roofs. So far, all he was sure of was that they had killed and butchered one I-5 steer and that they spent their days skulking around the adjoining hillsides. He watched them cut a bit of brush here and there to expose the rock beneath. He both heard and saw them tapping rock with small hammers each man had slung to their belts. They had all the appearance of prospectors, but still, Ivan felt there was more to it.

At times My Way hunkered beside Ivan. At other times he ventured off on his own, returning as silently as he had left.

When their explorations took them further afield the day before, the two men, being afoot after having left the horses at the I-5 Ranch, took to hiding under the tree to avoid the long walk back to the loft hideaway, in the hopes that the men would return in the morning. They did.

Ivan, growing up on the I-5 in a family that avoided mixing with others and having no particular love of cattle or ranching himself, had spent days and weeks wandering the hills. When he befriended Kiril, the two of them wandered together from time to time. Kiril seemed to know every hill and corner of the mountain, although he showed no real interest in any of it. His wanderings had no particular purpose as far as Ivan could discern. Of course, later, when it was found that the old man was somehow mixed up in the matter involving stolen gold coins and rustled cattle, questions arose in Ivan's mind as well as his friend Rory's. Together they had partially solved the matter but were unable to get to the bottom of the mystery that died with Kiril.

Now, Ivan's knowledge of the hills and hollows that made up the mountainside above the I-5 was being put to use. As county deputy sheriff, he forced himself to look beyond one rustled and butchered beef from his family's ranch. These men were up to something, but he had, so far, been unable to see what it was or where their wanderings were leading.

After another strange and, to Ivan, fruitless day of walking, crawling, and hiding while they trailed the four mysterious men, he abandoned the spruce tree and made his way in the semidarkness to the cabin. By the end of that day, he had been about ready to give up on the whole vigilance idea. The men had ridden back down to the cabin, leaving their unnoticed shadow to walk the long couple of miles. By the time he reached Kiril's small holding, Ivan had talked himself into taking more affirmative action. He scouted the barn and corrals to assure himself that all the men were in the cabin. With that evidence satisfactorily stored in his mind, he walked to the single cabin door. Two gentle, quiet steps put him on the door stoop, with the door handle close to hand, ready to twist and push. Following the teaching of his friend Rory, and even thinking the words Rory so often said, he led with his carbine. Stepping in, with a magazine full of .44-40 slugs and with the gaping muzzle of the weapon focused on one of the suspects in the case, had a quieting effect on any immediate resistance.

If the door had been locked by those inside, Ivan would be facing a different situation. A simple twist of his wrist had proven that the men felt secure enough in their borrowed quarters. A slight click was the only sound the lock made before the door swung open silently on well-oiled hinges. Four heads lifted from their dinner plates and turned toward the movement.

Looking at four hands holding four forks in midair almost made Ivan laugh. He settled for a grin.

"Evening, fellas."

As Ivan said those two words, he stepped to the side, enough to move him away from the door opening and behind the security of the thick log wall.

"If you men would kindly unbuckle your belts and drop them on the floor behind you, we could have us a friendly talk."

"And who exactly are you?"

The speaker appeared to be the oldest of the four and the one Ivan had pegged as the leader during his long hours of watching and trailing these men.

"Name's Ivan Ivanov. As to why I'm here and what interest I have in you men, there are really three answers. I'll only be giving you two of them right at this time. First, this is by rights my cabin and my land. And second, that's I-5 beef you're eating, and I own the I-5, along with a brother and my parents. So, you see, I really am serious when I tell you to rid yourselves of the iron."

He had initially thought of telling the group about being deputy sheriff but then thought better of it.

Very carefully and slowly, each man leaned far enough from the table to reach the buckle that would release their weapons. The man closest to Ivan held his belt in his left hand and raised it high enough to lay it on the table. He had been told to lay it on the floor, but Ivan didn't make an issue of it. One by one, each man followed suit.

"Push them all this way."

When that was done, Ivan stepped forward and worked his arm under the pile of leather and guns. He lifted it and, with three quick steps to the still-open door, he dropped the four handguns, their belts, and holsters on the ground outside.

"Now, the next thing is for you to dig in and lay one hundred dollars on the table. Gold or paper, either one."

"What's that for? That's a lot of money."

"Why, mister, that's so's we can say honestly that you paid a bit of rent on my cabin and that you bought that beef. Otherwise, I'll have to turn you in for rustling. I'd march you all down to the jailhouse and have the law hold you over till the judge can get down from the fort. And I might mention that the judge spent some years being raised on a hardscrabble ranch, struggling from meal to meal. He takes a dim view of stock stealing. So, you can see how it might just be easier to buy that beef."

The man who Ivan had singled out as the leader said, "Got to get my pouch from my saddlebag."

Ivan watched his every move as he bent to the saddle, but there was no effort made to pull a hideout weapon. The man stood and dropped the pouch on the table, saying, "This will go hard on us. We're not rich men. And, mister, you had better hope we don't find out that you're lying about the brand or this being your cabin. Facing you with an even break might change the situation considerably."

After pocketing the gold coins, Ivan said, "Well, I'm not lying. Not in either case. Now, while we're all here and so friendly, I'll help myself to what's left in that frying pan. That and a cup of coffee. And you can tell me what you're doing up here and what you hope to find. And while I'm dishing up, you can give me your names."

Reluctantly the names rolled out. The leader said, "I'm known as Chouse Ramble. This fella beside me is Grit Price." Pointing with his thumb to the end of the table, he said, "That there is Toby Whitelaw, Diego Ramirez."

Ivan stood beside the now-closed door while he ate, holding his plate with one hand and watching every move the men made. The carbine was leaning against the wall beside him. His Colt was within easy reach.

"Alright, now tell me what you're doing. I've been following you for three days. Seen you cutting brush and pulling growth off, baring the rock beneath. Watched you tapping on rocks but didn't see you taking any samples to keep. From a distance, you look like prospectors, but closeup, not so much. And, so far as I know, all the mining finds are further up into the hills."

Chouse Ramble sneered, "Lot you know! There's claims enough to north and south both. All along the river and up along Blackhorn Creek. Ain't much of a creek, comes to that, but it's a way of knowing where a man is. A dividing line, you might almost figure. You say you know this country. Don't know as much as you say you do, I'm thinking. I'm about ready to call you for a phony."

Ivan chose to ignore the man's challenging words in place of digging for more important information.

"Tell you what I'll do, fellas. You paid for the beef, so we'll say no more about that. Except if you take another, it won't be paid for in silver. I'll give you tonight and one more night in the cabin. Then I'll be wanting to see no more of you. Is that clearly understood?"

Again, Chouse Ramble spoke threats. Threats and a promise.

"You and your bunch don't scare me. Don't scare me at all. We run that other I-5 man off. Took off with his tail between his legs. And set that gun down and meet me man-to-man, we'll see who stays and who goes."

Ivan found a grin somewhere and flashed it at the braggart.

"That man you say you ran off is my brother. He left because he faced four drawn guns. Pavel likes his peaceful life, but don't let that fool you. He'll stand, and he'll be standing when the smoke clears. As to my father, he learned his guerrilla fighting in an old country. He's forgotten things you'll never live long enough to learn. And then there's me. You take your one more night here and then be gone. You just can't live through any other option."

With that, Ivan slipped sideways, lifting his carbine as he moved, and was out the door into the dwindling twilight. Choosing to take to the hills again, rather than the barn loft, he started up a known trail through a small draw. After a quarter-hour of climbing, he turned a slight bend and came to where My Way was sitting on a trailside rock. There might have been a small grin on his face, but it was hard to tell in the near dark. The Indian simply stood, and with a single word, "come," he led off.

They didn't go far before My Way veered off to the right and into a dense aspen grove. Ivan had always believed he was good on a trail and able to slip into tight spots as well as anyone. But when My Way eased through the close-growing aspens with hardly a twig moving, he was forced to rethink all that. The man was like a ghost, even in the bush.

My Way led the way into a rock overhang that would shelter several men if the need was there. He turned past a pillar-like rock at one corner and ducked behind to where a bed of leaves and moss lay. Without asking, Ivan knew that this was where My Way had spent the last couple of nights.

"Good place, My Way. I didn't know this was here."

"No one know."

Ivan acknowledged that truth with a nod of his head.

"I will gather some leaves for a bed before full dark."

THE WELL-SHELTERED CAVE, facing north, was still in darkness when the birds in the grove were waking the world to the fact that another day was dawning bright and clear. Ivan could hear something scurrying through the sparse grass at the foot of the trees. And somewhere off, a crow called. My Way slipped to his side, and the two men knelt silently together, tasting the morning, studying its risks. After a few moments, My Way slipped back into the darkness of the cave, and soon, a small fire was sputtering on night-dampened twigs and dried leaves.

Leaving the fire, and breakfast, if that is what it was to be, to the Indian, Ivan eased through the grove, stopping well before he would become easily visible. Again, he looked and listened. There was nothing. No sound but what nature offered. And then there was.

Horses. Too far away to see or to judge their number. Then a click of an iron shoe on a rock, a slight stumbling sound, and a gasped out, "Low branch!" If he had to guess, Ivan would have said the voice was that of Chouse Ramble. Grinning to himself, he thought, *You've got some learning to do if you're going to skulk around these hills.*

Another voice answered the first. "I know where the low branches are. What I want to know is where those sacks got off to."

"Why don't you shout it from the highest hill, you fool? Your voice can be heard for a half mile in these hills."

Those words came from a different voice. He didn't know which of the men it could be. At the cabin, he had only heard Chouse speak.

Ivan waited until he could no longer hear the clop of hooves on the soft trail before turning back to the cave. He bent to clear the entry and then stood fully upright once inside. The small space had taken on a good heat from the fire. There was already a nice bed of hot coals. Dried aspen burns fast, but the remnants build up quickly to form the hot bed that is ideal for cooking. My Way had skinned and gutted a rabbit, slitting it down the back. Each half was spitted on a green branch sunk into the floor of the cave. The aroma was just beginning to be released. The aroma and the juice that was dripping onto the hot bed of coals, causing smoke to rise, enveloping the meat.

Ivan caught the Indian's eye and grinned with a nod at the fire. He then asked, "Could you hear the riders going past from in here?"

"I hear."

There was no expression of feelings as he said the two words, but he grinned a bit as he rummaged around in the corner of the cave and stood, passing Ivan four small canvas sacks that could only be holding gold. Of course, at full light, he would check the contents, but his heart told him it would only confirm what he already knew.

It was only caution that kept Ivan from laughing out loud.

"Where did you find this, my friend? Those men sounded pretty upset as they rode past. I suspect this might have something to do with that."

Ivan immediately thought his long sentence might have been too much for My Way. If it was, the curt, "I

71

find," assured him that whatever the Indian's shortcomings were, his abilities would be more than adequate.

The two men squatted on their heels as they tore the rabbit, piece by piece, into chewable portions. They dug out what remained by holding the skeleton to their teeth and pulling out what they could get a hold of. When they were done, Ivan held out his hand for the remains of My Way's half. He walked to the entrance and buried the bones under a layer of leaves a few feet into the grove. My Way brushed out the remains of the fire and scraped it over the cave floor. A filtering of dirt would disguise it from all but the most observant visitor. They scraped their beds of leaves into the forest with the sides of their feet. Ivan was wearing boots. My Way was wearing moccasins, which left virtually no visible marks. Ivan had to go back over his work, using his hands to brush out the boot marks. The cave looked undisturbed when they left. Idly Ivan wondered why they had bothered. The chances of anyone else finding the cave or caring who was there before them were slim.

Ivan took off his shirt, leaving only his long-sleeved underwear to cover his upper body. With the shirt, he made a satisfactory pocket to hold the hide sacks. He tied this around his waist for easy carrying.

"Let's go get our horses."

My Way only nodded in response.

9

THE BAWLING OF A HUNGRY AND THIRSTY HERD COULD not be disguised. Or ignored. Nor could the shouts of the drovers.

Rory had said goodbye to Marshal Wiley just moments before, swinging into the saddle, headed for the Double J and Stevensville. When he heard the bawling of cattle, he stepped up his pace to get clear of the town and to a point where he might see what was happening. Once past the big livery barn, the last building to block the view to the east, he could see a small herd of whiteface cattle plodding their tired way toward the river. Through the dust cloud, he counted eight riders, plus a wrangler who was trying to hold a small remuda of spare horses. The smell of water was soon going to make his job near impossible but unnecessary, in any case. The animals, cattle and horses alike, would run for a short way and then stop at the river. As he watched, the point rider pulled off to the side and waved for the other rides to pull off as well. He sat watching as the cattle picked up their pace at the smell of water. Although still a good half mile off, he could see that these were young whiteface animals. They would have little inclination to break into a run, unlike their longer-legged longhorn cousins.

Studying the herd and then the riders, the bulk of them still at a distance, Rory thought he recognized one of the Double J blood-red bay horses. The finely bred animals had a look of distinction that was difficult to miss. If this was the boys back with their replacement heifers, new times were about to begin on the Double J. Idly, he thought, *I own half of those*. The thought wasn't typical of the way his mind worked. He seldom gave any thought at all to money or accumulating wealth. He owned half the Double J, and he still had a sizable deposit in two Denver banks and a smaller deposit in the bank in Stevensville, all from the gold he and his father had worked and suffered for over their three years in the wilderness. He wasn't careless with money, but he didn't horde it either. But, still, the idea that half the animals in the bunch now at the river were his did something unde-finable in his mind and heart. Perhaps he wasn't as detached from the ranch as he had once thought.

Rory stayed clear of the dust cloud enveloping the herd until the riders broke free. He then eased forward to meet the men coming his way. The cattle would stay by the river, contentedly slaking their thirst or pulling on the available grass until they were driven onward.

Henry and Thomas pulled together and pointed their way toward where Rory sat his horse. Henry, often the more expressive of the two, lifted his hat and hollered, "Hello, cousin. What do you think of your new heifers?"

Rory waited until the men were close enough for normal talk before he said, "Looking good, fellas, you should be able to have them on the J before full dark tomorrow. And welcome home. The folks will be glad to see you. You and the animals, both. I'm just heading that way and then down to town. I'll pass the news to the ranch. And I'll be happy to hear your story another time. Right now, you're busy, and I have to be somewhere else pretty soon."

"Tell the folks that all is well. We'll see them tomorrow."

With that brief greeting, the two cousins turned back to their jobs, and Rory pointed his gelding south.

AFTER ONE NIGHT in his own cabin on the ranch, with Kiril's dog guarding the door after wagging him a great welcome, Rory rode up to the marshal's office in Stevensville. Marshal Key stepped out to greet him.

"Morning, Key. Wondering if Ivan has shown back up yet. He was going up into the hills a few days ago."

"Hasn't come back yet that I've seen. He and My Way rode up to the I-5 like you said. He left no word on how long he'd be gone."

"My Way? The Indian rode with him?"

"I managed to convince him that Tempest would be under no threat here in town. I think he was glad to be riding again. And Ivan was glad to have him along once he was convinced that My Way talks enough English to make himself understood."

Rory glanced off to the early morning sky as if seeking inspiration or explanation.

"Maybe I'll just go ahead and ride up the hill myself. They may have shown back up at the I-5."

Two hours later, the Ivanov men were assuring Rory that they had seen nothing of the deputy or the Indian since they had ridden off a few days before.

"Left their horses here. Set out walking. Horses are still here."

Rory offered his thanks and rode off, heading toward Kiril's cabin. Once on the property the old man had left behind, Rory dismounted and, after very carefully looking all around, entered the small structure. The place looked much as it had before, except that the men bunking there had left dirty dishes scattered on the table. Rory left them as they lay and walked to the barn, taking a quick study of the chicken coop as he walked past. Nothing in the barn looked disturbed. Only the extra hoof-turned dirt in the corral and the liberal gatherings of fresh droppings indicated any recent use. There was no sign of Ivan or My Way.

Rory gathered up the reins and stepped into the saddle. Taking another careful look around as he rode toward the hillside trail, he was satisfied that there was no one anywhere around. If the four campers had intended to return, they would most likely have left their bedrolls or some other indication. There was nothing. Rory turned to the trail and continued on his uphill journey. To exactly what or where he wasn't sure, but he was going anyway. He missed meeting Ivan and My Way by less than one hour.

After several hours of walking, Ivan and My Way, carefully hidden away in the brush and forest, gave Kiril's cabin site a studied look. There was no sign of activity and no horses in the corral. Deciding that nothing had changed since they were last there, they moved on toward the I-5. That evening they were sitting at a table with the family. They intended to stay one night and move out early the next morning. This time, on horseback.

My Way couldn't be talked into spending the night in the cabin. When Ivan said, "As you like, my friend," My Way thanked Mrs. Ivanov for the meal with a nod of his head and left the cabin. He retrieved his blankets from the saddle shed and disappeared into the bush behind the barn. He was saddled and ready the next morning when Ivan emerged from the cabin.

Ivan retrieved the four gold pouches from the feed trough he had hidden them in and took them to his brother, Pavel, with instructions to hide them well. He and My Way then rode toward the same trail Rory had taken the afternoon before. Ivan hoped to somehow find the four men from Kiril's cabin and follow them. He wanted to know where they got the gold and what they were planning next. And he knew Rory would want that same information. He might have accepted their plea of innocence, but when My Way found the hidden gold pouches, that thought disappeared.

RORY SAW Mrs. Lander's BL Ranch in the distance but didn't bother riding in. He was looking for mining activity, not small ranches. He had never climbed the hill beyond the BL. To get to the Half Anchor, he had ridden more or less north of the BL and just a bit to the west, but in a different valley system.

He found his first sign of digging in a small, lonely, steep-sided valley a couple of miles above the Lander's spread. He would have missed the small diggings if he hadn't heard a hammer striking steel. He left the trail and followed a narrow path winding through the brush that led him to a small, open area. At first glance, he saw nothing. Only as he rode a bit closer did he see the opening in the hillside with the small pile of tailings at its mouth. Two men who had heard him coming were hidden behind their own tailings' pile, lying flat, with their rifles at the ready, following the sound of Rory's horse. About the same time the diggings came into view, one of the miners made a slight movement, which caused a flash of reflected sunlight to grab Rory's attention. He pulled his ride to a halt and studied the situation before him.

He had already decided that his best approach in the mining territory would be to tell right off that he was county sheriff. He slowly lifted his right hand into the air and said, loud enough for the hidden men to hear, "County Sheriff Rory Jamison here, men. I'm alone. I didn't know you were here. Just riding through. But I'd like to have a talk while I'm here."

A voice from behind the tailings pile said, "You got any proof of all that?"

"Got a badge in my pocket."

"You might have traded a beer for a badge in some saloon."

"I might have, but I didn't."

After a short pause, waiting for a response that didn't come, Rory lowered his hand and picked up the reins. He turned his horse halfway around and said, "I'll be on my way, men. Could be we'll meet again someday."

His horse had taken no more than three steps when the voice rose again.

"Keep your hands where we can see them and come on in. We'll have us a visit."

Rory turned the animal back toward the diggings but didn't move forward until the two men stood. One held his rifle more or less in Rory's direction while his partner climbed back to the top of the broken rock. Only when both men were standing at the mine mouth, and their rifles were tucked into their folded arms did Rory move forward. His carbine was secure in its scabbard, but his jacket was open, exposing both .44s. There was no sign of trust until Rory dropped the reins across the gelding's neck and stepped to the ground.

Slowly, carefully, so the men could watch his actions, Rory fished the badge from the small pocket worked into his canvas pants. With the little pocket half covered by his gun belt, the whole thing was a nuisance, but he wasn't wearing his usual vest, so he had nowhere secure to keep the badge. He held the bit of metal so the men could see it and waited. The miner who appeared to be the spokesman, glanced at the stamped badge and licked his lips. He looked at his partner and then into Rory's eyes. Nothing was said while ten short breaths could be taken. Finally, the miner said, "Alright, find yourself a comfortable rock and set by. I'll stir up that fire and see what I can do for coffee."

The man who had yet to speak, now said, "Name's Badger. This here is Rawlins. What's the sheriff doing up here? We've heard of no trouble up this way."

"I'm just nosing around. I haven't been this high on the mountainside before. I had some dealing with the ranches down below last year or so. Thought I'd just ride up and see what's happening. The news down in town is that there's a lot of activity happening up here. What can you tell me? Where do you get supplies and such? And have you heard of any strikes promising enough to bring the big boys in?"

Badger looked at Rory for a long time before he answered, "You aren't going to get many folks to talk about their finds. That's held as being private. You nose in too far, someone will take to sett'n you to rights."

Rory smiled in response and said, "I know you're telling the truth. But I wasn't asking about your operation. I'm asking about what you might have heard. I might as well tell you, too, that I worked gold myself for some years. My father and me. But that was panning. Digging old stream beds and panning out the sand. A few years ago, and far from here. I've never worked rock."

That seemed to open a slight bit of daylight on the conversation. Badger studied Rory through another short pause and said, "I expect gold is gold. Expect it spends about the same, too, no matter how it's come by. But I'm not telling any secrets when I say there's more than gold being found in these folds of rock."

"I've no personal interest in mining, men. I hold a share in a cattle operation down below. When I get tired of toting the badge, I'll probably find my way back there. Hammering on rock holds no attraction for me. But I admire you fellas that do the hard work and who know how to go about it. Seems to me, though, that it would take a site of knowledge to know one find from another. There're stories enough of men who were walking all over silver laden tailing while they kept digging for gold, having no idea what they had already found."

Rawlins nodded and replied, "Did my own share of that up on the Comstock. Walked away from a good claim with nothing in my hand but blisters and a broken pick. Next man made a fortune off my little bit of a claim. That was way back, before the war. Learned some though. Badger and me, we hope to be smarter this time."

The three men drank their coffee in near silence while Rory tried to figure out a way to learn more. In the end, he settled for asking where the men bought their supplies.

"You ride back the way you came. Keep on up the hill. Few miles along that way, you come to a heavily used two-track road. Connects this hill with a couple of the bigger towns to the south. Seems the fellas that started it all didn't want to tackle this hill for a trail. Decided to connect with the towns already up and running. You come to that two-track, you turn to the north. You'll come to a small settlement. Calls itself MacNair's Hill. Fella named MacNair started 'er up maybe one year back. Maybe a bit more. Runs the mercantile and the saloon. Few other operations close by. Does some assaying."

"Have you seen any other riders going by on the uphill trail?"

"Never seen any riders at all. Seems no one from down below bothers climbing higher than those few ranches you mentioned. Saw no one until just a couple of days ago, that is. Four hard-looking riders spotted us and came in to nose around. We gave them a Winchester welcome, and they decided to keep on riding."

"Thanks, fellas. I'll be riding myself. Anyone else down this little valley, or do you have it to yourselves?"

"There's been a few tapping on rocks here and there. Don't know if any have stayed. Don't even know how far this valley goes. Neither of us has bothered to find out. But no one's come this way in some time."

"I'll wish you good digging, men, and be on my way."

When Rory looked back just before he turned up the hill trail, the two men were still standing there, watching. Remembering how lonesome the claim was in Idaho and how he often longed for company, he thought, *Lonely business, this digging for wealth.*

Rory continued on the uphill trail until it joined the larger road. He rode down the two-track until, two hours later, it burst from the forest, exposing a widening in the rocky valley. There before him lay a settlement much larger than he had anticipated. He suddenly had the thought, watching the activity of the town, that these were county voters. He knew there was some activity up this way, but he thought of a few prospectors digging holes here and there. He never imagined there would be a town, so he hadn't extended his census work that far.

"Best leave it alone," he said to himself. *"There'll be other votes and other elections."*

Rory rode slowly down the center of the dirt street, taking in the sight of a collection of mostly newly built structures. The crudely painted sign at the entrance identified the settlement as *MacNair's Hill*. The town was much larger than he had expected. He had wondered as he followed the two-track wagon road, thinking the road was almost too good, taking too much effort to cut out of the bush if it was just servicing a few small one-man operations. But what he was riding into was a sure enough small village. There had been a considerable amount of work put into clearing brush and rocks, making the trail passable for wheeled traffic. And now he saw why.

Along the way, he had passed several hopeful mining operations and a few that were clearly abandoned. He hadn't stopped to visit. He waved at the few diggers that showed themselves and ignored the other operations as he moved on toward what became MacNair's Hill.

Welcoming the traveler to MacNair's Hill, the first building on the street was the mercantile and saloon, housed in a single, rambling, added-to wooden structure. On a corner of the structure, creating an odd angle that didn't match either the road or the side road that veered off toward the back of the big store, looking like an afterthought, was the assay office. Beyond that corner, a wide assortment of businesses had established themselves along the street.

The little settlement was busy with foot traffic on the disjointed, multilevel boardwalk. A few riders were coming and going. Judging by the activity around the few mine sites, Rory could see the population of MacNair's Hill would increase substantially when the day's work was done and men were let loose from their backbreaking toil.

There were a few large ore wagons being hauled by plodding teams of horses and in one case, oxen. He could see the beginnings of an ore-crushing hammer mill, known as a stamp mill, under construction further down the valley.

The buildings on one side of the road came just short of clinging to the steep mountain slope forming one side of the narrow valley. The two-track leading to the village had followed a fair-sized stream for several miles. There was another small source of water tumbling down the mountainside, joining the larger stream before it entered the settlement. A thrown-together log bridge allowed traffic to flow unimpeded by the gully that channeled the small stream. Most of the town itself was built high above the stream, which formed the base of the small valley. Only a few buildings, crowded out of the built-up, older section of town, were forced to build closer to the running water. Judging by looks and weathering, the oldest building in town would be less than two years old.

Much of the nearby mountainside was bare of trees, leaving only a scrabble of bushes and stumps. It was logical that builders would harvest their materials as closely as possible to their work, but Rory feared future heavy rains or snowmelts might bring some of the loose hillside down with the flow. The need for mine timbers, as the digging went deeper into the rocks, would take another large bite out of the hillside forest.

Many of the buildings had a sizable firewood stack beside them, indicating the expectation of a cold winter for those that stayed on and even more cutting of trees from the hillsides.

Most of the small buildings were built of logs, hurriedly and roughly piled together and chinked with mud and grass. Idly he thought, *Kiril would have cringed at the sight of such poor workmanship.* The brick structures would follow, provided the ore proved to be profitable. If the mines failed, the town would be abandoned and left to collapse, with the miners moving on to the next hopeful strike. It was also possible that the lumber and logs would be torn down to be rebuilt at the next cry of "gold."

MacNair's rambling structure was built of sawn lumber, undoubtedly hauled in from some larger settlement. The other option was that some energetic souls had whipsawn the boards. But there are few jobs more known for pure misery than being on the bottom end of a whipsaw. That option seemed unlikely.

Rory counted four team-hauled wagons, in addition to the two big ore carriers so common in established mining settlements. Perhaps MacNair's Hill was too young, the pay rock too scarce to justify the presence of more ore wagons. Or the cost was too high when ore was hauled over the miles to the closest stamp mill. He figured activity would pick up only after the local stamp mill was completed. The other possibility was that there had been no meaningful strikes.

Rory rode from one end of the short street and back, taking note of the livery, the tent hotel, the log dining room advertising *fine eats*, the miner's supply store, a butcher shop, the gun and saddlery shop, a hopeful but forlorn-looking ladies wear store, two saloons, one of which was attached to MacNair's multifaceted edifice. There was a small law office advertising *mining claims registration service*, and an even smaller sheriff's office, more or less in a line along the offside of the road, sided by the livery and corrals.

Joining the business buildings was a collection of shacks and tents that could have been anything from private homes to buildings built to protect a digging operation from the weather. Or from curious eyes. There were scattered shacks all up and down the valley.

The presence of the sheriff's office and jail surprised him. He did not expect to find established law in the tiny settlement. He pulled the horse to a halt and stepped to the ground. There was no boardwalk in front of the sheriff's office, and the typical half-barrel chairs were missing.

He turned the knob and opened the door. As the light streamed into the small space, he could see it was empty. Not even a chair or a desk. No stove or gun rack. No sign of ever being used. Just the stale smell of a long closed-up space where spiders and black flies ruled the day.

But there was a single iron-barred cell. The key was

hanging on a nail beside the door. Satisfied with what he saw, he remounted and continued his look at the settlement.

Rory had his normal, emergency camp fixings stowed in his saddlebags, but he could work up no desire to put a meal together for himself when there was a dining room close by, no matter how rough-looking it was. He tied off his riding animal and adjusted his gun belt after he straightened his clothes. Entering the small establishment, he was surprised to see that most of the tables were already in use. It was midafternoon. He had expected to be one of just a few early diners, or perhaps, even alone. He moved to an empty space at a long table that sat six to a side. Swinging one leg over the bench and then the other, he took his seat. Neither man already seated adjacent to his choice of seats made any attempt to move or give him space. A teenaged girl stepped behind him, reaching over his shoulder to remove the plates and cutlery used by the previous customer. She returned a moment later with a warm, wet cloth to wipe the oilcloth-covered tabletop down. As she was doing her job, the man seated next to Rory reached out and grabbed her wrist, pulling her to himself.

"Leave me be, Buck. You've been told before."

"Ya? And who's going to make me? Ain't none of these pantywaists around here going to stand up to Ol' Buck. Come on now, sit here on my knee while I drink my coffee. You're sweet on me and you know it."

Rory swiveled a bit sideways, taking a good look at the speaker. What he saw was a big, unshaven, black-haired man. He looked strong as an ox. Big hands, large, long arms. The sheriff figured he would stand well over six feet. He would be a formidable opponent. He had a hungry grin on his face as he spoke to the waitress.

Quietly, but with built-in intensity, Rory said, "I believe the young lady would prefer that you leave her alone. It would go better for everyone if you heeded her request."

Buck pulled his hand away from the girl's wrist and began a sideways, backhanded swing at Rory's head. Rory batted the hand away with his left arm. Before Buck could speak or object, he had a Colt .44 muzzle pressed against the bridge of his nose, midway between his eyes. Neither man spoke. Buck's eyes rounded and finally focused on the seat beside him. When he finally gathered up enough nerve to speak, he said, "You'll regret the day you pulled a gun on Ol' Buck, stranger."

Rory stood and then pulled the weapon away from the bully. He reholstered it, stepped back over the bench, and said, "Stand up."

Buck grinned at the prospect of a rough-and-tumble fight with just fists for weapons. He said, "You leave that Colt holstered, and I'll stand. Tear you apart. Teach you to stick your nose where it don't belong."

"I'm sure you'd try, but you're not going to get the opportunity. You're under arrest. Stand up."

The words caught everyone's attention in the small room.

Buck stood and sneered, "And who do you think you are? There's no law in this rock pile." He backed away a few feet as he spoke. He balled his hands into fists and bent his neck, pointing his chin slightly toward the floor as if braced, ready for what was to come. The chords of muscle stood out on his neck and in as much of his arms as his rolled-up sleeves exposed.

Rory dropped his badge onto the table in front of the eating men. He then said, "Rory Jamison, county sheriff. And like I said, Buck, you're under arrest."

Instead of standing down, Buck closed the few feet between himself and the sheriff with a roar and a wild swing that would have felled any man it connected with. Rory managed to raise one arm enough to cause the fist to slide past his head and lifted the .44 again. Wanting to bring the confrontation to an end before it turned into a brawl, tearing the small business space apart, Rory slammed the heavy Colt just above Buck's left ear. He tottered for a second or two before falling to the floor in a heap. Rory reholstered the weapon and said, "Can I get a couple of you men to give me a hand here."

No one moved. He asked again with the same result. But finally, one man in the far corner spoke up. "You're on your own, Sheriff. Buck's going to wake up fit to be tied. He'll have an anger on for anyone helping you. And he ain't alone. Always seems to be others siding him. Ain't none of us want'n to put ourselves in that position."

Nodding his understanding, Rory rolled the unconscious man onto his belly, grabbed a fistful of shirt collar, dug in his boots, and pulled until Buck's feet faced the door. Saying, "I'll be right back," he stepped onto the road and walked over to his horse. He stepped into the saddle and, in just a few seconds, was at the dining room door. Once on the ground, he took down his catch rope and began uncoiling it as he walked toward the dining room. One end of the rope was already tied to the saddle horn. The other end was worked into a loop. He pulled the door open wide and, with one foot, slid a block of firewood in front of it to hold it open. He then snugged the loop around Buck's legs just above his boots. He walked back out and took the reins in his hand. Slowly he led the animal across the road. He heard laughter as Buck slid across the dining room floor and out the door, bumping down the step to the boardwalk and bumping again as he dropped to the road. Rory held his pace down as Buck slid down the two steps to the road. He had no intention of hurting the man unnecessarily. Traffic stopped as sheriff, horse, and prisoner walked and slid across the road. Again, there was laughter.

Rory pulled the gelding sideways to the sheriff's office and stopped when Buck was close to the door. It was a struggle, but he soon had the bully locked in the single cell. The thought crossed his mind that perhaps that had been the easy part. The more difficult question was, what was he going to do next? The slight offense of bullying the girl didn't warrant guarding Buck all the way down the hill to stand before the judge. He decided to return to his dinner and think through the rest later.

Rory left the gelding beside the jail and walked back to the dining room. He was greeted by an empty room. It seemed the frightened men had either taken their meals in a couple of large bites or had left half-finished plates lying on the tables. The girl was busy gathering up the plates, scraping the remains into a wooden bucket. Rory smiled at her and said, "Sorry, miss. I didn't mean to drive your customers off."

"Don't worry. They paid, and they'll be back another time. That's all I really care about."

A voice from behind turned Rory toward the kitchen. Standing with her legs slightly parted, as if to give extra stability, and wiping her hands on a cloth, a slim but strongly built woman said, "I want to thank you, Sheriff. That bully lays his hands on Gloria every time he comes in here. It's got to the point where we asked that he not come back, but he just laughed. And as I heard one of the others saying, Buck's never really alone. Or doesn't appear to be. There always seems to be two or three men hanging around admiring Buck. It seems to me that

MacNair's Hill would offer slim pickings for thieves, but there's a gang of some sort here, nonetheless. I don't have any idea who all is involved or if Buck is involved. It could be he just has some admirers. You know, lesser men who need someone to look up to. But I do know that Buck's not the worst of them. He's simply a brute. There are men in town that truly frighten me.

"Now you sit down, I'll get a plate for you."

The two women stayed in the kitchen while Rory ate alone. Perhaps the news had gotten around already. At least, no one else came in. As he stood, digging into his pocket for a coin to pay the cost of the meal, the cook came again to the doorway and said, "You can put that back in your pocket, Sheriff. The meal is our thanks for taking care of Buck for this once."

Rory laid the coin beside his plate.

"No, ma'am, I'll not be known as a man who takes free meals on the strength of the badge. I'll pay my way and be happy to do so. Thank you for the dinner. The best I've had since leaving home."

As he walked out the door, he chuckled to himself thinking, *She doesn't know if I left home yesterday or a year ago, and it doesn't really matter.* He walked back across the road to the jailhouse and entered, cautious of what he might find. The warning about a crew that had somehow taken root in the small village made him cautious. There was no need. The prisoner was awake, sitting on the wooden bunk cradling his head in his hands, offering no threat.

"Well, Buck, I see you're awake. Glad about that. Now perhaps we can have a private talk. Just you and me."

"I ain't talk'n to nobody. Jest get that there key and let me out'a here."

"Why, Buck, we haven't stood you before the judge

yet. A man never knows what might happen standing before a righteous man of the court. Of course, we could avoid all that if we had that little talk I mentioned. Otherwise, you'll have to stay right where you are until I'm ready to ride back down to the fort where the closest judge sits. That could take some time. But you decide."

After giving Buck a full minute to think it over, Rory turned to the door. "See you in the morning, Buck."

"Wait. Wait. I can't sit in no jail that long. You get me out of here."

"I'll let you out, Buck. But you've got to do two things. First, promise me you'll leave Gloria in the dining room strictly alone. How about that, Buck?"

"Ya. Yeh. I'll leave her alone."

"I'm taking that as a promise from a gentleman, Buck. There must be something of a gentleman somewhere inside that big body of yours. Don't make me regret it.

"Now, tell me what's going on around town. I need to know if anyone is really finding anything. I need to know who runs the town. And I need to know if the talk of a working gang is true or not and what your part in it is."

The response was slow in coming. But, finally, Buck said, "A few small finds is all. One gold operation, named Hill One, that don't amount to nothing yet, but the ones that claim to know say the Hill's going to be big. The best around here so far is the Cam One. Works a few men. Small but steady showing of color. Strangers holding it now. Claim the owners sold out and moved on. Don't know if I believe that.

"Couple of finds showing strange rock, but no one seems to know if it's minerals or just colored rock. Strange stuff. Town is young yet. Could be good finds some day."

Rory soaked that information in before saying, "Someone's putting up the money to build a crusher. A stamp mill."

"Ya. That's probably MacNair himself. He seems to be behind most things. Some folks think he's behind Hill One. The talk is that he's somehow involved with the new owners of the Cam One too."

Rory nodded at this information before asking, "Who runs the town and the hills? I mean really runs it. There's always someone."

Buck wasn't eager to talk, but he wasn't keen on spending the night on the hard bunk either. Rory could easily see the conflict.

"I'll tell you what, Buck. I promise this conversation is just between the two of us. You can give up to your friends that you agreed to leave Gloria alone. That won't cost you any prestige. I'll say that's all we talked about if anyone asks. But you have to tell me about the town."

Seeing the merits of the offer and the hopelessness of opposing it, Buck said, "MacNair started 'er up. Not more than a year, year-and-a-half ago. There were already small mines in the area and a few small but worthwhile diggings further down the valley. Cam One had shown some color. Couple of hardworking men found the prospect and filed the claim. Canby, by name, brothers. Put the name Cam One to it. The story is that they sold to an investor. A moneyman. Sold it and rode out."

"But you have doubts about that story."

"The word is that the Canby brothers were steady. Good men and good miners. It don't seem likely they would give over a promising claim like that."

Rory carefully looked at the prisoner, trying to see any sign of falsehood. When the man's face showed nothing, Rory returned to the original question. Before he answered, Buck hesitated, rubbed his face, and massaged his neck.

"You do a man hard, Sheriff."

"I could have shot you."

Buck didn't pursue that line of talk. Taking a deep breath but returning to his talk of the town, Buck said, "MacNair was the first in the town to build anything more than a shelter against the weather. Built himself that poor excuse for a building. Brought in supplies from the big outlets down in Idaho Springs, Blackhawk, somewhere down there. Has money. Finances mines and such. Get a man most anything, give him the time to do it. Hoists, pully and rope, pumps, any of that, should a man need it. Finance it, too, for a share of the mine. Or so they say. I've had no need myself, so can't say exactly. Put that trail through from the big mining areas. Got a finger in every pot it seems."

Rory said, "I figured that since his name is on the sign at the entrance to town. But is he just the figurehead leader, or is he the real power controlling things?"

"Ain't really much to control, comes to that. If'n it ain't MacNair, I don't know who it would be. Ain't all that many folks around, you count 'em all up. Can't be more than a thousand in the whole valley, end-to-end. And most of them no more than day labor miners. Some coming and going, but I don't have the straight of that."

Rory hoped to slip the next question in discreetly enough to catch Buck off guard, but it didn't work out that way.

"Tell me about the gang you're part of, Buck. And where you get your spending money."

Buck's head rose slowly. There was a big grin growing on his face. Even with the swelling above his ear that was obviously still hurting, he had his wits about him.

"Sheriff, I ain't that dumb. You ain't going to fool me with some stupid question I don't know the answer to anyway. If there's a gang operating around the claims, I don't know anything about it, and I sure ain't a part of it. I know how people talk about me, but ain't any of it true. And like I already said, ain't no one making any money yet, so what would a gang of thieves want with this place?"

"Where do you get your spending money, Buck?"

"Don't need much. Got a little claim myself down the valley a ways. Half-hour walk is all. Work it a bit most every day. Shows promise in the exposed quartz, so I keep at 'er. Come up with a dollar or two's worth from time to time. There's more there, I know there is. Sell my findings to MacNair. Enough to keep me fed and clothed. Figure I might be going out for the winter anyway."

Rory stepped forward and lifted the key from the nail it hung on. He gave the prisoner a firm look.

"Alright, Buck, you can go. The last part of this conversation didn't happen. But don't you be forgetting your promise."

"I'll remember. I'll leave the girl alone. Man gets lonesome, though, you know what I mean?"

"I'm not interested in your feelings, Buck. Just keep your promise."

As Rory watched the big lug tramp across the street, he thought, *There's more to that fella than he lets on. It could be that some of the bullying is more for cover than anything else.*

94

10

NOT EXACTLY SURE WHAT TO DO NEXT, RORY WANDERED the single main street of MacNair's Hill, taking a slower and more careful look at the buildings, the surrounding shacks, and again, the almost barren hillside. *There's a price paid for everything*, he thought to himself. *This time the price is paid by the trees.*

Figuring his presence was known and already spread far and wide, he decided to meet MacNair. The boardwalk in front of the big mercantile held a half-dozen oak barrels. The barrels housed picks, shovels, axes, replacement handles, various timber saws, a small collection of pine lumber, indicating the scarceness of that commodity in the town, and a gathering of miscellaneous items. He climbed the two steps that led from the boardwalk to the store's entry door. The bell that tinkled with the swing of the door was a common feature of most western stores. He stepped inside, stopped, and took a good look around.

There was a sameness to western general stores everywhere Rory had been. The crudely built tables formed into aisles held stacks of work clothes, from heavy canvas pants to woolen shirts and cotton under-wear. Another table held winter coats, scarves, fleece-lined leather hats with fold-down earflaps, and a few knit sweaters. A shelf along the back wall held a wide selection of hats, from wide brim Stetson-style to older, traditional bowlers and the more modern, flat newsboy-style, so commonly worn by recent European immi-grants, and even more warm, lined pieces in several shapes and designs, ready for the cold months.

There was one entire table taken up with boots of every imaginable size and design. And, as expected, items were on display overhead, hanging from hooks screwed into the wooden ceiling. It appeared as if there was no wasted space in the cluttered mercantile.

All in all, Rory decided the store was justified only if there was a major strike with more people pouring into town. The few people already there couldn't explain the stock on hand.

"Help you, sir?"

That voice pulled Rory away from his examination of the store.

"First time here. Just taking it all in."

He said that as he was winding his way through the angles formed by the cluttered tables, approaching the speaker who stood behind the sales counter.

"Mr. MacNair, I presume? I'm Rory Jamison, county sheriff. Just taking a look around some country I've never ridden before. Since your name is on the town sign, I figured I should meet you first."

He held out his hand as he neared the counter.

MacNair shook the sheriff's hand and said, with a bit of a grin, "Good to meet you, Sheriff, but from what I've heard, I'm hardly the first you've met."

"Well, strictly speaking, that's true, Mr. MacNair. I suppose I should have clarified my meaning. You're the first I've set out to meet. The others just sort of happened."

MacNair agreed with, "Of course. Sometimes things will happen when we least expect them."

Rory matched the man's grin as he replied. "What I didn't expect, sir, is the village of MacNair's Hill. I have only recently been elected sheriff. Leading up to that election, I was tasked by the state people to canvas the county with the idea of forming a list of electors. I know I missed a few along the way, but I'm embarrassed to have missed this entire town. Most of the mineral claims are south of our county, so I didn't burden my horse with the task of carrying me up this high. I apologize for that oversight."

"No need for the apology, young man. None of us have been here long, and there are not more than perhaps a few dozen that could be considered permanent citizens. There's a lot of coming and going. We hold out hopes for longevity and prosperity, of course, but time and the quality of the ore will tell on that one, do you not agree?"

Rory chose not to pursue that remark, saying instead, "Most of my time since the election, and the year before that, when I was an appointed county deputy, was spent down below in the ranching country. I've little knowledge of the mining towns to the south. I expect they have their problems. But that will be something for the sheriff from another county to deal with.

"I probably wouldn't have come up here at all if there hadn't been a bit of a mystery further down the hill. It was following the trail of four men that led me here. I lost their trail, but the ride was not in vain, seeing that I now know that MacNair's Hill is a thriving metropolis in our county."

MacNair laughed at the description of his town, interrupting Rory's next thought for a moment.

"Just for interest's sake, Mr. MacNair, may I ask where you're from and how it is that you picked this particular valley to establish a town? There hardly seems to be enough mining activity or proven returns to justify the expense or your work and trouble. It's almost as if you're anticipating a big strike and the growth that follows."

MacNair appeared to be taken aback a bit by the sheriff's inquiries. There was clearly more to the question than what was evident in the simple words. He hesitated but, to show he had nothing to hide from the law, at least nothing anyone was likely to discover, finally said, "We are all from somewhere else, are we not, Sheriff? I suspect either you yourself, or perhaps your parents came from the East, and before that, somewhere in Europe, as did most of us. Some came recently and some earlier."

Hoping to move the conversation along, Rory said, "That's totally correct, of course. I don't actually know when my first relative landed on these shores or from where. There is talk in the family of the British Isles but nothing specific. My parents came west before the war and claimed a small piece of ranching land. We lost my mother and sister to the smallpox. Tiring of the struggle, Father and I rode to the Idaho gold fields. After he died, I made my way back to the ranch. An uncle was keeping it going on shares. I'll probably end up back there, by-and-by.

"My father wanted nothing to do with the foolishness of war. In any case, the popular prediction was that the war would be a short one, and it was a long way from Colorado to those eastern states where the blood was being spilled. In any case, Father believed that the nation would be needing quality beef and he wanted to be part of the solution to that need. He believed there would soon be a steady host of settlers heading our way. They would need both beef and breeding animals. He believed firmly that the settlers were the future of the country. I tend to hold that view myself, Mr. MacNair."

MacNair nodded, seemingly interested in this short recounting of settlement and heartache, and continued, "For myself, I left Louisiana behind before the war. I've never seen any reason to return. I left there with little I could claim as my own. Mainly my memories. Memories of a small plot behind the church that held the only woman I have ever loved, and some little knowledge of minerals gained during a couple of unhappy years in a college my parents insisted I attend.

"There appeared to be considerable risk in venturing into the goldfields, or travel in general, during the war, so I hunkered down in West Texas for the duration, working in a buffalo hunter's trading post. Learned the retail business and something of the cattle industry along the way, and generally suffered through the winds and extremes of each season as it came along, praying the whole while that I would survive long enough to see these beautiful hills and dip my fingers into the world of mineral discovery.

"As any observant eye could easily see, Sheriff, I am neither strong enough nor healthy enough to swing a pick or make my bed on the rocky ground. I must satisfy myself with a more distant relationship to the treasures God hid in these hills. Hence, the mercantile, the assaying, the little bit of consultation my short education can be helpful in. And there you have it. You now know more about me than, I dare say, anyone else in these hills."

Rory nodded in understanding, also noting that he had said nothing about owning a mine or investing in others. As he sized up the man before him, he agreed he didn't look fit for the difficult life of hard-rock mining.

When the inquiry of their heritages was satisfied, Rory said, "I'm guessing, Mr. MacNair, that the town has not seen the need to appoint a marshal or sheriff. The little building shows no signs of use, although it came in handy for me this afternoon."

MacNair laughed as he thought of the story of Buck being dragged across the street.

"It somehow seems fitting, Sheriff, that Buck should be the first to initiate the jail cell. He's not a bad man, but he can be rough and difficult to reason with at times. And he's not an easy man to know. Holds to himself most times and doesn't seem to crave fellowship, although he has his admirers and a few who sidle up to him at every opportunity. He breaks some quartz chunks out of his claim from time to time. Picks out enough pay mineral to put a few dollars in his pocket. I purchase the gold from him so he can eat and take the occasional drink.

"I hear there was some laughter as you dragged him across the road. He won't take that kindly. He'll forgive you for the dragging, but the laughter will gnaw at him.

"But to your question, no, we have not bothered with a lawman. The time will come, of course, but so far, what little problem we've had, which mostly involves the consumption of alcohol, we have handled ourselves."

AFTER A SHORT ADDITIONAL visit about nothing in particular, Rory left the store and wandered down the street with no specific goal in mind. MacNair had built a small saloon into the end wall of the mercantile, accessible by a narrow doorway in the store or a wider door leading onto the front boardwalk. Rory had taken that path, studying the small saloon as he was leaving.

As he strolled the walkway, his eyes were busy, taking in the surroundings and looking for anomalies, anything that didn't seem to fit. After walking a hundred steps past the last building, he stood, hands on hips, and studied the mostly untouched countryside. He was struck by its beauty and remoteness. But as he had said to Ivan days before, no one would take interest in this land other than lumber men or miners. Satisfied with what he saw, he turned back to the town. Rory had never been a drinker, but he was aware that much of the country's business was transacted in saloons. Privately naming MacNair's Saloon as a gathering point for working men and, perhaps, a rougher element, he decided to enter the second drinking establishment, boldly named Miner's Rest, the larger and more dignified of the two choices, if that title could be lent to a saloon.

A short visit might enlighten him in some way.

Some men patronized saloons to drink and visit, and some to gamble. But there were also those men who, although they might take a drink or two, were there to talk business with associates. Only rarely did a lady intrude on this mens' den of solitude. Rory's motivation was the gathering of information. He stepped into the dim interior and looked around. Like the sameness of general stores, there was little to choose from between frontier saloons.

In the big city, he had ventured into fancier establishments where the bar was a sculpted work of art and the tables and chairs of higher quality, the ceilings were of pressed metal, and the air pungent with cigar smoke. In those places, the shouting and loud laughter of the typical western saloon was missing. The drinkers were more apt to wear business clothes and speak more quietly and seriously with their tablemates.

In cattle or mining country, there were few men in business suits patronizing the drinking establishments. Work clothing, often soiled from the day's activities or many days' activities, was the order of the day. Pushing through the door of Miner's Rest, Rory could see the place could lay claim to little that was fancy. Still, he could see that an effort had been made. The short bar was built of sawn lumber hand-planed more or less smooth to hold down the incidents of slivers and finished with some kind of dark stain and a coat of varnish. The floor was rough-cut lumber covered with an inch or two of sawdust that needed to be swept out and replaced. The selection of bottles stacked behind the bar offered a wider choice in drinking than MacNair's establishment. Two kegs, one tapped, one waiting its turn, were cradled on a pinewood bench behind the bar.

Giving way to the difficulty of maintaining cleanliness that so much of the frontier suffered from, the drinking glasses were swished in a tub of scummy water between customers, but no one appeared concerned about the lack of hygiene.

At MacNair's, there had been more plug chewers than cigar smokers. The sawdust around each spittoon reeked with unpleasantness. The spittoons in Miner's Rest saw little activity, while the air was saturated with vile cigar smoke.

Rory grimaced and walked to the bar. The indifferent barman said nothing, just waiting. Rory ordered one beer, which would never be drunk, and carried it to a table near the front window. He sat facing the room, considering what to do next. One part of his mind was questioning why he had even bothered riding up the hill. But the more diligent portion of his mind wondered where the squatters from Kiril's cabin could have gone and where, for that matter, Ivan and My Way had gotten themselves to. And now that he had become aware that MacNair's Hill sat inside his own county and was, therefore, his responsibility, there would likely be more rides to mining country in the future.

The saloon boasted no half doors, as was so common in warmer climates, only a single swinging door that would protect the patrons against the snow and cold of the winter months. When that door opened, he couldn't help glancing up. The man that walked in was at least as large as Buck but far better groomed. The kind of man that would be noticed and perhaps admired in any crowd.

Rory's eyes tracked him as he stepped to the bar and ordered a beer. A few words were spoken quietly to the barman. Without comment, the server reached under the bar and lifted out a glass. He then picked up a clean towel from the backboard and gave the mug a careful wiping. Only then did he pull the handle on the spigot and wait while the yellow liquid rose in the glass stein, topping off with a liberal foam. The barman slid a small piece of pine board across the top, whisking the foam into a bucket placed there for the purpose, and set the mug on the counter. The customer nodded his head in thanks and turned, holding the mug before him. As if it had been preplanned, the man's eyes fell on Rory.

As the fellow took the few steps required to cross the small room, Rory unconsciously let his hand drop to his belt, slightly loosening one of his .44s, and waited. The wait was very short.

"Few things in this life are more apt to remind a man of his lonely state of being than taking a drink by oneself. Some things almost demand a degree of fellowship. May I join you, sir?"

Casually Rory flipped his hand toward the empty chair across from him as a silent nod of consent.

"Thank you, sir. Most hospitable of you."

Rory could see several heads turned his way as the visitor slid the chair back and took his seat. As if responding to a formal invitation that had been nowhere voiced, he held his hand out, saying, "Terrence Climber."

Rory, grinning inside at the certain knowledge that this man wanted something, responded with his name only, along with the customary handshake. He said nothing about being sheriff, although he was reasonably certain that everyone in the small room was aware of his status.

Climber took a small sip of beer, unnecessarily wiped his lips off with the back of his hand, and set the mug down.

"I take it you're not much of a drinking man, Mr. Jamison, judging by the fact that your stein hasn't been lifted from the table since you set it there."

Since Rory had taken the table several minutes before Climber's appearance, there was a degree of presumption in the statement, but Rory accepted it as a way of starting a conversation.

"I will admit to the accuracy of your observation, Mr. Climber, but a man can hardly take up a table in a business establishment and not expect to make a purchase.

And one thin dime is little enough rent for the table and chair as I observe the traffic out the window and the comings and goings of the town."

"Right you are, Mr. Jamison. I drink very little myself. One after my day's work is done, and that only from a properly cleaned stein. They keep a few under the counter for those that demand the extra effort. I don't expect there is anything that will kill a man in that rank tub of scummy water, but it's the thought. Would you not agree, Mr. Jamison?"

"I will have to acknowledge, Mr. Climber, that I haven't given it a second's thought. I'm sure I've drank and eaten worse on the trail more than once. But may I ask what your business is, sir? You are not dressed for mining, and your hands don't show the curl of a pick or double jack."

"Right again, sir. In fact, my business, as poor as it is, is the registering of mining claims on behalf of the miners who are too busy or who don't know how to do it for themselves. That, and the other bits of legal work as it comes up from time to time."

As Rory was studying his guest, wondering why he felt a bit uneasy about the situation, Climber said, "You're probably thinking there would be little work in a place like MacNair's Hill for services such as what I offer. You would be correct in that, except that I have small offices in some other mining settlements. I travel from one to the other. A bit like a circuit preacher. Together they allow me to keep my needs met.

"But you haven't told me what brings you to this mountainside settlement, Mr. Jamison. I'm sure you understand that your presence and position were generally known before you finished your dinner this afternoon. But now, the growing question around town is more specific. Are you here on a visit alone, or is there a crime problem none of the rest of us have noticed?"

Rory chuckled good-naturedly. "Gossip, often passing for news, travels where there is little else to talk about. That is a fact of life in the villages. But I have nothing to hide, so there's no loss."

With both men aware that the question of an unnoticed crime had not been answered, they allowed the conversation to idle along for a few minutes, touching on little besides the futility of most prospector's work, finalized by Climber saying, "Of course, it's the promise of the possible that keeps them going. And the example of the few that have succeeded."

Under different circumstances, Rory may have enjoyed continuing that philosophical conversation but not when his time on the hill was limited. In any case, he suspected there was more than idle chatter that attracted the lawyer to his table. Wanting to get to the meat of the visit, he turned the talk toward his tablemate.

"A man such as yourself, Mr. Climber, educated and all, knowledgeable in the law, could no doubt find more promising locations to hang out your shingle. I'm not sure I'm altogether convinced that it's the occasional registering a claim or two that attracts you to MacNair's Hill. What's your history, if you don't mind sharing, and what really brought you to the hill?"

That direct, challenging question was answered with, "I have emptied my tankard, Sheriff, and since you have no interest in what sits before you, how would it be if we were to go for a short walk? I could perhaps point out some of the highlights of MacNair's Hill. Maybe even tell you a story." He ended those few words with a smile.

Thinking back to the first time he had met Block Handly, he responded, "I like stories, Mr. Climber. True stories. I'll join you and buy you a cup of coffee later on in exchange for a true story."

"Done, Sheriff. Let us be out of this smoky hovel and into the clean evening air."

The two men strolled slowly down the boardwalk until the walk ended and became a jagged dirt path that wound along the fronts of the small stores. Lamps had been lit in most of the stores. There were few people in sight, but the storekeepers lived in hopes of one more paying customer before he locked the door for the night.

At the start of their walk, Climber had said, "Please call me Terrence. I am not comfortable with Mr. Climber. In the city, of course, the prefix is commonly used in what is known as polite circles, but here on the hill, it seems a bit presumptuous."

Rory was unsure if Climber was expressing his normal thoughts or if he was trying to impress in his use of language. He decided it didn't matter, he would pursue his questions in any case.

"And I am Rory, Terrence. I am as uncomfortable with the title of sheriff as you say you are with mister, so first names it will be. But I am still waiting for that story, Terrence."

"Yes, well, you will understand, Rory, that a man must be very careful telling stories. Stories falling on the wrong ears in a place like this can have immediate and, sometimes, quite final consequences. I have decided to trust you, Rory. I have known your name and something of your reputation for some time now and was told that you are a straight shooter and can be trusted. I was also advised that you would one day find your way to MacNair's Hill and to watch for you. I may need a fast horse and an hour's head start if I'm wrong in any of that.

"I've traveled some, Rory, and done a variety of things since leaving the East. A few of those things were done along the long, sometimes lonely roads that cross this huge land, and some while settled temporarily in one town or another. I plied my trade in West Texas for the better part of a year, although no one here knows that, and I never talk about it. During that time, I met a man who answered to the name of Block. I thought it a rather strange name at first, but once I got to know the man a little, the name seemed to fit. He is, indeed, a block of a man. Of course, it's still an unusual name. Have you ever heard 'block' used as a personal name, Rory?"

The statement and the question opened a whole new direction for the conversation. Rory immediately understood why Terrence insisted on going for a walk. There was no chance of listening ears being anywhere close as they stood quietly talking on the edge of town. Still, he hesitated.

Rather than offering a direct answer, Rory said, "It seems to me, Terrence, that the law has many tributaries, not unlike those winding flatland rivers. Certainly, a lawyer would be seen as one of those tributaries, as would a sheriff. Each brings something to the table in the fight against crime. So tell me, Terrence, are you a register of mining claims only, or, as a lawyer, are you in the fight against crime?"

"You're as smart and cagey as Block said you would be, Sheriff. And yes, I am referring to Block Handly, your partner or assistant in bringing down the notorious Lance Newley Gang of thieves. He did warn me, by the way, that you are sometimes given to bold but rash decisions and actions. He recommended that I keep my powder dry and my horse saddled. And to save me saying it again later, his offer to wrap you into the federal service still stands."

Rory ignored the mention of the federal service and said, instead, "Block is a relentless recruiter to his interests. If he has, in fact, recruited you, and do you have any proof of that?"

"Everything open and aboveboard, Rory. He recruited me but not to a formal position. I have no desire to carry a badge, nor do I think I have the necessary attributes. Simply said, I am not cut out to pursue criminals. But I believe I have, up to this time, and am still doing a reasonable job of working undercover, digging around for facts, names, and situations. I am not in these hills because I love the hills, as pleasing to the eye as the mountains are. I would just as soon admire them from a hotel room window in Denver. No, I am here because my training in the law fills a need and gives me freedom of movement. As for proof, you have all that is available. My word."

Rory seemed to accept this and continued the questioning, asking, "What is Block looking for, and what does he expect, or hope, that I might do?"

"Here's the crux of the matter, Rory. This could well be seen as a federal matter only. But that theory breaks down when the local actions are considered."

As if he wasn't sure how to proceed, Terrence stopped talking at that point.

Rory responded, "That's clear as the sky on a dark night, my friend. Make it plain. What are you investigating, and how does it impact us at the county level?"

11

"SERIOUS SUSPICIONS, RORY. NOT QUITE FACT YET.

"There's a lot of money floating around these hills. Money that originated somewhere else, not just from the diggings. The big boys go their own way, not needing anyone else. But there have been more mines than normal that have suddenly burst into full production, often enough with new owners. Production that cannot be attained without capital input, and new ownership that cannot be explained satisfactorily. To move an operation from a one- or two-man pick-and-shovel show to a full-fledged, functioning producer takes money and expertise, engineering. When that happens too freely, people are apt to take note. Now you understand I'm not talking dozens of mines. Mining is too complex for that. But even the three or four under observation is a significant number."

Rory let this statement fester in his mind for a few seconds before saying, "I've seen no sign of what you're talking about in MacNair's Hill. Of course, I've only been here a few hours and haven't ridden the extent of the valley yet. Is there an example of what you're talking about in the valley?"

"There are examples of new ownership, but as for suddenly becoming a large operation, no, not yet. But there are examples enough in the near vicinity. I'm trying to keep an eye out. That's why I keep moving from strike to strike, offering my legal services. We want to pin down the agents the money is funneled through. If they turn out to be legitimate, so much the better. All we have to this date are suspicions. But serious suspicions, you understand."

The story was clearly incomplete. That bothered Rory, who hated wasting time and would far prefer to be riding the grasslands than spending his time in the upper hills. He would need more than Terrence had offered, or he would be riding on in the morning.

"Why would the Federals care? People can spend their money any way they see fit."

"Awe, there's the truth of it all, my young friend. It's not the spending of money that has Block losing sleep, it's the source of that money. And there we have, at best, a broken trail."

Suddenly Rory thought he saw the more complete picture.

"Would this have anything to do with certain gold coins? Coins that are water stained and showing more tarnish than what is common on gold coins? Coins the government lost in a botched transfer of funds? Block seemed to be somewhat fixated on that."

Terrence laughed right out loud. He slapped Rory on the back of his shoulder and replied, "You're almost too smart and understanding to be wasting your time riding the county looking for bandits. Come. The dining room will be closing soon. I'll be wanting that coffee you mentioned."

Quietly, across the coffee table in the dining room, Rory asked, "Why would the Federals still care about a crime that's years old."

"That's another story, Sheriff. Shorter, but interesting."

12

RORY DROPPED THE BAR ACROSS THE SHERIFF'S OFFICE door and bunked down in the cell. After a fitful night's sleep, he walked to the stream and pulled off his shirt. The cold water felt good as he splashed it over his upper body and washed his face and hair. He allowed a couple of minutes for the fall air to dry some of the moisture off before putting his shirt back on. He needed to talk with Terrence again, and then he intended to ride on after taking a breakfast at the dining room. But he had one other thing to do. Or at least, try to do. He had long trusted his own judgment. His instincts. Could he trust them once more in a totally unlikely way? But food would come first while he thought that out.

He paid for the plate of meat and eggs and stepped onto the boardwalk just in time to see Buck coming from the brush across the streambed. Rory walked slowly toward where Buck would emerge from between the Sheriff's office and the saddlery and gun shop.

Buck stopped abruptly when he glanced up and saw the sheriff waiting for him.

"You leave me be, Sheriff. I ain't done nothing to trouble you nor anyone else."

"No trouble, Buck. I just want to talk with you."

"I got nothing to say to you."

"Well, Buck, that doesn't surprise me. But what if I have something to say to you? That might make a difference, don't you think?"

Buck looked doubtful, but he stopped, as if to listen to what the lawman had to say.

"The thing is, Buck, we need to have a private talk. Just you and me. I scrounged a couple of chairs for the jailhouse last evening. Let's go have us a visit."

Buck was anything but reassured, but he saw no way out. His head still hurt from the sheriff's reception the afternoon before, and he was a little groggy after waking from a sound sleep. He wasn't sure he was ready for a serious talk. But he entered the little building and took a seat. Rory followed him in and closed the door.

As he usually did, Rory started right in.

"Buck, I think you're a liar. I don't believe you. If it turns out that I'm wrong, I'll apologize."

Buck stood as if he was already done with this talk. Rory laughed and said, "Sit down, Buck, it's not what you think. What it is, Buck, is that I don't believe you're the man you show the town. I don't think the heavy tangle of a beard and long hair, dirty clothes and such is the real Buck. I noticed yesterday, when I mentioned a part of you being a gentleman, that you might have sat up a bit straighter, and you lost a bit of the scowl from your face. And when you spoke in somewhat fractured English, you had to put it on. It's not natural to you. Actually, you have a good command of the language when the ain'ts and such are removed.

114

"Many men are hiding out in these hills or on lonely ranches for their own reasons. I won't ask what yours is.

"But let me get right down to it. If your diggings are really providing for your needs, that's great. It gives you a reason to stay on at MacNair's Hill and helps in what I want you to do."

"I ain't doin' nothing for you nor for any other star toter."

"Well, let's think about that for a moment. I'm the county sheriff. I have no authority in town unless it impacts on the wider population. I can't be everywhere at once in this large county. I want you to take on the county deputy sheriff's position for MacNair's Hill. And we'll ask MacNair about you doubling as town marshal. You will stay right here in town. You'll fix up this jailhouse until it's comfortable to spend the winter in. You'll receive regular pay from the county, through me or my other deputy. And a stipend of some sort from the town. Your job will be to watch the goings-on up here on the hill and report to me if you see anything suspicious. In the dining room, there was talk of a gang operating and that you were a part of it. I doubted that when I heard it, and I doubt it now. Are you a member of a local gang, Buck?"

"There ain't no gang here that I ever heard of. Not enough in this whole entire valley to attract a gang of thieves. And I'm no thief. I never took one dime from anyone. I'll beat anybody that calls me a thief to my face. Anyway, we talked about that yesterday."

Rory's smile was growing as his premonition was being proven, piece by piece, to be valid.

"No, Buck. Your beating days are over. Your time pretending to be a bully is done and behind you. A lawman doesn't beat on folks. Now, let's get you down to the bathhouse and then to the barbers. Then we'll go to MacNair's and get you outfitted in better clothing. After that, you and I will have a long talk about how being a deputy works and what the county will expect from you."

"Now, just hold on a minute there. I ain't agreed to no such a thing."

"I think you have in your mind, Buck. You're just having trouble getting the message to your feet. Stand up now. This is your only chance. Let's not waste time. I'm anxious to ride back down the hill. I'll pay for the haircut and the clothes and buy you lunch after. But you have to decide."

Buck steadied his gaze on the young sheriff but didn't say anything. Rory gave him another half minute and then stood.

"Come on, my new friend. We're off to that tent hotel. They're advertising hot baths. It's time. Let's go."

Buck, still not having thought it all out, stood and followed Rory out the door and down the road to the hotel. He left Buck alone while he soaked in the hot water but finally had to tell him that was enough. Clearly, Buck was enjoying the experience.

At the barber shop, Rory sat on a chair while Buck gingerly eased into the barber's fancy, raised chair. The barber threw a cloth over Buck and asked, "What will it be?"

Buck was trying desperately to hold to his wounded approach to the change being thrust upon him. In answer to the barber, he pointed at Rory and said, "Best you ask him. I don't seem to have any say in my own life anymore."

Trying to understand that strange statement, the barber looked over at Rory. His answer was, "Trim the beard down till it's neat and combed out. Then shorten the mustache. Put some effort into the haircut. Don't just hack it off. Buck is going to be the best-looking man in town if you do your job well."

An hour later, sitting in the dining room having an early lunch before the crowd arrived, Rory thought that in spite of Buck's sour looks, he was really enjoying the feel of the new clothing and the shortened beard. Rory caught him running his hand over the pants and shirt several times and fingering the shortened beard. The question was, of course, whether or not the new Buck would really become Buck, the deputy sheriff. The answer wouldn't be known for some time.

It was probably a good sign of his acceptance in the community, if nothing else, that Buck was minding his manners and that Gloria didn't seem to recognize him.

As they were eating, the door opened, and Ivan and My Way walked in. Ivan glanced across the room and immediately said, "Sheriff..."

He was cut off by Rory saying, "We are in the midst of our dinners here, sir. If you have business with me, you can come to the sheriff's office across the street in about one hour."

He followed that short speech with a pleading look, hoping Ivan would catch his meaning.

Ivan turned to look at My Way and said, "We might just as well eat while we're here."

My Way made no response which Ivan took as approval. They selected a table toward the rear of the small room and took their seats. Gloria came from the kitchen at the sound of the voices. She looked first at Rory and Buck and then turned to see a stranger and an Indian sitting close by. The sight of the Indian stopped her in her tracks. Ivan noticed and, hoping to jump ahead of any refusal of service, he said, "He's with me."

Gloria hesitated, still staring at My Way. Finally, she turned to the kitchen for advice from Mila, the cook and owner of the establishment. The two women walked back into the dining room within seconds. Mila looked first to Ivan and then to My Way. With a grin on her face, she spoke directly to My Way.

"I won't have any loud whooping or scalping of customers in my dining room. I hope you understand that, sir."

From behind the first half-smile Ivan had ever seen on the man's lips, My Way said, "No whoop. No scalp."

Mila patted him on the shoulder and walked back to the kitchen.

AN HOUR LATER, Buck had left to dig out the gun belt and Colt 45 he had left with the gun shop for safekeeping. He was then going to rent a horse, saddle Rory's mount for him, and wait for Rory to arrive. Clearly, the sheriff had wanted to be alone as he talked with the stranger and the Indian.

IN THE SMALL JAIL BUILDING, Rory and Ivan were seated on the chairs. My Way was content squatting, his back against the wall, holding a position Rory knew he himself could never hold for more than a minute without serious pain.

Rory had apologized for his abruptness in the dining

room, explaining that it was best for Ivan and My Way to remain unknown.

"I arrived yesterday and announced right away that I was sheriff. But I still have no real idea what's going on up here. Maybe nothing. If you fellas aren't known as lawmen, you may have more opportunity to snoop around. I plan to spend the rest of the day with Buck, but I'm feeling the need to go back down the hill. I've been away from the towns long enough. I'll ride down tomorrow."

Rory thought it best if Buck didn't know who Ivan and My Way were, so there were no introductions. He did, however, make them all separately aware of Terrence's involvement and swore them to secrecy, also advising that Terrence could be used to pass on messages. With a simple nod at Rory, Ivan and My Way swung onto their animals and rode out of town.

When Rory was convinced that Buck would do his simple job peacefully and honestly, he left him at the marshal's office and rode once more to the law office. He still wanted an answer to his question from the night before.

"Afternoon, Terrence. You ready to tell me another story? I have a story, too, but you first."

Terrence looked up from the paper before him on his desk and said, "I'm assuming you're referring to the question of seeking out a trail as cold as the one with the gold coins at the end."

The question needed no answer. Rory simply waited.

"The truth is, Sheriff, that the man pushing this is the same one who botched the transfer of those trunks right from the start. He now holds an important position in the Capitol but still has the one blemish against his name. That blemish is holding him back in his climb to the top. He has a long reach and a long memory. He is able to move the checkers around and apply pressure as well as anyone could. He wants the bad guys caught and named. If some are dead, he still wants them named. This isn't going away."

Rory ran that through his mind for a moment and replied, "It has nothing at all to do with me. But I wish Block all the success in the world."

With a smile, Terrence said, "I'm not so sure it won't involve you, my young friend, but we'll wait and see. But now you have a story for me."

"It's a very short story."

Rory then told Terrance about Buck as well as Ivan and My Way. Terrence took the news of Ivan and My Way without comment, but the mention of Buck was met with raised eyebrows and a quizzical look.

With those explanations behind him, Rory dug into his pocket and drew out a gold piece—a marred and stained gold piece. Without comment, he lay it on the desk. Terrence raised a single eyebrow by way of a question. Rory responded, "I was given that as part of my change after paying for the new clothes for Buck."

"MacNair?"

"Nowhere else."

Terence leaned back in his chair and drew in a long breath. He then reached out and fingered the coin. After a short time, he grinned and said, "I believe I said something about you getting drawn into this thing."

Frustrated, Rory stood, slid the coin off the desk, and put it back in his pocket. With his business completed for the time being, he rode downhill. It was late in the day, but he thought he could make it to Kiril's cabin before dark.

13

RORY RODE INTO STEVENSVILLE IN TIME FOR LUNCH AT Ma Gamble's dining room. When he pulled out a chair opposite Marshal Key Wardle and sat down, Key set his fork back on his plate and smiled a welcome.

"Good to see you, Sheriff. We've missed you."

Rory returned the smile and said, "Who's we?"

"Oh, you know. Me and the town and your family. And the federal agent who's been hanging around for days now, asking questions and wondering when you'd be coming back."

Wondering if he was ever going to be free of the Federals, Rory asked, "Is his name Block?"

"No. He named himself as Simon. Simon Webb. Not a friendly man. A bit rough, if you take my meaning. Seems to think we're all kind of unimportant, back-woods types. That it's only what he wants that matters. He and I had to disagree on some things. Now I'm not sure what to do with him, so I'm glad you're back."

Rory carefully studied the sheriff. He had resumed eating. He seemed calm enough. But he had most certainly left a question hanging in the air. A question that had to be answered, and quickly, if Rory's suspicions were anywhere near correct.

"What exactly did you mean, Key? What to do with him. You need to explain that."

"Well, he was causing such a fuss he had half the town upset. Going from one store to another looking for you. Insisting you were hiding out somewhere. Demanding that you be sent out. Wouldn't listen to anyone. Bullheaded, I'd say. You met my father, Sheriff. You will understand that I know something of bull-headedness."

"Key. None of that answers the question. Where is the man now?"

"Him? Why he's in the jail where I put him yesterday. Figure to charge him with disturbing the peace. Maybe some other things. But wanted to talk to you first."

Rory sat stunned, staring at the young marshal. Then he started to laugh. When he had settled down again, he shook his head in amazement and glee and picked up his fork to begin eating. A few more minutes wasn't going to change much. But before long, he and Key were walking across the road toward the jailhouse. As they walked, his mind was on Key, this young man who had been appointed town marshal.

Mulling on Key's actions, he thought that perhaps being raised in a remote area where a boy became a man at a young age, and having a father who bristled with authority, wasn't an altogether bad thing.

Key unlocked the door and stepped in, followed by Rory. Key sat behind the desk. Rory took a couple of steps toward the cell. The unhappy man looking back at him was about average in height, slim but strong enough looking. His face was narrow, ending with a somewhat pointed chin. His eyes were glaring with anger and hatred.

"Good afternoon, Simon. I'm Rory Jamison, county sheriff."

He picked the cell door key off the peg it hung on before saying, "How would it be if you come out and sit down, Simon. We'll have us a talk."

Rory opened the cell and pointed at a chair. "Have a seat, Simon. Do I understand it correctly that you're a deputy federal marshal? I believe that's what you told the town marshal. The problem there is, of course, that you've given no one any way of proving who you are. Who or what, for that matter. We'll have to sort that out, won't we, Mr. Webb."

Simon stood in the open doorway and said, "We'll sort nothing out. I'll have you and your foolish young marshal up on charges of interfering with a federal investigation. I'll not sit down, and I'll not talk with you. I'll have my weapons back, and I'll have you both stand down while I pick up my gear. Then I'll be leaving this dust-blown excuse for a town."

Rory stood and, with a simple push, ushered the man back into the cell. The door clanged shut. With an oath of outrage, the deputy shouted, "Open that door. You have no authority over me!"

Calmly, Key said, "Mr. Webb. I don't pretend to know much about the law, but I know you can't ride into my town claiming to be a federal deputy, for which you refused to show any evidence, and tear the town apart. This is my town and my jurisdiction. Sit down and shut up while we try to figure out what to do with you."

Key stood and beckoned to Rory. "Got something I want you to see, Sheriff."

The two men left the jailhouse, and Rory followed

Key to the livery. He walked directly to the tack room and indicated Webb's saddle. Tied across the rear housing was a bulky set of saddlebags. The bedroll was snugged tightly on top of the saddlebags. Key undid the buckle on one bag and lifted out a change of clothing and then an old newspaper. He fished through a few miscellaneous items and lifted his hand out holding a small canvas sack. Turning toward Rory, he undid the tie string, turned the bag over, and dumped several ten-dollar gold pieces into his hand. They were all tarnished like the ones that had given Rory more than enough to do for the past while.

Rory stood in wonder. As if talking to himself, but so that Key could hear, he said, "Will this thing never stop?"

"How many are there, Key?"

"Seventeen."

"That's a lot of money."

"More than I've ever seen before."

Rory took the sack and the coins from Key. He dropped the coins back into the sack, tied the string, and hefted the sack to feel the weight, thinking of the tale behind the coins.

"Key, let's not mention these coins to Webb. He won't take time to look for them now. He'll be too anxious to put the town behind him. Saddle Webb's horse. Bring him around to the jailhouse. I think we'll just turn Mr. Webb loose. We're not going to do anything but stir up dust holding him any longer. There's another way to approach this."

Rory tucked the coin sack into his coat pocket as he was walking back to the office.

He walked into the jail and opened the cell door.

"Mr. Webb. You're free to go. Your horse will soon be outside, saddled and ready. Get on him and ride. Your

gun belt is draped over the horn. Your rifle is in the scabbard. Both guns are unloaded. Leave them that way until
you've made some miles from Stevensville. You've worn
out your welcome in our town and county. If you ever
return, it had best be with a different attitude. Key
treated you pretty gently. I may have taken a different
approach. Take that as a warning and ride."

Without a word, but with his lips pressed firmly
together, the released prisoner stepped past Rory, out
the door, and took the reins from Key's hands. He
climbed onto the saddle, ignored Rory but looked down
at Marshal Key. "I'll see you again, kid."

Key had the maturity to keep his mouth shut, but he
returned the comment with a steady stare that held
intensity the likes of which Webb had seldom seen.

Webb turned onto the town road and put his ride
into a slow lope. Key and Rory watched until he was out
of sight.

Rory rode to the Double J for an evening at home and
all the benefits that promised. Before retiring for the
night, he wrote a lengthy letter to Oscar Cator. He wrote
another to Block Handly. This one he would fold into a
small box Eliza had found for him. He would add the
sack of gold coins. He would pass the letter and the
package directly to the stage whip in the morning. It was
possible that Block and Oscar would have their notes in
hand before Webb returned to the city.

A FELT duty had Rory making a quick ride up to the fort. Wiley Hamstead, still becoming familiar with his position as town marshal, was standing in front of his little office when Rory rode up and stepped down. Wiley took the reins and tied the animal. He stepped a bit to the side and ran his hand down the animal's neck.

"Sweated up pretty good, Rory. I take it you've made some miles this day."

"We have for a fact, Wiley. Walk to the livery with me. You can bring me up-to-date as I'm caring for my animal."

"Not much to tell, Rory. A couple of drunks that were full of remorse, embarrassment, and sore bones after a night on the floor of the cell. Craziest thing you ever saw. The two of them got into a fight right there in the cell over which one would get the bunk and which the floor. Upshot was they both slept on the floor. Judge fined them ten dollars, which neither man could pay, and sent them on their way. We probably won't see them or the fine money again until next payday.

"Grady Stiles wants to see you."

"Alright. I'll see him right after I finish with the horse and find something to eat myself."

WALKING INTO STILES EMPORIUM, Rory stepped to the side of the service counter. Grady was wrapping an order of clothing in a large sheet of brown paper torn from the roll kept for that purpose. The woman who made the purchase was watching every move. Rory stepped back a bit when he realized the woman saw him as a potential threat, as if he might reach in and grab off one of her purchases. Grady completed that task by tying a wrap of sturdy string around the package, then waited on one more customer before turning to Rory.

"Good to see you back, Sheriff. I heard you were intent on visiting the high country."

"I was, and I did. More going on up there than I knew about. I missed the little settlement of MacNair's Hill for our census. I had been led to believe there were a few hopeful prospectors digging around, but there's much more than that. I'd say the few that are there are there to stay. Until their efforts prove futile, at least. There's been a bit of color found. Someone is building a stamp mill. That shows faith in the findings. Quite the town."

Grady had no comment on that subject. He moved right into the thing he wanted to talk to Rory about.

"Fella here some days ago looking for you. Name of Simon Webb. He didn't make any friends during his visit. When Marshal Wiley explained how we like a quiet town, he climbed back on his horse. We haven't seen him since. You know him?"

"Met him a couple of days ago down in Stevensville. The town marshal had him locked up. Disagreeable sort of fella. Made a lot of noise but refused to prove his claim to be a federal agent. Young Key, the town marshal down there, somehow got the drop on him and put him behind bars. After explaining that he was no longer welcome in town, we let him go. He never did get around to saying why he was looking for me."

Grady nodded at this information before saying, "Good. Sounds like you have that one under control. Now tell me about this MacNair's Hill."

FEELING the need to ride back up the hill, Rory rode directly to Stevensville and then from there to the I-5, a convenient jumping-off spot for the climb up to gold country. Along the way, he did another thorough search of Kiril's cabin and land but could find no sign of occupancy since his last visit. He rode into MacNair's Hill late in the afternoon. Buck was standing in front of the office as he rode up and dismounted.

"Afternoon, Buck. How goes it?"

"Got myself appointed town marshal. Town never seen fit to get no badge, but the word got out. Expect pretty much everyone knows. Ain't had to shoot no one yet. Nor even threaten to. Got something we need to talk about, though. Come inside where we can sit out of the sun. Fall sun seems to stream down that valley after it's circled behind the mountain. Hot for this time of year."

Rory grinned at the thought of this former town bully talking about the setting sun. Someday he hoped to get Buck to talk about himself, but he knew better than to push that topic.

Settling onto the two chairs Rory had rustled a few days before, the two men stared at each other as if each was waiting for the other to begin the conversation. Rory was determined to outwait his new deputy. It took a full slow minute, but finally, Buck started to talk.

"I still ain't altogether sure this is what the Lord had in mind when he put me on this earth, but here I sit anyway."

Surprised at the statement, Rory said, "Why, Buck. I'm surprised, and pleased, to hear you referring to the Lord for our placement in life."

"All I mean by that is if I'm in the wrong place and He ain't happy about it, I could end up getting my tail feathers shot off. Then I wouldn't be happy either.

Course I'd also be dead, and no one knows for sure what all that really means."

"Well, Deputy, you still have your tail feathers, so why don't you tell me about your first few days."

"Took the first day to get settled in here. Found an old cast-iron stove someone had thrown aside. Dragged it down here and set 'er up. Cut a hole in the side wall for the chimney, as you can plainly see. Smokes into the room a bit, but it works. Then I hammered some old boards together for a cot. Covered it with hay I talked the liveryman out of and bought me some blankets. Should be alright till the weather gets real cold.

"Walked down to my claim and dug around a bit. Ran across a nice seam and dug 'er out. Don't rightly know if it goes anywhere, but there was a handful of pay rock in that one big chunk. Busted it out and sold it to MacNair. Fella working the claim next to mine seems to have hit it big, if what he's working on continues into the hill. One or two more like that will bring in the big boys with money. They'll buy everyone out for small change and make a fortune themselves. I ain't selling, though."

"I'm glad for you on the claim, Buck. But have you seen anything to worry you around the town or district?"

"Nothing a lawman could do anything about with only suspicion to go on. Four fellas rode in a few days ago. Just after you left, actually. Stabled their horses and disappeared into the saloon. They've done nothing suspicious that I've seen but waste their time. But you understand, wasted time is time you might have made a big hit in gold country. Not many fellas just sett'n around. Everyone's working. Folks used to think I was just lazing about, but I done a sight of work on that claim. Got another registered claim further up the hill

129

too. No trail nor horse path. Have to climb 'er on foot. I staked 'er and registered it through that legal man what does those things for prospectors. That Terrence fella.

"Seen those two that called you out in the dining room that time. The tough look'n fella and his Indian friend. Just seemed to be rid'n about, snooping into everything. I hunted out where they were sleeping in the brush and put it to them direct. I wanted to know what they were doing. Said they were looking for a likely claim. I don't believe them, but I let it go. They rode out yesterday. No idea where to."

Rory listened carefully and thought clearly before he said anything. Finally, he felt confident enough to say, "You're off to a fine start, Buck. Good for you. Now, what do you say to a bit of dinner? I've been riding on creek water and promises since morning. My stomach is beginning to question my wisdom."

THE DINING ROOM was busy with only a few chairs left and no spaces at the long tables. Rory barely had a chance to glance across the room when he heard a voice holler out of the din of clanking cutlery and conversation. "Over here, Sheriff." He followed the voice to a corner table with two empty chairs. Seated in the third chair was Terrence. Rory led Buck over, and both shook hands with the lawyer.

"Join me, boys?"

"Kind of you, Terrence. Kind of makes up for the time you joined me in the saloon a while back."

Both men were smiling. "Kind of the same, I'd guess."

They settled in with Terrence turning to Buck and asking, "So how were your first few days, Buck?"

Buck was still a bit intimidated by anyone that reeked of authority, or at least he made out to be, but he managed to say, "Alright, I guess. No problems."

Wishing to encourage the much-changed man, Terrence responded, "I've seen gold camps before. Sometimes things are not exactly as they seem. You keep your eyes open and your wits about you. Don't look for unnecessary trouble or challenges and you'll be alright. And try to line up a couple of men who will side you when trouble comes. With any luck at all, perhaps we can keep this camp peaceful."

The conversation wound on as they ate their dinners, with Rory calling an end to the meeting with, "Men, I like to go for a bit of a walk after dinner. Alone, if you don't mind. I do my best thinking when riding or walking alone."

Terrence, getting in one last question, asked, "Anything special you're thinking about, Sheriff?"

"The main thing right now is my realization of how large this county is. Down on the flatlands, this lawing all seemed pretty doable. But when we add in the uphill side with more growing ranches and now this mining activity, the job seems almost overwhelming. Well, it is overwhelming for one man. Having Buck up here eases my mind a bit, but it's still a big territory. It will do with some thinking. Good evening, men. Buck, I'll roll my blankets on the office floor later if that won't crowd you too much."

He walked away without waiting for an answer, turning his words into a statement rather than a question.

14

THE NEXT MORNING, LEAVING BUCK TO MANAGE HIS OWN plans for the day, Rory saddled up with the idea of scouting out the upper end of the valley. Avoiding the dining room and the inevitable conversations and questions his presence would draw, he rode over to the saloon. He hadn't yet eaten there, but the word was that the bartender's wife was an excellent cook. He hoped he could take his meal in peace.

After a satisfying breakfast, he pushed his plate away in order to pull his last cup of coffee closer, reflecting on the plate of side meat, eggs, fried potatoes, and the two slices of toast—a rarity anywhere on the frontier. From the crowded premises, he could logically conclude that a lot of miners, who would feel more comfortable at MacNair's when they wanted a drink in the evenings, had discovered the woman's talents. He decided he'd return if he stayed in town. He slid the price of the meal and an extra coin under the edge of his plate and went to his horse. He tightened the cinch and mounted.

The mountain valley he followed ran on a northwest

angle, judging from his internal compass as well as the position of the rising sun over his right shoulder, and rose to form an easily followed basin between the two larger hills. Almost immediately after putting the town limits behind him, he started seeing workings on both sides of the trail. Most were exploratory holes, soon abandoned after a few days' work. But two were active, with small crews hard at work. Another was being worked by a single man who didn't bother looking up as Rory went past.

One-quarter mile beyond the town limits, work was being done on the ore crusher. It was far enough advanced for Rory to become curious about how it worked. He rode closer, taking in the entire building site as well as the machine itself. Studying the round vertical rods with large cast-iron cylinders attached to their bottoms, he logically assumed that the lifting and dropping of these heavy weights would be the heart of the crusher. There were five of these rods standing side by side inside a metal and timber enclosure.

He pulled his horse as close as he could without bothering the workers, hooked his knee over the horn, and sat back, intent on watching the proceeding. Immediately two thoughts entered his mind. The first was what hard, heavy work was involved in the construction. That led him to consider the follow-up work of shoveling the ore chunks into the hopper and removing the crushed product away to the tailings pile after the valuable ore was extracted. Those thoughts were quickly followed by relief that he wasn't one of the crew.

He had been there several minutes when the foreman quit shouting orders at the crew and sauntered over to confront Rory.

"Help ya, mister?"

"I hope I'm not in your way, sir, I'm just curious about what this is and how it works. I have a general idea, is all."

"And who are you, and why would any of that matter to you?"

The question was clearly belligerent. Rory let the challenge go and answered civilly enough to mollify the foreman.

"As to who I am, my name is Rory Jamison, county sheriff. I'm not here because of your work or mine. I'm just interested in exactly what this is and how it works. I'm more familiar with cattle and ranching country than I am with hard-rock mining. Other than that, I'm just looking the valley over. Kind of familiarizing myself with the workings. I spent some years in a gold panning claim, so I understand a bit about the mineral, but these rocky hillsides are pretty much a mystery to me."

As it had done with the two miners the week before, mention of having worked the creeks mellowed the foreman just a bit.

"Called a crusher or a hammer mill by some, but more accurately, it's a stamp mill. After you listen to it working for a while, you'll think up all kinds of other names for it. None of them friendly. You can easily see those bins on the back side of the frame. That's where the wagons back in to shovel the quartz rock into the big hopper. It's the quartz that carries the gold. The chunks of useless host rock are picked out back at the mine. Only the pay rock is brought to the mill.

"The operator opens the ore chute to let in just the right amount of ore, and the stamps crush it to small bits. You can see those slots built into the metal frame. That's where the escape screens will go when we're finished. The crushed ore, looking a bit like large sand, makes its way through the screens while more ore is continually let into the crushing pan. The fines are released into another chute, where water washes them over a big table that we haven't put in place yet. The table is painted with a thin covering of mercury. The gold is attracted to the mercury and scraped off, and you've got yourself a collection of pay dirt. Then it's just the cleanup—separating the gold from the mercury and recapturing the mercury so it can be used again.

"The whole thing is powered by a steam engine. You can see the crew over there putting it together, ready to be mounted on that concrete footing.

"Of course, there's a bit more to the process than what I just said, but I've told you the gist of it."

Rory thanked the man and rode away, trying to imagine the din those five heavy stamps would create. And he had been told that many mills had ten or even twenty stamps. He had heard about some mills being built within town limits, where they would hammer out their misery day and night. He couldn't imagine such a thing, but he was sure he would prefer the peace and solitude of the Double J Ranch given the choice. He was also considering that there was a large investment being made on an unproven field and wondered about it.

He rode on until he finally saw no more digging taking place. He had spoken to none of the miners, not having any particular questions he hadn't had answers to already. On the return ride, he stopped to talk with a miner that appeared to be quitting for the day.

"Afternoon, sir. About ready to shut it down for the day?"

"Hard work, being alone. Six hours is enough for one morning. I'll take a break, have a little nap, and be back at it for the afternoon."

Rory rode a bit closer and introduced himself. The miner's response was, "Halverson, here. Heard there was a sheriff up here looking around. Heard, too, that Buck, he that owns that hole next to mine, was taken on as deputy. He's a better man than most give credit for. He'll handle the job alright."

Pointing, Rory said, "That's Buck's right there?"

The answer was simply a nod. Rory took a closer look at the beginnings of a mine that represented Buck's work and hopes and waved at Halverson, saying, "Good luck on the digging."

The miner had turned back to his work. If he saw Rory's wave, he ignored it.

~

HE ARRIVED BACK in town in time for lunch. *Spend most of my time in one dining room or the other.*

15

AT NOON THE NEXT DAY, RORY WAS JUST RETURNING FROM a visit with Terrence when an excited Buck hollered across the road, calling him over to the office. Buck, with no horse, walked the mile to his claim each day. He had alternated between walking and a slow run on his return that morning. When Rory met him in the office, he was sitting in a chair, trying to recover his breath. He took three or four more deep breaths and blurted out, "That claim next to mine. The one I told you had made a strike. There's a whole crew there this morning, and no sign of Halverson, the fella that owns the claim. When I walked over and asked what was going on, I was told I was on private property and I wasn't welcome. I might have stood up to the one fella, but there were seven or eight of them there, and each one armed. Three or four look like miners. Looked uncomfortable with gun belts hanging on their hips. The others have all the appearances of toughs. Gunslingers. When I asked where Halverson was, I was told again to get off the claim. Something not quite right going on down there."

Rory thought for a moment and then said, "Go rent a riding animal. The county will cover the cost. Then stay here until I return."

Rory walked across the road and down the boardwalk to MacNair's place. He entered and went directly to the rack of weapons for sale. MacNair joined him there, asking, "Look'n for something special, Sheriff?"

"Yes. I'll be needing a couple of shotguns. Double twelves, if they're available. Used is fine. The price is the thing, not the looks of the weapon."

"I have just the one. Ten dollars, and she's yours, and a box of shells to go with it."

"Alright, I'll take it. I'll check at the saddlery for another."

WITHIN MINUTES RORY was walking back to the jailhouse with the double tucked into the crook of his arm. The box of shells was held firmly in his other hand. He had loaded the gun before leaving the emporium. At the jailhouse, he passed the gun to Buck and asked, "Do you know how to use this?"

The smiling Buck responded, "Just aim anywhere close to your target and let 'er rip. How hard can that be?"

"Alright, but be careful. I loaded both barrels. You'll notice that the hinge is a bit wobbly. Not much, but maybe enough to be a problem. We'll have to take care."

With Buck's ready agreement, Rory said, "Sit tight," and left the building again, leaving the door open behind him. The walk to the saddlery was short, and the visit was quick. Before long, Rory was back in the office with a reasonable match to the gun bought from MacNair.

This one he loaded after lifting two shells from the box on the desk Buck had found somewhere. He snapped the breech closed. Neither weapon would fire until the hammers were pulled into their cocked and ready position.

Rory had no idea what Buck knew about firearms, so he risked giving offense by repeating his previous warning.

"Buck, we'll leave the hammers uncocked until we get right to the mine. These guns have considerable use on them. They both feel a bit loose in the joints. We don't know how trusty the mechanisms are. We don't want them going off unexpectedly. And when we cock them, we'll still hold our fingers outside the trigger guard. And we'll hold the barrels pointing a bit over the men's heads in case a hammer somehow falls. It's easy enough to lower the aim if that becomes necessary. All agreed?"

Buck agreed with a nod and picked up one gun.

"Alright then, let's ride, Buck. I want you to remember that the weapons are for our safety and for leaving a message with the men we're confronting. A message they're sure to understand. Hopefully, we can tell the gunslingers from the pick-and-shovel men. We're hoping we don't have to pull the triggers. I'm hoping the sight of four barrels loaded with buckshot will bring out the wisdom in the men. A man has to be a fool to stand against a shotgun, but if someone does, don't waste a warning shot. You won't get a second shot off if you do that. If there's time when something happens, follow my lead."

The daily walk for Buck took nearly a half-hour when he wasn't in a particular hurry. On horseback, that time was cut to just a few minutes. Rory pointed his gelding directly at the gathered gang and stopped within easy shotgun range. He turned the horse a little to his right to allow a clear shooting path to his left. Buck followed that lead. Every man on the claim stopped what he was doing and stood looking at the two lawmen. Perhaps it was the shotguns they were looking at.

"I'm Rory Jamison, county sheriff. Buck here is deputy county sheriff and town marshal. I'd like if you men would unbuckle your belts and drop your weapons. Then we can have a talk."

The man who had run Buck off less than an hour before said, "We got nothing to talk about, and we're not dropping our weapons. You have no cause to confront us this way. We're only doing a job of work we were sent here to do."

Rory answered, "You see, there's the problem right there. You don't own this claim, and you have no right to be working it. Now, drop the weapons."

The leader said, "You got it to do, kid."

"Well, I've done it a few times before, and I'm still here. Don't want to do it again but it's your choice. It could be you've never seen the path of destruction a twelve-gauge leaves behind it. Take my word for it. You would have just no chance at all.

"Now, there's no need for anyone getting hurt here this morning. We just have some questions for you, and we'll be expecting answers. Now, if you pick-and-shovel men would drop your weapons and move to the side, I'd appreciate it."

Four of the seven men in sight moved to the side, unbuckling their belts as they went. Rory thanked them and then, looking at the three remaining men, said, "I'm assuming you three are the guards to make sure these men do their work and that no one interferes. It's you I want the answers from."

He looked at the men who had stepped aside.

"You, blue shirt, go harness that team I see over there and get that wagon ready to roll. You others had best get a bit further away. I wouldn't want any innocent men spilling their blood for a dollar a day and a hard bunk in a filthy tent. Red shirt, you gather up those belts and bring them to me. Come to the off side of this horse."

It was less than one minute later that red shirt held the belts up to Rory. He took them one by one and draped them over the neck of his gelding. With that done, the pick-and-shovel men shuffled aside. One man went to help harness the team.

Rory looked again at the gunmen.

"Now or never, men. Whatever you've got going here or whatever your boss has promised you, it isn't worth dying over."

A hard-looking gunman standing behind the leader said, "I'm out of it, Herc. Even at forty a month, I'm not standing against no shotguns at twenty feet. There'll be another day."

The second man said, "That speaks for me, too, Herc."

Herc, nearly trembling with anger, had no choice. He reached for his belt buckle, never taking his eyes off Rory. In a touch of bravado, he said, "Kid, you don't want to ever be where we're alone and you without a shotgun." Rory ignored the comment.

With blue shirt holding the reins to the team, the wagon load of men was soon settled in front of the jailhouse. The wagon's passing through town, with seven unhappy men crowded into the back and Buck riding behind, holding the shotgun at the ready, caused a bit of a stir as it moved along. Many eyes followed its travels, wondering what was happening.

At the jail, Rory instructed the pick-and-shovel men

to sit tight while Buck ushered the three gunslingers into the jail cell. With no prompting from Rory, Buck had each man drop, one by one, from the tailgate they were seated on and stand while he searched them for weapons. Only when he was satisfied with the collection of knives and hideout guns forming the small pile on the wagon's tailgate, did Buck point at the door with the shotgun. There was no need for further words.

Before turning the miners loose, Rory asked each his name, where he had been recently working, and who had hired him. He jotted this information in the tablet he carried in his shirt pocket.

"Alright, men. I'm trusting that you're honest men put to a dishonest job. You must have suspected something was wrong when you were surrounded by gunmen, but we'll let that go for now. Don't cause trouble in my town. If I come for you again, you're not going to enjoy the experience."

The men wasted no time crossing the road and heading for MacNair's Saloon, leaving their weapons behind. Rory dismounted and entered the jailhouse. Buck had been busy. He turned a piece of paper on the desktop so that Rory could read it. There were three names, and then a fourth a bit lower down. Buck said, "Claim that's their names. I have some doubts, but it will have to do. The one below is the moneyman that hired them. Rory read the names slowly, especially the fourth, scrambling for familiarity. But he had never heard any of them before. Another part of his mind was noting Buck's almost script-like penmanship. He salted the information in the back of his mind to discuss with Buck another time.

He read the names aloud. "Herc Branson. Tidy Sampson. Montana Red. Creative, if nothing else, fellas. I suspect Buck is correct. These aren't the names on your baptismal certificates, but they'll do for now. You'll probably be hung and buried with these names someday. Now, just to set your minds at ease. We're not charging you with any crime today, depending on what you tell us. Tell us who hired you and where Halverson is, and we'll unlock that door."

Herc said, "Halverson, if that's his name, we weren't introduced. Left out walking last evening after we got there. I mentioned the buyer's name, and he just turned and walked away."

"Which way did he go, Herc?"

"Not into town. He was heading further up the valley."

"Alright. Now, who and where is the moneyman? It says on this sheet Emmett Streetly. Is that the right guy, or is he just the front man?"

"That's who hired and paid us. Don't know any more than that. We never met anyone else. If he's fronting for someone, you'll have to find that out for yourself. We know nothing more."

"Last question, men. Where can I find this Emmett Streetly?"

"He hired us out of the saloon down in Hovel Hill."

Rory smiled a bit and said, "Strange name. Never heard it before. Is that another gold camp?"

"Right prosperous gold camp if you were to ask me. Named before the big strikes, I'm guessing."

"Is this Emmett a moneyman around the claims and the town, or is he just a runner?"

"You already asked that question, kid, using different words. Answer's the same."

"And Hovel Hill is where?"

"You follow the two-track south out of town. Maybe

three hours ride on a solid gelding, and you'll be at the Hill."

"Alright, men. You're free to go. I'd advise that you look more carefully at job offers in the future. Even a blind man could see that you were working on a steal. Buck will give you your unloaded weapons. Don't do anything foolish with them. And as a word of advice, I wouldn't doubt that you'd find some other town more to your liking. Probably even some other county."

With that, he lifted the key off the peg and unlocked the cell door. He stood aside as the men filed out and picked up their gun belts. Without a word, they left the small room, heading for the livery and their horses.

Rory and Buck walked to the dining room and ordered lunch. As they were waiting for their meals, Rory eased into the topic of Buck's handwriting.

"Buck. Looking at your handwriting, I'm guessing that you're even further from your origins than I at first guessed."

When Buck simply stared at the table, choosing to make no response, Rory let it go.

16

RORY HAD BID BUCK FAREWELL AS HE MOUNTED HIS gelding, heading for Hovel Hill. On the way out of town, he pulled the gelding to a stop in front of the tiny law office of Terrence Climber. The lawyer saw him coming and stepped outside.

"Afternoon, Sheriff. What's in the wind this crisp fall day?"

"Hovel Hill. You know it?"

"Sure enough. I've got an office there. Don't use it much, but I keep it just the same."

"Emmett Streetly. You know him too?"

"Know him and like him. Great guy if you're just looking for someone to have dinner with. Interesting to talk to. A bit shady, otherwise."

"Is he the moneyman or just the front man, the delivery boy?"

"Well now, Sheriff, that's a question no one seems to have an answer for. Doesn't work. Doesn't mine. Sticks close to town most days. Goes on what he calls his 'ride abouts' from time to time. Could be gone overnight or even a couple of nights. Never talks about those rides, and if he's asked, he clams up. I do know he's been through to MacNair's Hill a few times."

"Does he seem real friendly with MacNair himself?"

"Can't say. I've never seen them together."

"Did the news about Halverson get to you, or should I tell you about it?"

"I heard. It's a small town. News seems to float through the air, and it never takes long. No sign of the man?"

"None I've heard of."

"You turn those men loose? I saw them riding past."

"They're free to ride. I had nothing to hold them on except bad judgment, and that's not a crime."

The two men fell silent, studying each other as if waiting for something. Finally, Rory told the lawyer about the incident down in Stevensville.

Terrence grinned and finally said, "Simon Webb. Wrong man in the wrong job. He hasn't the temperament or the judgment for law work. He can shoot a pistol, though. I'm glad it didn't come to that with you."

"Do you think it's logical for him to have a sack holding seventeen tarnished gold coins in his saddlebags?"

That question set Terrence back some and drew nothing but silence from him. After the silence wore on a bit, he finally said, "Can't imagine Block putting him on that job. The gold coin mystery calls for caution and easing into the evidence, not charging around like a bull in springtime."

"Thanks, Terrence. I'll see you when I get back."

As Terrence watched him ride away, he thought, *Good kid. Smart. I'd hate to see him get his tail in a crack.*

17

AFTER A BIT OF A POKY START ON THE DAY AND A FEW
short side trips to examine digging operations, Rory
arrived in Hovel Hill too late for any meaningful work.
He took the time to ride from end-to-end of the little
village and then rode further into the valley, following
the *thump*, *thump*, *thump* hammering of the stamp mill.
Even a few seconds of listening to the ground-shaking
racket convinced him that his initial thought was accurate. He preferred the quiet of the Double J. Still, he
wanted to watch it work.

He sat his horse close enough to see the workings of
the mill without getting in the way of the miners and
mill operators. No one came near, and he didn't stay
long. He was soon back in town looking for a restaurant
and a hotel. He found the restaurant without a problem,
but the six-room hotel was full. Knowing no one could
make a living renting six rooms, he figured they
depended more on the attached saloon.

He turned back to the restaurant and entered. Here
there were no long tables with bench seating. He spotted

a small table along the back wall with a single chair on either side. He wound through the other diners and took a seat facing the room and the door.

He laid his hat on the empty chair and looked over the crowd of men. No one was paying him the slightest attention, which suited him just fine. And then there was. His eyes had swept past the interior of the room without expecting to see anyone he knew. But as he reversed his glance, he found himself looking right into the eyes of Herc Branson. The two men held each other's gaze for a brief few seconds before Herc turned back to his food. Rory was not totally surprised to see the man. He thought the gunman may have ridden further, hunkering down for a few days to allow the Halverson mine episode to cool a bit.

This was where the gun crew had been hired, and obviously, this was where they had returned to. They must feel safe in Hovel Hill. Remembering Herc's threats, he knew he would have to be careful.

After a satisfying dinner, he walked his horse to the livery and treated him to a gallon of corn and a good rubdown. The hostler didn't offer to help. As he was working on the gelding, a familiar voice said, "Now you see here, My Way, there's a sensitive and diligent man. Holds true to his respect for a good animal. Might be the kind of man we could share the loft with. What do you think of that, My Way?"

Rory gave time for the Indian to answer, but My Way saw no need to comment. He dragged his brush over the gelding's back once more, working his way toward his off-side hip. That move put Ivan and My Way directly into his line of vision. He grinned at the two men, saying, "Haven't seen you for so long, I thought you went to your blankets in the bush and a bear ate you."

"No bear," said My Way. He so seldom spoke that both Rory and Ivan were surprised at the comment. They were even more surprised to see a rare grin forming on the Indian's lips.

Ivan said, "You see there, My Way. It was only two days ago we saw this lawman. It must mean he misses us and wants to stay close."

It never took Rory long to get serious. "You fellas been up here a couple of days. That's a long time in a place this small. What have you found out?"

Ivan said, "Found out that there's a whole lot going on up here that ain't necessarily to the advantage of the small miner. Haven't been able to sort any of it out. Sorting it out, right down to the bare facts, is what I mean to say.

"Saw a couple of coins your friends down in the big city would be interested in. Thought to buy them off the storekeeper but decided to show no interest. Might hold to our mine-search story better if I said nothing."

Ivan's statements caught the sheriff's attention. He looked over his two friends as he quickly mulled on the statements. Finally, he said, "Is there somewhere we can talk? I just got to town. The hotel is full. Did I hear right? Are you sleeping in the loft?"

Ivan answered, "We are. Getting mighty cold of a night now, though. The hostler is friendly and trustworthy. Let's go to the office. There're chairs and a nice little woodstove there. We can have our visit in comfort."

Ivan opened the office door and led My Way and Rory inside. The hostler was taking his ease, leaning back in a well-worn rocking chair. Ivan said, "Cain, this is a friend of mine. Meet Rory Jamison. Rory, this is Cain Glidden. Hostler and former miner. A good man to know."

Ivan made no mention of Rory being sheriff.

Cain didn't bother to stand, but he did hold out his hand.

"You'll have to pardon me for not standing, Sheriff. And for not offering my help with your animal. I can get up and walk a bit, if need be, but I'd as soon not. Rockfall a few years ago put paid to my prospecting and mining. Pretty near put paid to everything else too. Now, mostly, I sit and hope to collect enough livery fees to keep body and soul together. And don't look so surprised, Mr. Jamison. Your name is known to me. And not from these two who are trying to hide the fact that they're deputies snooping around for information. The deputies are new to me, but I've known your name for a year or more. I kept watching for you when you were gathering names for the county vote, but you didn't make it up this high."

That whole short speech was cloaked in a satisfied grin. The hostler looked at both Rory's and Ivan's startled expressions and laughed.

"News doesn't get into these hills quickly, Deputy, but it does eventually get here. I heard weeks ago about the sheriff and his deputy trying to sort out Kiril's death. Well, not his death exactly. That appears to be from natural causes of some sort. It's the fallout of his death that has caused a bit of a stir. And before you ask again, yes, I knew Kiril. Not well, you understand. Just from stabling his horse and talking a bit a couple of times.

"More recently, I heard the deputy was riding with an Indian. An Indian that says little but sees much. That came from some fellas who had been down below for a few days and were passing through. But don't worry. I doubt anyone else in town knows."

Rory, always on guard, said, "If you know, how can you be so sure no one else knows?"

"Because I get my news from a friend. A trusted friend. He hears just about everything. Knows things. Sees things. Drives a freight wagon up from Denver to each of these towns. Winter will put a stop to most of it pretty soon now, but until then, he's a fountain of information."

The hostler then turned toward Ivan and My Way.

"And don't you two worry about the four you chased away from Kiril's cabin. They told me about you when they stalled their horses, but they didn't know about your being deputies. Come to think of it, they didn't mention the Indian. Perhaps you weren't seen, My Way."

Rory was suspicious, and he didn't mind if the hostler knew it.

"Mr. Glidden, you've convinced Ivan that you're to be trusted. Now convince me. I could use a friend in town, so I'm ready to be persuaded."

"The best proof I have, Sheriff, is that you're still alive. There are men and places in these valleys where your identification could have a different outcome. You take those three you chased out of MacNair's. Herc Branson and them. They'd as soon shoot you as look at you. Of course, they know about you being sheriff, but not about Ivan and My Way. It's best you boys keep to your story. You're cattlemen looking to explore the gold mine business.

"Now, Sheriff, you can either trust me or not, but if it's not, I just can't say where else you might go for information."

Rory had made a decision as the man spoke. He was not absolutely sure, to the point where he wouldn't be careful, but then, he was aways careful.

"Mr. Glidden. I'll take what you say as the truth, reminding you that I'm not a good one to cross either.

Now, what I need to know first is, who is Emmett Streetly? Or perhaps my question should be who and what is Mr. Streetly?"

Cain's eyes opened in surprise. He paused a moment before saying, "I see you have done some homework, Sheriff. Asked the right questions, I might say. And I might also guess that Herc did a bit of talking."

"It's hard not to be serious with the twin barrels of a double twelve pointed in your direction."

"Yes. I've never experienced that particular situation, but I can easily imagine. Well, to your question, Emmett Streetly is a friend of mine. A friend to many folks here in the Hovel and up and down the valleys. If you were to ask on what basis we were friends, I might have to simply say we're two men in a very small settlement. Men with no families nearby. Men of similar backgrounds and likes. If you were to ask if I trust him, I would have to say that I do, as long as I can see him and know what he's doing. He has another reputation, beyond friendly, in his dealings. But I don't question him on that."

Offering recent news, Rory said, "He's the moneyman that sent Herc and his friends to MacNair's Hill and the diggings of a miner named Halverson, a miner that had recently made a substantial strike."

Cain leaned even further back in his chair and studied Rory. He blinked several times and seemed to be sucking on his teeth before he said, "News. It's all about hearing news of events. So we're left with a question. Where would that news come from? It's not like a miner to shout his finds around the town. So where else could it have come from?"

Under his breath, Ivan said, "The assayer."

Rory was quick to look his way with, "Say that again, Ivan."

"What I said was, 'the assayer.' Who else would know? Or who would be in a better position to know?"

Cain was grinning at the quickness of the answer.

Rory accepted the suggestion, with his mind looking back on MacNair himself. That brought up another question for Cain.

"Does Streetly have money, or is he fronting for a moneyman?"

"Now you're getting down to it, Sheriff. The right question demands the right answer. And I don't have that answer. He always has money, but that's just enough to play the big shot in the saloon or around town. He's never shown any more wealth than that."

Rory lifted one of the tarnished coins from his pocket and showed it to Cain.

"Have you ever seen Streetly with any of these?"

"Just the once. Paid his livery bill with one. He had gone out to the city for several weeks in late winter. Returned when most of the snow was off. Owed for all that time. Paid with the tarnished ten piece. I thought nothing of it. Just another coin to me."

"Do you still have it?"

"No, Sheriff. I turned it over in exchange for my winter account over at the mercantile."

18

BEFORE CLIMBING DOWN FROM THE LOFT THE NEXT morning, Rory looked over at Ivan, who was just pulling on his pants after digging the bits of hay out of his underwear and his hair. Rory was dressed and ready to go. My Way had dropped to the floor of the barn a half hour before.

"Ivan, I have a job of work, I'd like if you and My Way would take it on. Miner down MacNair's Hill way, fella named Halverson, is missing. He was run off his claim by some toughs. Those toughs call Hovel Hill home. I asked them to leave Halverson's diggings. After thinking it over a bit, they decided it would be the prudent thing to do, given the circumstances. I saw the leader, one Herc Branson, in the restaurant last evening. He saw me, too, but neither of us said anything. He and the others were hired and paid by Emmett Streetly. He's also from Hovel Hill, but I haven't met him yet.

"I'd like if you and My Way would ride down and scout around a bit. Branson said Halverson had simply picked up his coat and headed further up the valley when he was told to leave the claim. He may be alive, or he may be dead. As far as I could see, there was no other digging at that end of the valley. He could be hunkered down waiting for an opportunity to strike back, so don't take any chances. Don't assume he'll be happy to see you. But bring him back to town if you can."

Ivan asked, "Mind if we get some breakfast first?" He was grinning as he said it, knowing the answer already.

Rory dug into his pocket and lifted out a few coins. Holding them out to Ivan, he said, "You must be near enough broke by now. I'm not too far from it myself. I'll have to ride down pretty soon and raid the county account in Ambrewster's bank.

"If you can find Halverson and get him back on his own claim, we'll call that success for now. I'm going to try to find Emmett Streetly. Then we'll see what happens from there."

They separated before leaving the livery. Ivan and My Way had saddled their horses and were ready to ride after breakfast. Rory rapped lightly on Cain Glidden's door and entered when he heard the invite.

Cain turned the handle of the coffeepot toward Rory as a silent invite. Rory filled a porcelain mug that had been washed and placed upside down on a shelf above the stove. He looked at the hostler and smiled. "Good morning. And thanks."

Cain adjusted his position on the rocker, looking for some relief for his broken and poorly healed hips. He looked as if he was struggling between saying what was on his mind and holding his silence. He finally said, "Figured you'd be back after the others rode out."

Rory answered, "I hoped you might have thought of something I should know."

"Good choice of words, Sheriff. I'm thinking you're

an educated man. You talk well, and you choose your words carefully. I've a bit of education myself. I know the signs in a man."

"I'm as educated as a man can get, learning his letters and doing his numbers sitting at the kitchen table or in a tent on a day that's too rainy to work the stream. My father was a reader. Always trading for books. He read them and passed them on to me. I guess I've read a hundred books or more. Some great. Some that should not have been published, but I read them all anyway."

"Should not have been published. You mean like that magazine on the table behind you?"

Rory turned and dug the magazine from under a small gathering of newspapers and a well-worn copy of Dickens's *Barnaby Rudge*, one of the author's lesser-known efforts. He turned the magazine right side up and read the lead story title. In large print, almost overshadowed by the garish pictures of smoking guns and dying men, along with a half-dressed woman hanging on to the only man left standing, was the title, "Sheriff Rory Leaves No One Standing." He looked and then looked back up at the hostler. The man was struggling to hold back his laughter.

"You didn't really think you'd escape those vultures, did you?"

All Rory could think to say was, "Where did you get this?"

"Came on the last supply train from the big city. They'll be all over the country by now."

Rory flipped a couple of pages and then dropped the offensive tablet back onto the table. With an inward shudder, he brought the conversation back to where he had intended it would be.

"I'd appreciate if you could tell me more about

Emmett Streetly. Where he lives, or where I might find him? Who he associates with? Have any mines up here mysteriously come down with new owners, with the old owners disappearing? And was Streetly involved? Any other thoughts along that line you might have."

Rory hadn't seen Cain smoking the night before, although he could smell the residue of stale smoke in the room. Now the man pulled a pipe from his overalls' pocket and fished under even more newspapers to find his tobacco pouch. He took his time cleaning and then refilling the bowl, glancing from that task to Rory and then back to the pipe. He struck a match on the side of the cast-iron stove and lit up. He blew a gray cloud into the air and sighed as if the smoke was satisfying his every desire. He looked back at Rory before he said, "You ask a lot, Sheriff. I live here and make my meager living here. You're going to saddle that gelding and ride back to Stevensville and the Double J. And don't look so surprised. Keeping track of things is the kind of hobby a crippled man can enjoy. Visiting and listening and remembering. I've known your name since that mess up at Pierre, Montana. I forget who told me about that. Some rider that needed shelter for the night I'd suppose."

He puffed on his pipe while Rory waited. Starting in the middle of a sentence, he finally said, "Probably. Probably some mines have changed hands. Like you say. Little place like this. Takes a sight of ore to make 'er pay. Support the town. Man with a pick and shovel ain't going to make that happen, no matter how big his dreams have grown. Some just hang on because their dreams won't let them do anything else. Most sell out to those with the money and expertise to expand the mine. And most of those will take the money and go tapping on rock again, here or somewhere else."

"Can you suggest a mine or two that changed hands and who the original owner was? I have no concern about mines changing hands. My concern is for the men who didn't want to sell but did anyway and are now gone, leaving no message behind."

"Fella named Bittern. Sold The Blue Bell. Last year that was. South maybe the most of a mile, mile-and-a-half. Nearer into town by a bit is Bobby Hepburn's Gray Lady. Named for the color of the rock the quartz is embedded in. No one seems to know what the gray rock is, but it's different from most. That's all anyone knows for sure. Chambers had The Hobbit. That's almost right here in town. I can't tell you any more than that. If the owners sold willingly or not is always a question in an area with no law. You'll have to take it from there yourself."

That bit of information came freely enough. Rory figured it was because news like that could never be kept secret. He could have gotten the same information from the waitress over at the restaurant.

"Thanks. Ivan and My Way rode out this morning. I told them I'd cover their stable bill. I'll be here at least another day. I'll make everything right before I leave."

The hostler had no comment on that arrangement. Rory saddled up and rode across the road for breakfast. As he was leaving the restaurant after eating, a man called to him from where he was sitting in a top buggy. Rory studied the movement on the street before making his way to the buggy. There sat a heavy man, weighted down with pounds that would not have accumulated on a working man. He wasn't an overly tall man. Probably about average. But he was thick in the shoulders, and the thighs of his legs stretched his pants almost to the breaking point. His hair was long. His light beard was blond, easing into gray. The face hair did little to hide the double chin. The smile on his face didn't match the grim cast of his eye. Rory thought, *This could be a dangerous man.*

"No need to worry, Sheriff. I'm alone. I hear you've been asking around about me. Climb up here and let's have us a visit. I'm Emmett Streetly."

"Good morning, Mr. Streetly. Yes, in fact, I've been hearing your name mentioned more than just a few times. I've got a couple of questions. I'm hoping for informative answers. And thanks for the invite to sit, but I'm happy here on the boardwalk. There's no one close by, so I'm sure we can keep our talk confidential, if that matters.

"I heard your name for the first time a couple of days ago, Mr. Streetly. It was in connection with a mine down in MacNair's Hill. A mine owned by a Mr. Halverson. The story was that the mine had somehow magically changed hands overnight, with Mr. Halverson simply picking up a few of his things and walking off into the forest. That's the story I got from Herc Branson. That, and the fact that it was you that hired Herc and a couple of other toughs and a few miners. Is that what happened, Mr. Streetly? Is that how you remember it?"

Streetly looked off down the road and paused before answering.

"I'd say at least some of that is true. Mr. Halverson was pleased to take an immediate profit and turn the hard work over to others. Someone with the ability to bring a larger mine on stream. As to what Halverson did after that, I have no idea. I wasn't there.

"What I do know, Sheriff, is that you used a rather heavy hand to deal with something you knew nothing about. You ran my crew off with no evidence of wrongdoing, and the owner has now lost a couple of days of production."

"He's going to lose more days too. There will be no digging on that site until I can find clear and provable evidence that a sale took place. I need to find Halverson to do that. It would be best all the way around if you didn't send any more men to that site.

"Now, I've been given the names of other mines in this area that have somehow changed ownership, with none of the original owners being seen after the sale. Your name came up in regard to all of those matters, Mr. Streetly. You've been a busy man. I'm going to need the names of the new owners in each case, Mr. Streetly. I'd appreciate you providing me with that information."

"The owners are not inviting publicity, Sheriff. I can't give you any more than you already think you have."

"Ownership is public information, sir. The new owners would have had to register the claims in their names. Can you tell me if they did that themselves, or did they use the services of Terrence Climber?"

Streetly was beginning to look angry and defensive. He covered his distress with, "You have all you're going to get from me, Sheriff. Except for one piece of advice. Go easy. Walk softly. Let sleeping dogs lie, and then ride out, back down the hill, knowing it's good to be alive."

"That sounds more like a threat than advice, Mr. Streetly. Goodbye for now. I'm sure we will be meeting again."

Streetly lightly lashed the rump of the harnessed horse and drove the buggy away.

19

RORY WATCHED THE BUGGY UNTIL IT DISAPPEARED AROUND the corner and then stepped into the saddle. He turned the animal to the south, planning to visit the three mines Cain had mentioned. He would stop first at The Hobbit and ask about Chambers, as well as the new owner.

Cain had said the mine was almost in town, and that proved to be good information. Rory only had to ride a few hundred yards, then off the trail by a bit, and he saw the sign identifying the mine. The first thing he noticed was a steam drill. He had never seen one previously, but he knew what they looked like. The machine was idle at the time. Several men were working at the mine face, perhaps twenty feet inside the hill. A half dozen others were gathered in a bunch outside, not working but with their tools close by.

Rory rode in and said, "Foreman around?"

"That'll be me. What'll it be for ya?"

"Rory Jamison. County sheriff. Looking to find Mr. Chambers."

"Chambers ain't here no more. New owners."

"That's interesting. Can you tell me where Chambers might have gone to?"

"No idea."

"Alright. Then tell me who the new owner is and how I might find him."

"No idea on that either. I just work here, do my job, take my pay, ask no questions."

"Well, sir, that's convenient. Who do you call when something goes wrong or when there's a problem?"

"Streetly. You'll find him down to town I expect."

"And does he bring your pay out to you as well?"

"Does everything for the owner. Now you had best be moving along. The boys have packed a string of holes inside. They're about to blow 'er. I can pretty much guarantee your horse won't like it."

"Thank you, sir. Be careful with that stuff. I'm told that powder doesn't know friend from foe."

With that, he turned the gelding and trotted south on the trail. The foreman was undoubtedly correct, the horse would not react well to an explosion and flying rock. When he heard the solid *whump* of the powder going off, he was far enough away that his gelding did nothing more than wiggle his ears.

IT WAS another short ride to the Gray Lady. He asked the same questions there and got the same answers. The Blue Bell visit provided no new information. Streetly was a busy man.

He rode back to town with much to think about. The first and primary question was, where were Hepburn, Chambers, and Bittern? And how was he going to go about sorting it all out?

20

It wasn't a long ride back to MacNair's Hill. Rory was there in time to find Terrence Climber still at his law office. As he dismounted and headed for the door, he wondered, as he had before, what the man found to do all day long. There didn't seem to be any legal issues to deal with, and the new mines that needed registering were few.

"Afternoon, Sheriff."

"Afternoon, Terrence. It's chilly today. I had to dig my heavy coat out of my bedroll. Reminds me that winter is not going to be long in coming. Do you sit out the cold months up here, or do you head out until spring?"

"Maybe another couple of weeks, and then it will be Denver for me until the snow is off again."

Rory laid out the information on the three mines at Hovel Hill.

"Did you reregister any of those mines? Do you know who the new owners are?"

"No, I didn't, and no, I don't. I've heard about the sales, of course, but no one came to me for help."

"How do I find out who the new owners are?"

"You ride down to the big city, and you get your state friend to pull some strings for you. If you can cut through the red tape, you'll get your answer sometime before spring. Get to the right man, the top man, and you might get the information right away. Otherwise, it could take a while."

Rory sat studying the man. The information had come freely enough, but still, he wondered if there was more to it.

He placed his hat back on his head and stood.

"I'll see you again soon."

As Rory rode off, Terrence was left wondering what this young sheriff's next step would be and where it would all end.

AT THE LIVERY, as he was brushing down the gelding, he tried to sort out his feelings toward Terrence. He was involved somehow. He had claimed to be working undercover for Block Handly, digging into the tarnished gold coin matter. But was he more than that? Was he into something else? Something that would benefit himself directly. He certainly wasn't making any kind of a living from his legal work.

His mind then turned to Ivan and My Way, wondering where they were and what they had managed to find out. And he was wondering where Buck was. He had seen no sign of him at the sheriff's office.

Looking out the big sliding barn door, he decided there was enough light left in the day for a ride to Buck's mine. With Halverson's diggings close by, he might catch an answer or two.

Fifteen minutes later, he heard the sound of a hammer striking steel. Buck was hard at work and didn't see or hear him as he rode up and dismounted. Rory watched until Buck completed what he was doing. He wasn't drilling holes for powder. He had neither the funding nor the knowledge of mining to begin blasting. He settled for chipping out ore-bearing quartz when it was visible and pounding away more host rock when the quartz appeared to be leading further into the hillside. It was backbreaking work, no matter how a person looked at it, much of it done kneeling among the already broken rock debris.

Buck straightened from his work and eased his back. The movement brought Rory into view.

"Hey there, Sheriff. I didn't see you ride up."

With a smile, Rory answered, "Didn't hear me over all that racket either."

"You got that right. But that little bit of pounding is nothing compared to a steam drill grinding or hammering away. I'll come out and we can have a sit-down."

In reply to Rory's telling of the situation at Hovel Hill, Buck had nothing new to report. He ended that statement with, "No more sign of either Halverson or those fellas that were working his mine."

"My deputy and his Indian friend are up valley looking for any sign of Halverson. I'm going to ride that way now. You can get back to making yourself rich."

Evening had almost turned itself into night when Rory rode upon a strange sight. The first sign of human presence was two staked-out horses. Rory recognized them as belonging to Ivan and My Way. He dismounted and walked carefully toward a bit of splashing water he could hear. The stream the town was built above originated higher into the mountain above where Rory was standing. He pushed his way carefully through the willow and aspen bush and started to laugh. There, not fifty feet from where he stood, the two searchers were sitting in the cold water, far enough apart for decency, bathing away the odor that even Rory was now picking up. The odor appeared to be rising from the heap of clothing cast off by Ivan. My Way was further away. Although he sat naked in the stream, he had his buckskins in the water with him.

"Looks cold for bathing, fellas."

Ivan answered, "And you can believe it's colder than it looks. Now if you throw me those clothes so's I can wash them up a bit, and give a man a bit of privacy, I'm for getting out."

Rory moved back to the horses and waited. It wasn't long before Ivan appeared, still wet but dressed back in poorly washed clothes that still carried a wisp of the unpleasant odor. My Way had pulled on his wet buckskins and moccasins. The two men stood there trembling with cold. Rory looked the men over and said, "I'm sure you're going to tell me what this is all about."

"It's about a dead man. A dead and decaying man. A man some varmints had been working on. Probably wouldn't be as far decayed or smell as bad if the varmints had not opened him up. Awfullest thing I ever did see. Or smell. It was the smell that led us to him. I thought a body would last longer in this cool weather."

Emphasizing the situation as they had found it, Ivan restated, "Stink must have been from the varmints digging into his insides. It was Halverson. No doubt about that. Shot in the back, dead center. He never would have seen it coming and didn't have a chance. There's no doubt it was murder.

"Body pretty well stripped. No sign of his rifle or bedroll. But there was a letter in his shirt pocket. It took all the determination I could dig up to get that close and find the letter. My Way and me, we piled rocks over the body, left him where he lay. Awful business."

Hardly knowing what else to say, the trio rode in silence to Buck's mine. At their call, Buck hid his tools behind some fallen rock, put a foot into Rory's stirrup, and took a seat behind him. Even as big a man as Buck was, the gelding could easily carry two as far as town. Buck's face had fallen dramatically when Rory told him of the dead Halverson. His only comment was, "He was a good man."

In town, Ivan, struggling to get simple words out through his chattering lips, managed to say, "Rory, how about you go over to the mercantile and buy me some clothes? I'm not sure even a washing with strong soap will help these ones. Get some for My Way too. He may wear them, and he may not, but I'd like for him to have the choice. The most either of us got done in the creek was make it so's we could ride into town without folks raising a vigilance committee to drive us away. I'm going for a hot bath. With soap. I'll wait there for the new duds."

Rory made his way to MacNair's to make the purchases, but his mind was on the murder. There was no other logical suspect than Herc Branson. But he had no real proof. All he had was what a lawyer would call circumstantial evidence. Even that was thin. But on further thought, he remembered the couple of times he had put men behind bars. There was something about steel bars and a clanking door that gained a man's attention. He would ride back to Hovel Hill in the morning and see what he could do.

As he was set to ride away Ivan called him back. My Way, who was easily recognized by his buckskins and the feather in his hair, was out of sight behind some tethered horses. Ivan turned his back so the four men tying off in front of the mercantile couldn't see or recognize him. Without turning around, he said, "You see those four over at MacNair's? Those are the gents that made themselves comfortable in Kiril's cabin. I was wondering what had become of them. Seemed to ride up the hill and disappear. But that's them, sure as shooting."

Rory studied the men as they stepped up to the boardwalk and then into the store. Making his decision, he said, "You and My Way try not to show yourselves. I'll just go down and pick out those clothes you need. But keep your weapons handy."

Rory dawdled away a full minute adjusting the girth strap on his saddle, allowing the four mystery men to enter the store well ahead of him. The last man in failed to push the door completely closed. As Rory approached, a small gust of wind blew it open. He quietly stepped inside. The store was empty, but there were voices coming from the back room. He reached up and gently tipped the little bell so he could close the door in silence. He then eased his way to the curtain-shrouded archway separating the store's two rooms, close enough to hear but not close enough to cause suspicion if he was seen. He was fingering a shirt taken from the table that fronted the dividing partition.

"You fools! What are you doing here?"

"Well, one thing we're not doing is shouting so's all the town can hear. I thought you were smarter than that, MacNair."

At half his original volume, MacNair, sounding as if he was squeezing the words from between clenched teeth, said, "You were told to get away and stay away. I'd have Streetly contact you if you're needed."

"Ya, well, what we need is money. Streetly said you'd have it here and ready. We dealt with Halverson for you, so pass it over, and we'll be gone from here."

"That makes five fools I have to contend with. You four and Streetly. I just paid you for The Hobbit and The Blue Bell not so long ago. You broke already?"

"You paid us, alright, and it took you long enough to get around to it. Then you paid us in gold when we clearly told you we wanted spendable cash. Anyway, that gold got stole. Someone took it, and it's gone. Now we need real money for Halverson. And we need it now."

"Oh, that's just sweet. It got stole. Someone took it, and it's gone. I'm dealing with idiots."

Rory had heard all he needed to hear. Knowing there were four toughs just feet away, and he had no idea if MacNair would take a hand if guns were drawn, he stepped quietly to the door. He had no wish to face those odds. Holding the bell again, he opened the door and walked away, leaving the door open.

Taking his horse by the reins, he led him across the street and tied off again in front of the jailhouse. Although the sun had dropped away behind the mountain, Buck was enjoying the last of the day's warmth sitting on a chair he had dragged outside. Rory stepped into the building and hauled the other chair out.

The two men sat in silence for a bit before Buck said, "You weren't in the mercantile for long. Too crowded?"

"Just didn't think I'd be welcome right at that time."

"Which could mean almost anything."

"Right you are, Buck. Could mean almost anything. But the meaning is perhaps narrowing down a bit."

Buck decided Rory would say more when he was

ready. He let the conversation drop, instead saying, "I take Halverson's death hard. Talked with him several times. Private sort of fella. Never said anything at all about home or family. The mine claim looks good. Should prove up. Should be worth some money. But who the claim would go to with his death, I have no idea."

Rory had heard stories like this all his adult life. "Not uncommon on the frontier, Buck. Men come west intending to make a strike or establish a ranch or business and then send for their families. I expect there's more than just a few wives and parents back east who will wonder all their lives what happened to their husband, father, or son. Sad thing, but there it is."

The conversation drifted a bit before Rory asked the question that had been on his mind for days.

"I stopped where they're building that stamp mill. Interesting project. And expensive. Foreman had no idea who was paying the bills. He only knew that the payroll was always on time, and the push to complete it seemed to never stop. Emmett Streetly saw to the payroll and other costs. He's an even busier man than I first thought.

"I don't see the need for the mill in the valley. None of the mines are at that stage. What am I missing?"

"You're missing that trail up the hill, back there to the south. Up the hill and down another fold in the land. Ore from up there that assays high. Very high. Shows enough promise to keep the Hill going and put new money into development."

The way Buck's voice dropped off and he was chewing on his lip made Rory wonder if he had more to say. He kept quiet, waiting. The wait wasn't long.

"Cam One mine. Canby brothers, Tip and Craig, owned it."

Again, Rory waited for more but finally nudged the conversation along, saying, "You spoke their names as if they were past tense."

"You got that right, Sheriff. Both men disappeared. No one can find out who owns the Cam One now."

"There seems to be a lot of that going on up here. I've never heard the like."

"You're correct again, Sheriff. A lot of it going on."

After a moment, Buck let his tipped-back chair fall to the dirt and slapped his hands on his knees. He stood and said, "I'm for taking on some sustenance."

Rory joined him. Somehow the hours of the day were measured between meals.

21

RORY DIDN'T WANT BUCK INVOLVED IN HIS EVENING'S planned activities. He had a feeling there would soon be other opportunities for that. After Rory laid out the plan, Buck took his bedroll and an extra blanket and crossed the stream on a fallen log. He settled in where he had spent so many other nights before meeting the sheriff.

Ivan and My Way had entered the dining room when Rory and Buck were eating. Ivan and My Way were dressed in the new clothing Rory had purchased on his second trip to the emporium. No one had ever seen My Way in western clothing before. Rory expected he would be back in his buckskins as soon as they dried sufficiently.

They ignored each other, but Rory managed, with a tilt of his head, to indicate to Ivan that he should come to the jailhouse a bit later in the evening. When that time came, Rory dimmed the lamp and pulled the wooden shutters on the single window closed. They were as private as they could be in the little town.

Ivan started the conversation with, "I expect you have

a plan, Sheriff. A plan that involves four men, all well-armed. I expect, too, that you've been hatching a way for those men to be escorted into this single cell without placing yourself or others in too much danger."

"That's the plan, and that's the hope, Ivan. Now let's get down to it. You and I have taken some risks and come out well in the past. That's not always how things end. If either of you want to stay out of this, I'll understand. Especially My Way. He was brought into your plans, Ivan, hoping he would help you with tracking. It's not fair to expect him to do more than that."

Turning to look at My Way, and still not knowing how much the Indian understood, he said, "I'm going against four men this evening. I have no desire to put you at risk, My Way. You're welcome to join me, but if you want to slip into the forest, I'll understand."

There might have been a slight turning up of the corners of his lips when the Indian said, "I stay."

Out of curiosity and to help think the thing through, Ivan asked, "Do you know where the four are hunkered down?"

"They're over in MacNair's Saloon right now. I'm hoping to take them when they leave. Quietly and without any shooting."

"Then one of us should be outside watching."

"How about three of us outside watching, all in different locations?"

After some discussion, Ivan stayed in the darkened jailhouse with the window shutters open, Rory stood in the narrow alley that led to the back of MacNair's store, and My Way simply disappeared into the darkness, carrying his Henry rifle and with his skinning knife prominently displayed behind his leather belt.

MacNair's Hill was a small settlement where most of

the men worked long, hard days. No one stayed up much past the dinner hour. By nine in the evening, MacNair's barkeeper blew out the lights and prepared to lock the door. Three who had been playing poker, gambling for matchsticks, left first. The four Rory wanted came last, one of them staggering to the point that another was holding him up. The drunk began singing, but he was soon shut up by the others.

The clouded moon gave barely enough light for Rory to see Ivan gently close the jailhouse door and slink along the front of the building and then along the saddlery and gun shop. There was no sign of My Way.

It wasn't a sure thing, but Rory figured they were headed for the livery loft, although he had clearly heard MacNair telling them to get out of town. Their horses were on the street. If they led them to the livery, the lawmen would wait a bit. Take them when they were unsaddling. If they mounted, they would be stopped immediately.

They untied their animals, and three of them mounted. The fourth was still trying to get his foot into the stirrup when Rory tapped him on the head with his Winchester. The man fell silently to the road with his horse taking a few startled steps. Rory had been finding some satisfaction in taking men alive and the only way to do that seemed to be if they were unconscious. It was sometimes risky, but he preferred it to killing.

The rider who appeared to be the leader must have heard something or seen a shadow move. He was suddenly alert and reaching for his belt gun. He was stopped and pulled from his horse when Ivan leaped, grabbing him around his shoulders, and pinning his arms to his sides. The two men fell to the ground and rolled over several times before coming to a stop with

Ivan on top. The horses were whinnying and stamping every which way. One of them shouldered Ivan off the downed man, allowing him to get to his feet. Ivan was struck once, by a hurried and not very effective punch before he gained his feet. Rory was watching the fight, and the fourth man, while trying to drive the two frightened horses off.

Using just one hand, holding his Henry in the other, My Way took hold of the third rider's arm and pulled. With the man lying on his back, the Indian straddled him, holding his arms down by simply kneeling on them, he drew his knife, and pressed the point against his adversary's nose. Already terrified at the thought of fighting a fierce-looking Indian with a feather in his hair, the fella crossed his eyes and forced them downward. He could see just enough to know the knife was positioned where it could take his life with a simple flick of the Indian's wrist. The knife and the sight of the Indian holding it were enough to take away any fight left in the man. He lay still, hoping for rescue.

Out of nowhere, it seemed, a rope whirred through the air, with the loop falling over the fourth man. The coil failed to drop over the man's shoulders, ending up tightening around his neck. A firm, unsympathetic pull had the man leaving his saddle. He landed on his feet, ready to fight. That desire faded when a thundering blow from Buck's big fist made a mess of his nose and lips, dropping the man into the dirt of the road.

Rory watched this happen and smiled wordlessly at Buck. Buck grinned back at the sheriff and said, "What? You thought I'd stand by while my town was under attack?"

Rory didn't bother responding.

With the horses finally running off a few feet, Rory

could see that Ivan was in a fight for his life. Both men were armed, but neither had been given the opportunity to lift a weapon. Rory thought to assist Ivan, but the two opponents were moving in unexpected directions so quickly that he feared hitting Ivan if he shot.

With a quick, sudden move, Ivan's opponent was free of his grip. His hand flashed down and then back up with his Colt at the ready. Ivan, never worrying about being a fast draw, dove to the side, hitting the ground shoulder first and rolling. He twisted, clearing his holster. A shot hit the ground startlingly close to his head. But by then, he had his own weapon in his hand. A second shot from the standing man came even closer than the first, but it was the last shot the man got off. Ivan's first bullet hit his enemy just above his belt, slanting upward. The second, taken as the man folded over, entered his forehead, ending the match.

There were now four men on the ground. One was dead, one was unconscious, and two were thoroughly subdued. Knowing the shots would waken the town, Rory said, "See if you can grab those horses. Let's clear up this mess before we have company."

They needn't have worried. The sound of gunfire was enough to keep everyone lying low wherever they were spending the night.

There was one exception. At the mercantile, Buck noticed a shadow cross one window. MacNair was up and watching.

Within minutes the men were disarmed and dragged into the single cell in the marshal's office. The drunk Rory had tagged with the barrel of his Winchester was still out cold. He now lay on the single bunk in the cell. The other two were standing, silent, but their anger and their fear showed plainly on their faces. Ivan and My

Way grouped the horses, taking them to the livery and stalling them. The dead man was laid out behind the marshal's office. Buck had wandered outside, leaving the questioning of the captives to Rory. For reasons of his own, he was watching the mercantile. Rory noticed but said nothing. Nor had he said anything about what he had heard coming from the back room of MacNair's store.

The slim moon, visible an hour before, was now shrouded in cloud. The street and the little town were as dark as they would ever be. There were three lamplights visible. None of them lighted the road. One hung on the livery wall where a tall man could reach it, outlining the big doorway. The second was dimly leaking past the ill-fitting shutter on the marshal's office window. The third, also shaded by a cloth hung over the window, shone from the mercantile. Buck, standing in the street listening and watching intently, could hear small noises coming from the mercantile, as if MacNair was shuffling boxes around or searching for something.

Rory had the list of names Ivan had taken when he rousted the four men out of Kiril's cabin. He laid it out before him on the desk and said, "Alright, which of you is Chouse Ramble?"

One of the men said, "He's dead."

"I take it he was your leader."

"He thought so."

Rory said, "Well, we'll let that go for now. Grit Price, speak up."

When that man identified himself, Rory looked at the other standing man and said, "So you're either Toby Whitelaw or Diego Ramirez."

Toby Whitelaw kicked his still unconscious partner and said, "No good for nothing Mex. Could never hold his drink. Should have got shut of him months ago. I'm Whitelaw."

Rory looked the three men over and was about to speak when there was a disturbance on the road. It started with a banging door. That was quickly followed by the sounds of ironshod hooves, slowly at first and then spirited on by a shouted command. The horse burst into a lope and then a full-out run. The attempt to run was cut off when another shout, this time of fear, broke the silence of the town. What no one could see in the darkness was MacNair being tackled and pulled from his horse. With the speed the animal had already attained, Buck was only going to get one chance. If he missed, it would become a horse race through the darkness of the night on a poorly defined road.

As the animal started to run, MacNair was startled by the dim outline of a man standing directly in his path. Buck, waiting, had timed his leap. When the horse shied slightly to the side, turning so that MacNair was brought closer, Buck took his leap. He wasn't fussy about what he grabbed—shirt, coat, arm, head. He just wanted a piece of the store owner. If he could get him off the horse and onto the road, the rest would present no problem. What he managed to grab was a fist full of coat. He'd closed his fist on the canvas fabric and didn't let go. At first, he was dragged along by the running horse as MacNair dug his feet into the stirrups. But Buck's heels quickly fell to the ground again where he could dig them in and haul MacNair out of the leather.

As MacNair flew through the air, Buck stepped closer. He had lost the grip on the coat, but it no longer mattered. MacNair was his now, and he wasn't getting away. With a scream of pain, fear, and indignation, the storekeeper hit the dirt. Buck bent over, grabbed him by the hair, and yanked him to his feet. "No. No. No," was all MacNair could say.

Whether he was fearful of a beating or because his run of crime was at an end would never be known. He only knew he was being beaten for the first three or four punches. Quickly losing consciousness, he didn't hear or take notice of Buck saying, "You thieving, murdering excuse for a man. I've been waiting months to put my hands on you."

He continued hitting him until someone grabbed his arm, saying, "Hold on there, big boy. Let's leave something for the lawyers and the hangman."

It took every ounce of Buck's willpower to heed Rory's advice. Finally, knowing that the advice was good, he loosened his fist from the coat and let MacNair drop unconscious to the ground. Buck stepped back two paces and leaned over, putting his hands on his knees and breathing deeply. Ivan and My Way were there by that time. They and Rory stood silently, allowing Buck to collect himself.

Into the silence, Ivan asked, "Where will we put the storekeeper? It might be smart to keep him separate from the others."

My Way ventured his first opinion since Rory had met him.

"Maybe I take him. Bury him. No one find."

It took a moment for Rory to grasp what the Indian was saying, but he finally answered, "I could be tempted, My Way. But I think we'll be better off and learn more if the court deals with him."

Ivan brought MacNair's horse back, and together, he and Buck threw the man across the saddle. Rory looked on and finally asked, "What do you have in mind?"

"I'm thinking it wouldn't hurt Terrence Climber to lose a bit of sleep. We'll store this crook there."

Rory said, "Alright. You and My Way take him over there. But watch Climber. I'm only half satisfied with what he tells me. Stay there and guard MacNair. Buck, you go back to the jail. I'm going shopping."

No one knew what he had in mind when he said shopping, but they parted without asking the question. It wasn't long before Rory arrived back at the jail with a small bundle of light twine, not strong enough to hold a horse but plenty strong enough to hold a man. When Buck looked a question at him, he responded, "I don't think MacNair's going to miss this bit of rope."

The Mexican, Ramirez, was finally awake and sitting on the edge of the bunk. He was bent over with his elbows on his knees, holding his head in both hands. Without pity, Rory said, "Think of it this way, Ramirez. You're alive. Your boss is lying on the ground out back of the jail. Now come on, stand up. I'll talk to you first."

The Mexican looked at him as if this couldn't be happening. But finally, he stood.

"Open the door, Buck. If either of the others makes a move toward the door, shoot him. Don't kill him. Just shoot him a little bit."

Ramirez wobbled into the room, and Buck closed the door behind him. Rory asked, "Buck, how are you at tying a hobble?"

"No one better."

Rory passed him the rope and said, "Do it."

While Buck was busy hobbling the Mexican, Rory said, "Alright, you three. Listen up. I'm going to take you one at a time to the livery. Buck will make sure you can't run, and I'll tie you firmly when we get to the barn. What we're going to do is, we're going to have us a talk. One of you is going to explain everything to me. The first one that talks will get a break in court. I'll vouch for that. Think it over, fellas."

With that, he tied Ramirez's hands behind his back and led him out the door. With the tight hobble, the walking was slow. As he was walking down the wide, center aisle, he banged on the hostler's door. At the shout of, "What," Rory said, "Sheriff Jamison here. Stay inside. Don't come out."

The Mexican was tied into a back stall in the dim light of the lantern that Rory had brought in from the doorway. He was more than eager to tell what he knew. Rory listened, and when Ramirez promised that was all he knew, Rory led him back to the office. Buck tied him to a chair to keep him from the others while Rory led the hobbled Grit Price to the livery. The result was the same, except he was able to provide information Rory suspected the others had held back from the Mexican. The process was repeated with Toby Whitelaw, with the same result.

They were each eager to purchase a better chance in court, even at the expense of their friends.

On the way back to the jail, Rory said, "Sell your souls for an ounce of gold and sell out your partners with hardly a thought. A fine bunch you are."

22

By MORNING THE NEWS WAS ALL OVER TOWN. THERE WAS no longer a reason to deny Ivan and My Way's connection with the sheriff. And it had become clear to the town, too, that Buck was not the bully derelict he had been made out to be. Rory had first put the pieces together, but it wasn't until he was asked directly that Buck told his story. He and Rory were sitting alone in front of the marshal's office.

"Well, first, Sheriff, I have to credit you for figuring it out. At least the beginnings of the tale. I've told you about the Cam One mine. Very prosperous. They have a mound of rich quartz rock ready and waiting for that stamp mill to be completed. The Cam One was owned by the Canby brothers. Tip and Craig. Tip was my father. I'm Richard Canby. I only tagged onto the Buck name when I arrived here in town.

"Dad and Uncle Craig disappeared months ago. Just gone. No explanation. When I made an inquiry with MacNair, who was the only logical person to ask, the answer was that they had sold the mine, taken a big profit, and had ridden out. He tried to pass the disappearance off as just another couple of wandering prospectors taking the easy money and moving on. But neither Dad nor my uncle were like that. And in any case, if they had taken a big profit, as MacNair said, they would have come home. They were both family men. Responsible and grounded family men.

"I didn't question MacNair to the point where he would take offense or have any particular reason to remember me. I rode out and didn't stop until I was further down the line where the big gold camps are. I sold my horse and disappeared into the bush. I grew out my beard and hair, purposely allowed my clothes to wear out and get filthy, waited four months, and then walked back to MacNair's Hill. I was now Buck, the crude town bully. I purposely made a nuisance of myself with Gloria, hoping to keep it under control while acting my part. I was hoping no one would think me anything but a bum.

"But I was watching MacNair the whole time. I walked miles through the bush, first, looking for bodies or graves, hoping I wouldn't find any. And I was watching the activities up at the Cam One. New owners came in, bringing steam drills and a powder man with them. They put down tracks and wagoned in ore carts. The stamp mill was started.

"Once each week, MacNair would arrive driving a wagon loaded with provisions for the camp. That might have made some sense, except that he was far too curious about the mine. I saw him at the stamp mill too. Again, too, often to make sense. Then, when I saw Emmett Streetly in town every couple of weeks, I started putting it all together. Streetly would go first to MacNair's, pretending to be just another customer. But from there, he would ride to the Cam One and then leave town. Recently he has been adding a trip to the stamp mill site. Each time he comes, he passes the pay envelopes over to the foremen at both the mill and the mine. I had to make me a long walk up to Hovel Hill and ask some careful questions to find out who Streetly was, but I finally got the answer. Turns out he's the front man, delivering the payroll and doing the bidding of the moneyman at several mine sites. That had to leave MacNair as the moneyman."

Rory hesitated to ask, but he finally admitted it was time.

"Did you ever find a grave?"

Buck answered quickly enough, but Rory could see the hurt in the man when he said, "I did. Double grave. Shallow. Depending more on piled-up rocks than the digging. My father and uncle together. Just dumped into a hole not more than a foot deep. Not much left by the time I found them. It was the first time I really felt hate. We were always a hardworking but easygoing family otherwise. But I changed, looking into that hole in the ground. I had to rewrite my letter to Mother three times, knowing the first two showed my hate. Mother would never approve of my new attitude."

"Perhaps you can put some of it behind you over time."

"Perhaps, Sheriff. Perhaps."

Rory wondered about sharing his own story but decided to leave it alone.

As THE TWO had been talking, Ivan and My Way were at the small barn and corral behind the mercantile, outfitting MacNair's buckboard for the long trip to Denver. They had led the storekeeper's wagon team from the livery, harnessed and ready. Work had been stopped at the Cam One and the stamp mill. The small miners had finally heard all the gossip they could handle for one day and gone back to their claims. Mila and Gloria had fed the prisoners in their cell and in Terrence Climber's back room. Terrence was holding MacNair under guard. Climber would join the others on the wagon trip, offering to handle the team.

Rory slipped away from the others and went to the mercantile. There he looked through every possible hiding place but found no stash of money until he pulled a wooden box from under a pile of sacked flour. He was attracted to the box because it seemed an unusual place for it. It was hidden until he moved the front row of sacks.

Opening the box, he was startled to see wrapped bundles of paper money in several denominations. Hundreds, if not thousands of dollars. Along with the paper money were several canvas bags of coins. Beside the silver coins and the one bag of regular gold coins, he found another containing tarnished coins. The tarnished coin mystery had been bothering him almost from the day he had returned from the Idaho gold claim. He hadn't been able to sort it out but perhaps with MacNair in custody in Denver, along with the other three prisoners, the lawyers could get to the bottom of it.

Tucked into a big envelope under the sacks of money were written records of payroll at both the mine and the new mill. On another sheet was the running total of supplies delivered to the camp and their costs. There was another columned page with numbers on it, all listed under three abbreviated headings. Rory had no idea what the headings meant or referred to.

He fastened the lid back in place and toted the box out to the wagon, telling Ivan to take special care of it. He then went back into the store and found MacNair's living quarters. A thorough search turned up nothing of note except a list of names and addresses that meant nothing to the sheriff, but he took it along anyway.

It was nearly noon before the entourage was ready to hit the road. All the prisoners were hobbled and tied to the wagon frame. Climber took up the reins and urged the team forward. Ivan and My Way took their positions, one on each side of the wagon and just a bit to the rear. They were armed with their normal Colts as well as their carbines, but they had added the worn shotguns Rory had purchased a few days before. These they held on their laps, loaded but not cocked. None of the prisoners made any sign of trying to escape.

Rory rode ahead, saying, "I'll see you in Hovel Hill."

23

Riding into Hovel Hill, Rory could see that activity had slowed for the lunch hour. He stepped down in front of the single restaurant. He opened the door, scanning the crowd for Emmett Streetly. The man was not there. He stepped back into the saddle and rode to the location that had been pointed out on a previous visit as Streetly's shack.

The buggy Streetly had been using was pulled up beside the little house. A single gelding stood with his head hanging in the small corral. There was a harness draped over pegs on the side of a tiny barn. Rory stepped down and tied his gelding. Streetly had seen him riding in and opened the door.

"I'm surprised to see you come for a visit, Sheriff. It seemed unlikely I would ever see you again after the way we parted the other day."

"Get some warm clothes on and grab your coat and hat, Mr. Streetly. We're going for a ride. You'll need to harness that horse too. And do it quickly. We're due to meet some folks."

"Well, now, I hadn't really planned on going for any ride with you, Sheriff. I think I'll just take a pass on that offer."

"And I think you had best step outside where I can see your hands. Do it now."

Streetly decided that it sounded as if the sheriff meant what he said. He never carried a weapon on him in his own home, so he was unarmed. He couldn't expect to do anything but what he was told to do. But he would have his chance. He was sure of that. There was always another time, another chance.

With the horse harnessed and Streetly in the buggy holding the reins, Rory surprised him when he approached with a coil of rope.

"Hold out your hands."

"Now see here, Sheriff…"

"No talk. You had your chance to talk. Now it's my turn. And we'll have that talk when we have you behind bars in Denver."

Streetly made a motion to leap from the buggy, but Rory pulled a Colt and said, "Streetly, with your bulk, I doubt if you would even get up if you jumped to the road. And if you did, you couldn't outrun a wounded pup. Now sit still. This is going to happen. Fighting will only make it worse."

Rory wasn't as adept at tying a hobble as Buck had been, but Streetly wasn't going to be doing much walking anyway. The hobble was good enough to assure Rory of that.

"Now, give me your hands."

When Streetly complied, Rory tied a tight loop over each wrist but left some slack between the hands. He wanted Streetly to be able to handle the horse.

"Alright, now we wait. And I'll just take a little look inside your house while we're waiting."

He took the reins from Streetly, walked to the side of the horse, and tied the animal to the broken-down fence. He then did a thorough search of the small house finding nothing but a couple of sheets of paper divided into three columns the way the one found in MacNair's had been. He folded it to fit into his shirt pocket and left the house, bringing Streetly's gun belt and carbine with him. These he laid in the back of the buggy, well away from where Streetly could reach them.

"Drive up to the southbound road."

There they sat in silence for nearly a half hour before the wagon and its outriders came into view. The wagon kept moving when Rory waved them along. Streetly pulled in behind and followed. Rory brought up the rear, riding just off to the side where he could see everyone.

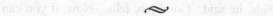

Two days later, with the help of a couple of restaurants along the way, and the loan of three cowboys from a ranch east of Idaho Springs, the weary entourage pulled to a stop in front of the Denver city jail, and Rory stiffly stepped to the ground. He made his way inside, where a young jailer looked quizzically at him. The young man was holding a Henry rifle in his right hand with the barrel resting on the desktop.

"Help ya?"

"Rory Jamison. County sheriff from up north a ways. Got some prisoners we need to keep safe for a day or two."

The jailer stood and looked out the window. Somehow, even with those movements, the Henry never moved away from Rory. It took the full of a minute for the jailer to assess the situation. Finally, he turned back, laid the Henry on the desk, and said, "City police usually take charge of decisions. I have no authority."

Rory was far too tired to worry about formalities.

"Let's try to be helpful here. Do you have a couple of empty cells?"

"Yes, but…"

"You go open the doors and stand out of the way."

With that, he went outside and spoke to all the guards at once.

"One at a time, fellas. Let's ger 'er done."

Within a few minutes, the wagon and buggy were empty, and the cells were full. Rory thanked the jailer, saying, "There. That wasn't too bad, was it? You just keep those doors locked and the Henry handy. I'll be back soon with the men who have the authority over this bunch."

Outside, he said, "Good job, fellas. Now, if you can find a livery that has room for the animals and a place to leave the wagons, you can go get settled into a hotel and see about hot baths if that's to your liking. Ivan knows what hotel we've used before. He'll make the arrangements. A room each, Ivan. I'll get myself over to the federal marshal's office and be back just as soon as the paperwork is done."

24

RORY MANAGED TO HOLD THE FEDERAL MARSHALS OFF until the next morning, pleading exhaustion and the lateness of the hour.

The next morning, he paid the cowboys and thanked them again. The other men hung around to see if their testimony was required. They had all completed their morning meal, but Rory hung around drinking coffee, waiting for Block to join him. The man was late, and Rory had to tell himself to keep his thoughts to himself. Not everyone kept rancher's hours. Ivan, My Way, and Terrence Climber went outside, telling Rory they would just walk around a bit and be back soon. Privately, Rory had asked Ivan to keep an eye on Climber. The man had been a help, and his story sounded good, but Rory was holding some private questions. He would need Block to assure him of the man's status.

Block entered the restaurant like a west wind just fresh off the mountains. He bowled his way through and around the tables and chairs, heedless of how he inconvenienced other patrons. He hollered, "Sheriff Jamison, how good it is to see you again. And I hear you brought in a wagonload of bad guys. Good on ya."

He had been holding his hand out since he entered the restaurant. By the time he got to Rory's table, in his excitement, he practically pulled Rory out of his chair, grabbing for his hand while he embraced Rory's right shoulder with his strong left hand. The finger pressure on Rory's right hand might have moved a lesser man to tears. The thought to squeeze back flitted through Rory's mind, but he finally simply pulled his hand away and said, "Good to see you, Block. I kind of thought you might have gone back to Texas by now."

"If there's any fairness left in this world or any of the Lord's love left to me, I'll never have to go back to Texas. Denver isn't perfect, but it's several steps above that windblown excuse for cattle country."

Rory had been half joking, but he could see that it would be unwise to pursue the topic. Instead, he said, "Block, I've been away from town far too long. There's no one left in either Stevensville or the fort but the town marshals. I've got to get back. If you and whoever else is handling the lawyering of the cases I bring down here could take my statement, I'd like to ride out before noon."

When the two men sat down, they automatically began to speak more confidentially. The many faces that had been turned their way lost interest and went back to their own meals.

"Tell me what you've got."

"I don't want to have to tell it twice. Oscar Cator is supposed to be here by now. Let's give him another few minutes."

The two men visited about nothing in particular for a quarter-hour before Oscar arrived. His arrival was almost subdued compared to the federal man's entry. Oscar wasted no time, except to say, "Bertha will be sorry to have missed you."

Rory didn't respond, instead saying, "What we've found involves county, state, and federal, as I size it all up.

"There's been murders and thefts up the hill. Place called MacNair's Hill and just a few miles away at Hovel Hill. We brought in the murderers, along with their confessions, three men each blaming the other and claiming the boss, who was shot and killed in the capture, was the only one who knew there was to be, as they called it, 'more than just a bit of rough stuff to move some prospectors off their claims.' I didn't believe that when I heard it, and I don't believe it now. That happened in my county.

"The state involvement, I believe, will have to be in the straightening out of stolen claims and putting the murderers before a judge. We have a judge up at the fort, but no lawyers that could handle the situation. It's better here in the city.

"The state and federal, both, will be involved in the tarnished gold coin thing again, and I hope to never see or hear about stolen coins again. I haven't yet questioned the one I believe to be the ringleader. There was no chance and no privacy. But he's here and safely under lock and key, so you can talk to him any time you wish. Here's what I know about him.

"His name is MacNair. He started a town where there were yet no actual paying claims. Built himself a big store and opened an assay office when there was no need for either. Just up the road at Hovel Hill, all the services a prospector or miner needs is available. I was suspicious of the man from the start. I don't believe he's the top man, though. That man, whoever he is, has access to all that stolen gold. There's little doubt that he's either found a bank that will take it in deposit, issuing clean money in exchange, or they've melted it down. The gold value is very close to the face value of the coins. Even with the coins we've found over the past year or so, there's nowhere near enough to purchase herds of cattle or gold mines in the hills. That would have to be done with bank transfers or something of the kind. The coins we found are almost like a token of some sort. As if the thieves wanted to hold some just for the holding. I'll leave that for the lawyers.

"We brought in a man named Emmett Streetly. He's down at the lockup too. Streetly's the one who runs between the various actors on that rocky stage. It took almost a week of skulking around, but we finally zeroed in on the information that MacNair holds the funds, Streetly delivers them on paydays for the miners, and the three others we brought in carried out the dirty work of driving prospectors off promising-looking claims. Streetly does the same things in both towns. MacNair will try to say he didn't order any killings, but I know for a fact that isn't true. And the three killers will testify against him, if for no other reason than to try to save their own skins. I told the three when I was taking them one by one to question them in private, that I would speak on behalf of the first one that spilled the whole story. My problem is that they all spilled the whole story. And the stories matched perfectly each time. The short story seems to be that MacNair is working with some-one. Someone who has a source of money. And here and there, among the various thefts and other skulduggery, a gold coin or two has shown up. I'm sure hoping you can make the connection and put a stop to the whole thing, although thinking about how much money could have been in those stolen bank boxes, I suspect the thief must be about at the end of his resources.

"One more small item on that, though. I saw a small bunch of cattle corralled at the butcher's on the way down here. Branded Big C. That's Webster Cunningham's brand. Big C from West Texas, the man who purchased the three herds from Stevensville that the phony judge rustled. You might recall that the phony town marshal is in the state prison. You might want to go have a talk with him. Those Big C cattle did not come from my county, so that problem belongs to someone else.

"Now, if you can stand one more complication, MacNair had a big stash of tarnished gold coins in the box he stored his payout money in, more than just the token amount the phony judge had. There must be a reason for that. That box of money is locked down over at the city jail. I'll leave it to you fellas to decide what to do with the money and the men. I just want to get back to town."

Block, serious now, asked, "Anything else, Sheriff?"

"I brought Terrence Climber down with me. I told him I needed him to drive the wagon. Which was true. But I also didn't completely believe his story, so I thought it best to make sure I knew where he was."

Both of Rory's tablemates burst into laughter. Block leaned back in his chair and grinned at Rory, saying, "I love it. We put a trusted man up there looking for gold coins, and you gather him up along with the real culprits. It's priceless. Any other surprises?"

"Well, I got a written list of mines that suddenly came for sale. There's a list of names too. Names and who they are and what their involvement is. A few I would have liked to bring down the hill, but the wagon was full, and I already had to hire some cowboys to help with the guarding. Any more prisoners, and it would have been easier to move you fellas up the hill instead of bringing half the population of two towns down here."

"How are things standing up there now?"

"Good question, Oscar. I think it's all under control and will stay that way if your work down here can be sorted out quickly. You'll need to work through that list of mines to try to find the real owners. I shut several down and drove off the crews. I know for a fact that there are dead prospectors, and it seems unlikely you'll ever find the next of kin. It's probably worth a shot, though.

"I deputized a man named Buck Canby. He's claiming the Canby brothers, owners of the Cam One mine, the only operating and profitable claim at MacNair's Hill, were his father and uncle. The men are dead. Buck found their graves. Ivan and My Way found the grave of a fella named Halverson. There are probably others. But the only way to sort it out is for you to get those men down to the state pen and start pulling fingernails out or whatever it is you do. They'll confess quickly enough if you promise to put the noose away. Talk to Climber. He knows the Buck story."

Block took a long breath and slowly let it out before he said, "I am truly afraid to ask, but I guess I should anyway. Who is My Way?"

"That's Ivan's Indian friend."

"Alright, I guess that's enough."

The two lawmen looked at each other. Finally, Block said, "I'll gather up some Federals, Oscar. Do you have anyone around that might be able to help us move that bunch?"

Within a couple of minutes, they had worked it out, but Rory needed to know one other thing.

"Who or what is Simon Webb?"

Block shook his head as if he had just remembered something.

"I should have told you right off, Rory. Simon was a federal marshal until he became more of a hindrance than a help. I fired him a couple of months ago, but he won't stay fired. Keeps letting on that he's still at the old stand. I half believe he's tied up in the gold coin and stolen cattle matter somehow. But I couldn't prove it. If he comes at you again, don't trust him. He's a liar. He's proven to be dangerous. And he's dynamite with a short gun. Be careful."

THE COWBOYS HAD LEFT for home right after breakfast. When Rory pulled everyone else together, Ivan led them to the correct livery barn. He saddled Rory's horse while the sheriff was squaring up the tab at the hotel. Within a half-hour, Rory, Ivan, and My Way were heading north as fast as rested horses could take them. Block and Oscar Cator were making arrangements for the transfer of the prisoners.

25

RIDING INTO STEVENSVILLE THREE ABREAST DOWN THE dirt street, the tired and distance-worn lawmen looked toughened almost to the point of hardness, as if no force on earth could challenge them. The riding, the nights on the ground, the scant food, the evil they had faced down, had pushed these men beyond lawmen. It had pulled them into trust and friendship. My Way no longer hung back, riding behind the others. He still didn't speak much, but when he did speak, the others listened.

People stood on the boardwalk watching them arrive. No one else could hear it, but a man standing in front of the dining room said to his friend, "I'm glad they're on our side."

Key Wardle came from the marshal's office. He stood watching until the riders were within easy voice range before he said, "Welcome home, men. Good to see you."

"Good to be here," Ivan responded.

Sonia Ivanov watched from inside the dining room, not sure which of the men she was most happy to see. That her brother was well and home was, of course, a welcome thing. Then there was Rory. She found herself comparing him to Andy Speth, the bank clerk she had been riding out with. Andy was a good man, and she knew the comparison was unfair but still…

Tempest Wardle left the ranch supply store and walked across the street to stand beside her brother in front of the marshal's office. She had a greeting for both Rory and Ivan and then turned to My Way, her special Indian friend. She had never touched the man since his recovery from the injuries, not even to shake hands, but she said, "Good to see you back, My Way." As usual, the Indian remained silent, but she thought there might be a lightening in his eyes.

She then turned back to Ivan.

"How was it, Ivan? You rode up the hill on one trail and came back on another. I'm assuming there's a story between those two trails."

Ivan was a bit taken aback by this forward woman, but still, there was something magnetic about her. And they seemed to understand each other even without speaking beyond a brief hello. They were both raised on remote ranches. Both a bit town-shy. And both a bit rough around the edges. Ivan didn't even know where the idea or the words came from, but he heard himself saying, "A bit of a story, I'd say. Perhaps this evening, after dinner, we could walk some. Talk some."

Tempest was as startled to hear the words as Ivan was when he heard them coming from his mouth. But she did manage to say, "I'll walk over to the marshal's office later. But I'd rather ride than walk."

Ivan just nodded and turned into the office.

Town Marshal Key, Tempest's brother, studied the two with a dawning wonder.

Rory rode for the Double J Ranch, and home.

26

LEAVING IVAN AND MY WAY AT STEVENSVILLE, RORY, after the usual noisy and welcoming family time the night before, rode for the fort early the next morning.

As he rode, he was reflecting on how much could happen in a short time. Before he rode up the hill, ending at MacNair's Hill, he had taken notice of the change in the weather and the turning of the leaves, edging into fall. It seemed he had been away for many weeks, but the leaves were virtually the same as when he had ridden away. Thinking more seriously, he realized he hadn't been gone all that long. But so much had been crammed into that time. His mind wandered back into what had called him into the law business, that being the phony judge trying to pull a theft of cattle on the Double J Ranch. That had led to the gold coin matter and then to the financing of stolen gold mines. In effect, using stolen government gold to take over and expand mines stolen from murdered men. He knew he would never sort it all out. The tangle of criminals involved was more than any amateur sheriff could hope to understand. Kiril's part fell into that category. It would be enough if the crimes attached to the tarnished coins simply stopped, and he could put it behind him.

He entered the fort riding alone. Few people noticed him. But one of the watchers was Horace Gridley, the eastern rancher that was under the control of two murderers until Rory had taken a hand. Gridley's daughter, Julia, and Rory had found themselves attracted to one another after the fight was put behind them. But the problem of distance was laid before the two young people, preventing any regular association.

"Hello, Sheriff."

Rory looked toward the sound to see Horace standing on the boardwalk with a big smile on his face. Rory, with practiced ease, laid the left rein against the gelding's neck. The horse turned to the right and delivered Rory right to where Horace, now joined by Julia and a young man whose looks told the world he could be no one but the son of Horace Gridley.

"Good morning, Horace."

He tipped his hat and said, "Julia."

Julia returned the greeting with a smile and then said, "Sheriff, you haven't met my brother. This is Rory Jamison, Doc. He's the one that…"

She was interrupted by a laughing Doc, who responded, "I know, I know. He came out of nowhere, riding a shining, noble steed, rescued the world and the fair young maiden, tipped his hat and rode away, saying, 'why shucks, ma'am, 'tis nothing at all.'"

Julia wasn't sure if she should be angry or flattered. She chose neither, settling for a somewhat less than shy study of the young sheriff.

Doc reached to shake Rory's hand, still smiling. "Truly, Sheriff, I'm glad you were there, and I'm sorry neither my brother nor I were available to help. It's good to meet you."

The group visited for a few minutes, finally parting with Rory's promise to ride out that way just as soon as the opportunity presented itself.

The welcome from Wiley Hamstead was not as exuberant, but it was still friendly enough. Wiley had been appointed town marshal only a couple of weeks before and was still feeling his way into the job. The two lawmen took up their half-barrel chairs on the board-walk and exchanged tales of their past couple of weeks. They were sitting like that when the stage came boiling into town, scattering everything else on the street, causing men to swear at the whip, and women to scream in fright.

Wiley rose from his chair and rushed across the road. The stage stopped, as it always did, in front of the hotel. Rory tagged along behind. Wiley rounded the sweating and stamping team and confronted the driver.

"Tate, now I'm new on the job, and I may not have understood, but I'm recollecting that the town fathers told you and the other whips to slow at the edge of town and walk your team in. Was there some part of that you didn't understand?"

"Well, sprout, you may have that right fer a normal sit-eation. But this ain't no way normal. I got news, if'n yer ready to listen."

When no one responded, Tate said, "The pure fact is that the station up on the border was raided yeste'day. Keeper and his wife both shot. Killed. Horses stol'd. Next station south wasn't touched. But third stop, the last before the fort, here, was wiped out this morning, hostler and keeper both killed, horses stol'd, barn and station burned. I'm thinking whoever it was what did the deed will be here at the fort today, unless they simply ride off with their horses. And since the stage company barn and corrals is out of town by a bit, those horses will be a temptation."

Rory, who had long been familiar with Tate, spoke before Wiley had a chance to respond.

"That's valuable news and a good warning, Tate, but you could have walked in like you're supposed to, without scaring everyone off the street, and still given the news. I appreciate the information, though. I'll just take a ride out that way. See what's going on. Now you had best cool off that team. It looks like you've run them a good bit."

"You young fellers think ya knows it all. Why, I was driv'n team afore you was born. I've keer'd fer more horses..."

Rory smiled at the whip and turned away without listening for the rest of the lecture. As he and Wiley were walking back to the little jailhouse, Wiley asked, "What do you think, Sheriff? Should I get a few men together and go out there?"

"No. You stand by here in case there's a ruckus of some kind in town. I'll ride out to the station and have a look-see."

RORY RODE around the stage company's big barn and corral complex, with the stacked hay ready for winter and the many horses penned up. He couldn't imagine horse thieves entering a town as big as the fort, but then, he'd already seen some strange things done by those who lived on the other side of the law. There was nothing at all to steal at a stage station except the horses, and those could be taken without violence by a skilled horse thief. So why kill the hostler, the station agent, and his wife?

He remembered the station agent at the border site. The agent and his wife both. Good folks. If it was horses the thieves wanted, why kill the agent? And to kill a woman was almost beyond believing. The remembering of the kind couple they were and their welcome for him when he was doing the voting list survey put him into a melancholy mood for a few minutes.

After circling the stage property, he rode to the big barn. Dismounting, he walked inside, and found the hostler in the tack room cleaning and oiling a harness. After introducing himself and repeating Tate's warning, Rory said, "If the raiders come here, I want you to get out. Keep a saddled horse somewhere close by and climb on it at the first sign of trouble. Ride for town. I don't think the raiders will enter the town."

The hostler responded, "Well now, I'll have to disagree with you on that, Sheriff. This isn't just where I work. This is my home. And a rather decent home it is for a barnyard. My old papa is liable to rise out of the grave and come smack me across the ear if he knew I was leaving my home for someone else to defend. No, sir. I just can't do it. I'll be here, and my much abused and scratched Henry will speak for me. I'm too old to be looking for a new job or a new home. But I promise not to get in your way, young man. There are hidey-holes and openings to the outside in this old barn and around the stacks. You'll find me a help or my name ain't Ol' Tom. That's what they call me, Ol' Tom. I took offense at the name for some time, but now I just let 'er go.

"As for Tate, I expect he'll be back right soon. He shouted a warning as he drove right past the team I had ready for him. I expect he'll be back any time now for his new team. He can't go on south with worn-down animals. Tate, he ain't no coward neither. If the thieves should show up while he's here, he'll take a hand."

Rory was a bit flustered and didn't know what to do or say. If the thieves were coming that way, there wasn't much time. But they may not come that way. They had choices. The horse thieves may have already been satisfied with their bunch and were headed over the mountains, or the east, to the settling-up farmland. There would always be a market for a well-broke team that could be put to plow work. Rory knew there were trails and passages through the mountain that would drop horses and men right down into Utah. There could as easily be a market among the Mormon settlers as among the Nebraska settlers.

But if the gang hoped for a larger take, they would undoubtedly show up at the company barns soon. They couldn't afford to hang back, leaving the town time enough to organize a defense. With a quick caution to Ol' Tom to please not shoot him, Rory stepped into the saddle for another look around.

When everything looked quiet and peaceful, Rory decided to ride north a short way. But before he left, he went to Ol' Tom and said, "It might be a good idea for you to leave that harness for another time. Take yourself some baling wire and wire every corral gate shut. Do it so's it won't be easy to undo."

Without a word, Ol' Tom stood and walked away. Rory watched long enough to see the man pick up a pair of pliers and walk out of the tack room. He assumed he was going for a roll of wire.

Rory had barely cleared the stage property before he saw dust on the northern horizon. A goodly cloud of dust moving south. He watched long enough to see one man in front showing the way for a band of perhaps thirty horses. Just two stage-relay stations wouldn't have had that many available. The gang must have started even further north, up into Wyoming. Or they may have ridden into the hills to the west. There were a few ranchers working long, hard hours attempting to establish themselves in those round-topped, high-up hills. Their ranch horses would be a temptation. And that would explain the time lost between the stage company raid and their arrival at the big barn and corral setup.

As he watched, three men peeled the horses off to the side of the trail and bunched them. Five riders continued south. They would be at the barns in only a couple of minutes.

Rory turned and ran his gelding back to the barn and shouted a warning to Ol' Tom. Tom shouted back, "Jest the two more to do."

Rory figured Tom was going to finish the job no matter how he warned him to seek cover, so he said no more.

Not wanting to lose his own gelding, Rory ran him inside and stripped the saddle and bridle. With a mane hold, he led him to the back door and slapped him on the rump. The horse took off running. Rory knew he wouldn't run far, but he also knew that no horse thief was going to get close to him. The Double J, blood-red bay horse wasn't quite a one-man animal. He allowed George to climb on his back. But anyone else trying would gain experience and little more.

Rory ran back carrying his carbine, aiming for the defensive spot he had picked out earlier. From there, on the raised mezzanine, higher than the barn floor but not so high or confining as the loft, he could see all over the corral yard. Immediately below him and off to the side, was the wide door opening to the main aisle between the many stalls. And he had a back way out if hot lead started to seek him.

As the five riders swung onto the stage property, Tom was just wiring up the last gate. One of the five lifted his carbine one-handed and drove lead at the old man. The shot slammed into the big gate post with a resounding thud. With no sign of hurry, Tom wound three more turns into the wire, pocketed the pliers, then turned toward the shooter, lifted his Colt, and replied with all six leads. With a loud yelp, the shooter dropped his carbine, grabbed for his flying hat with one hand, missing completely, and jumped from his dying horse. When he was standing on the ground, he pulled his own belt gun and turned to where Tom had been, but the old man was no longer there.

There was no more shooting as the crew waited for the now hatless man to open the corral gates. It had all been planned, this raid, right down to the minute. But if the gates couldn't be opened, the entire plan flew to pieces. They had no wire cutters, and they wouldn't have time to go stall to stall in the two barns, loosing animals and driving them outside. And with the old man shooting at them, it was an unlikely project anyway.

Into the silence of frustration, Rory shouted to get the thieves' attention.

"It's no good, boys. The gates are all wired shut, and you're under our guns. Give it up. Throw down your weapons and ride this way with your hands in the air. Do it now, and you might live through the day. Of course, I don't mind one way or the other. I expect you're going to be hung for murdering those stage folks. Or one of us can just shoot you dead. Your choice."

Rory didn't figure the gang would know if he was

alone or with a whole posse. But he knew he had a clear shot out the little mezzanine doorway, and he had three stacked-up hay bales between the riders and himself. They were heavy, tightly packed bales that tested his strength when he moved them. But he did move them, and he doubted any lead would penetrate or penetrate with enough power left to cause harm.

The thieves were milling around on their high-strung horses, with everyone talking at once. At least one man voted to turn and gallop away. As his partners and Rory watched, the rider jerked up straight in his saddle, grabbed his chest, and rolled backward off the rump of his horse. One boot hung on to the stirrup for just a few seconds, and then he fell to the ground. There was no further movement. A thundering roar accompanied his fall.

A raspy voice that Rory recognized immediately as Tate's hollered, "I hope you don't mind, Sheriff, I borrowed your Big Fifty out of the jailhouse. Just like old times, me and a fifty."

Turing his attention to the remaining riders, Tate hollered, "What do you think, boys? You can run, but I'll take two down before you're out of range."

To prove the point, the fifty roared again, this time knocking a horse to the ground. The rider was unable to clear the saddle before the horse gave in to gravity. Now there was one dead thief, one on his feet, having lost his mount, one with his leg held fast beneath his downed horse, and two still a-saddle. The two mounted men studied the odds for a second or two and then whirled their horses away, riding further into the yard to put the high corral fences between them and the fifty. Unknowingly, that action put them closer to Rory. He took advantage of the situation by shooting another horse. He hated shooting horses, but he hated shooting men even more. Ol' Tom wasn't burdened by such emotions. He now held the horseless rider's carbine. When the action had been on the other side of the corrals, the man Tom had unhorsed first caught up the dead rider's mount. He was now trying to escape. With a quick flip of the weapon to his shoulder and barely time enough to line up the iron sights, Tom knocked the man off balance. Tom had no clear idea where the shot hit, but he could plainly see that the man wasn't going far. He had fallen immediately over the saddle horn and then laid his head on the animal's neck. Blood was literally pouring onto the saddle skirting. Even as he and Rory watched, the man gave up his grip on the horse's neck and slowly fell to the side. His partner kept riding, never looking back.

The one man who rode away from the stage company corrals joined the three who had dropped off before. The four of them pushed the stolen horses into a full-out run, heading east.

Tate, Ol' Tom, and Rory came together at the end of the aisle between two corrals. One dead man was further out, toward the county road. The one Tom had shot was on the other side of the corrals. The one Rory had shot the horse from under, was making a vain, foolishly hopeless effort to run after his partners, who were already almost out of sight. But the fella with his leg firmly caught under the dead horse was right there before them and was going nowhere. When the men came in sight, the downed man lifted his Colt and threw it away. He did it plainly, leaving no room for misunderstanding. His fight was over. The hope of selling enough horses to buy him a soft, warm bed for the winter was gone, along with every other hope he had leaned on during his life of crime.

Rory, Tom, and Tate made a tight semicircle around the terrified man. No one said anything for a half minute. Tate broke the silence.

"You wanted horses. Why kill those good people, and one of them a woman?"

"That was Desmond. Crazy to kill. We never should have been riding with him. Crazy in other ways too. That was him that rode out of here without trying to help me, or Cab, either one."

Rory said, "These men are stage company employees. It was them you were stealing from as much as the company. Without horses, they can't do their jobs or make a living. I'm Rory Jamison, county sheriff. And you're under arrest. Now tell me your name."

"I'm known as Brownie."

While Tate and Ol' Tom held the downed man under their weapons, Rory went to retrieve his gelding. Once in the saddle, he grabbed a rope from a peg at the end of one stall and used it to drag the dead horse off the downed man. As the horse slid off, the scream from the man told everyone there that he was dealing with a broken leg.

Rory suggested, "Tom, perhaps you could find a wagon and get a team rigged. I'll go round up that running thief before he wears out his boots. When I get back, we'll load these two horse thieves onto the wagon, and you can take them to town. See if the doc can put that leg back to rights. I'll be wanting to run down those others before they make it into Kansas."

Pushing the gelding, in the hopes of bringing the

27

Rory tongue-clicked his gelding into a run, hoping
to catch the horse thieves before they got too far away.
He had his normal bedroll and heavy coat that was never
removed from his saddle except to wear it. But his food
provisions had not yet been replenished after the long
trail to Denver, bringing the wagon load of criminal
suspects to prison. He lifted his canteens, one at a time.
The first was full, the second felt half-full. It would have
to do. There wasn't much water in the eastern part of the
state, but perhaps he could find enough to give the
gelding a sip before he got into a running chase with the
escaping thieves. The chances of having to camp out
were slim, but he liked to be prepared.

It's impossible to hide the trail of four riders and
thirty driven horses. The cloud of dust on the eastern
horizon told Rory the herd was being driven a little to
the south. Not wishing to be seen or to confront four
desperate horse thieves head-on, Rory swung a bit to the
north, forming a bit of a *V* in their more or less parallel

trails. The dust cloud would keep him oriented. What he was looking for was a line of bush or a waterway of some sort that he could drop into. But first, he had to catch up to the escapees. His gelding was reasonably fresh, but the thieves' animals must be near their breaking point. They had been running when he had first spotted them arriving from the north, and they were still running. No horse can keep that pace up for long.

Pushing the gelding in the hopes of bringing the matter to an end, Rory could see that he was gaining. He found himself wishing that Ivan and My Way were siding him. He liked the easy way they all worked together, sometimes with hardly a word spoken or necessary.

A solid half hour at a good pace, not an all-out run, but fast enough, took Rory to the point where he was looking more south than east as he watched the dust cloud. He had caught up but had not yet passed the fugitives. Perhaps the gelding had a bit more in him yet. Taking a chance on his own dust being seen, he angled south, closing in as he rode. He wouldn't go too far, just close the gap a bit. He was still looking and hoping for a blind of some sort. A brush-shrouded waterway, a bit of bush, a steep change in the level of the land, a series of rolling hills. Anything that would allow him to gain the closeness he needed without being seen.

After another quarter-hour of riding, he thought he saw his chance. Ahead just a bit, there was a line of trees and low brush that might indicate a small creek or a slough of some sort. He couldn't be sure. But he had to bring the chase to a conclusion. His eyes had been telling him for the past while that the dust cloud was moving more slowly. Perhaps it was an indication that the fugitives' horses, as well as the stolen animals, were giving out. Or perhaps that was wishful thinking.

Praying the gelding still had some reserve strength, he used his spurs lightly. He seldom used spurs. Sometimes he wondered why he even bothered wearing them. But right then, he needed a few minutes of speed, and he wanted the gelding to understand that. Risking exposure, Rory nudged the animal more to the south. The line of bush was half a mile away. If his plan worked, he could wrap this thing up with no more loss of life. If the plan fell apart, there could be a different outcome. One he didn't dwell on.

Now the line of trees was right before him. And then he was among them. Pulling the gelding back to a trot, he glanced over his right shoulder. He had drawn ahead of the horse herd by several hundred yards. He was close enough to see the positions of the drovers. There were four riders in total, one on each side near the front of the herd, riding point, and two at the rear, one on each corner, bringing up the drag. Several of the horses had broken formation, causing the herd to be a bit ragged, but generally, they were all holding to the group.

He could see there was a small channel of water. Whether it was a flowing creek or just a low spot that caught the periodic rain that blessed this dry land, he didn't know. It didn't matter because the horses wouldn't care. With the smell of water, the horses would become unmanageable. He needed to get his plan in place before that happened.

He turned to ride as directly south as possible while not leaving the shelter of the bush. The sound made as the gelding crashed his way through the low growth would never be heard over the thunder of one-hundred-fifty steel-shod hooves.

He knew his plan was risky. If it worked, he might save lives. His own, as well as the thieves. If he failed, this could be the last ride for one or more of the thieves or himself. Pushing this out of his mind, he turned sharply right, again spurring the gelding into a burst of speed. His estimate of distance was not perfect, but it was close enough.

He materialized out of the bush like a phantom come to life. With a continuous shout, waving his arms wildly, and firing one Colt .44 over the heads of the horses, he watched as a beautiful thing happened. A few of the horses charged right past him but most turned, some to the south, some to the north, and some making a complete reversal of direction, turning right back against the two rear drovers.

The point men were taken out of the fight immediately. The stolen horses, frantic with Rory's shouts, the gunfire, and the sight of the charging gelding, simply bowled them over. Both men were unhorsed. From what Rory could see in his very brief glance from one side to the other, neither had made any attempt to rise from the turf. Their own horses had joined the stolen band and were swirling frantically, but aimlessly, through and around the previous gathering spot.

The two drag riders were surrounded by frantic animals—their own and the remnants of the loose band. One rider was still in his saddle. He was totally focused on staying there while his unruly horse twisted circles beneath him. Momentarily, he was no threat. But Rory knew experienced riders would soon have their animals back under control. He had only seconds. Pouching the

Colt and lifting his carbine, he swung toward the saddled rider. Timing his approach to the twisting of the horse, he laid the barrel of the rifle across the head of the thief. Idly he wondered how many times he could do that before he bent the barrel of the weapon. He had used the carbine in the same manner a couple of times before.

Blood burst from the man's ear while his hat fluttered to the ground. With a frightened bound, the horse surged to the side, throwing his rider out of the saddle. Rory leaped from his own saddle and disarmed the unconscious thief.

Hoping the man was out of the picture for a while, Rory returned to the saddle before seeking out the other drag rider. This was Desmond, the thief Brownie had blamed for the killings. Whether or not that blame was the whole story, Rory could easily see that Desmond was a man to be wary of. He seemed to be unhurt in spite of being thrown from the saddle. He rose from the ground with his hat pushed half to the side and jammed down over his eyes. He used the barrel of his handgun to return the hat to its proper position and free his eyes. He turned in a full circle looking for someone to shoot. When his eyes fell on Rory, it was too late.

Rory's big gelding's chest filled Desmond's vision with horror. He tried to turn, with the idea of leaping out of the way, but he didn't make it. The last thing he knew or felt was his feet leaving the ground as the gelding smashed him back and down. His gun flew out of his hand, and his hat disappeared. He sunk into unconsciousness before he fell fully to the ground.

Reasonably sure Desmond wasn't going to rise and continue the fight, Rory turned to the point riders. Neither had risen to their feet. Hurting badly, they lay where they had fallen. The several horse hooves that had driven over them had broken bones in at least one of the men and taken all the fight out of both of them. Rory stepped down and disarmed each of them anyway.

The horses had found the water and were content to drink and graze. They needed no herding.

28

As always, Rory had a few feet of light line in a saddlebag, but nowhere near enough to firmly truss four men. Feeling he was the most dangerous of the group, Rory rode to where Desmond lay, stepped to the ground, and tied the still unconscious man's hands behind his back. He did the same for the other drag rider. With that done, he dropped a loop of his saddle rope over the rider's feet and, as he had done with Buck up at MacNair's Hill, dragged the man down to where one of the injured men lay. Laying them side by side, he rode back and dragged Desmond to the same spot, holding his gelding to a slow walk.

He walked the horse to where the other injured point man had folded, unconscious, onto the grass. He was now conscious and hurting. Rory looked him over before asking, "Where are you hurt? Any broken bones?"

"You might ask where I don't hurt. You're a rough man. And who are you anyway? What's this all got to do with you?"

"I guess I was too busy to introduce myself."

When Rory completed his introduction, he said, "I'm going to need your name. First name will do until we get you to town."

"Bart."

"Alright, Bart. Can you get up and walk?"

"Give me a lift."

"No, if you can get up, you can get up by yourself. Of course, I could throw you belly down across a saddle and tote you to jail that way."

Not liking the sound of that and seeing no mercy in Rory, Bart rolled onto his hands and knees and, with a mighty effort, was soon standing. Standing and complaining of the pain and the sheriff's roughness.

Rory said, "You haven't seen roughness yet. Stop your complaining and walk."

When the four men were in one place, he used the last of his line to tie both the feet and hands of Bart. He tied him tight. The man named Tappan was left untied, but with bones broken, he wasn't likely to go anywhere.

The two unconscious men were showing signs of waking.

Rory went to the conscious men first, patting them down for more weapons. Each of the four had a belt knife but no guns. He then searched the saddlebags. He found ammunition but no other guns. He left the men waiting while he walked around picking up the dropped handguns. He unloaded them and dropped them, now harmless, into saddlebags. The carbines were unloaded and returned to their scabbards.

"Fellas, I'm going to catch up your horses. If any of you tries to run, I'll simply shoot you. I'm right out of patience for this one day. Now sit here quietly till I get back."

Time had worked the skittishness out of the saddled

horses. Rory managed to pick up the reins one by one, tying them to the bush and, when he had all four, leading them back to the men.

Pushing and prodding and promising worse things to come, Rory got the two unconscious drag riders awake enough to climb onto their saddles. He warned them to hold on and ride. Any attempt to run would result in their death. They seemed to believe him.

Bart helped Rory lift Tappan to the saddle. He screamed in agony but was able to settle down and find a more comfortable position once he was in the saddle.

Rory got their attention. "Listen up, men. We're going to the fort. There's a cell and a judge there just waiting for the likes of you. It's been a long day. Let's not make it any more difficult than it already is. One of you take the lead. I don't care who. You'll ride one behind the other. If you break that line, I will shoot you. Bart, you stay close in case Tappan needs help staying on the saddle. Now let's ride. No running, no trotting. Just a good, steady walk. And no talking."

The stage horses were left at the water. Ol' Tom could round up a crew to bring them back.

29

Rory was starting to feel like a circus ringleader. He had ridden into one town or the other so often trailing tied down, injured, or dead criminals he had almost come to think all fugitive chases would end that way. He hadn't thought of the position of sheriff or marshal as town entertainment, but there they all were, lined up along the boardwalk as the news spread like wildfire. Stores were emptying out, and men were coming from the saloon with shot glasses and beer steins in their hands. Someone cheered, and someone else hollered, "Way to go, Sheriff." Before long, there was a rhythmic clapping following him along the street. Wiley, the town marshal, came from the office and studied the situation.

The sheriff had been gone all afternoon and half the morning before that, chasing too many bandits for one man to tackle. But here he was, riding the drag behind four thoroughly beaten and bedraggled men. He would have liked to ask about the stolen horses, but that was irrelevant at the moment. He would find out later, but the truth was that Rory had stopped at the stage company's barn to speak with Ol' Tom. Tom promised he would get a crew together first thing in the morning. The horses weren't going to leave the water.

Tom also confirmed that the man injured in the fight at the barn had been taken to the doctor's, and the dead were in the back of the undertaker's small building. Everything at the barn was back to normal. The stage company was already at work finding replacement stage stop crews and making plans to rebuild.

Rory said, "To your right, boys. You can see the jailhouse. That's your new home until we can stand you before the judge. That will give you a bit of time to think through your life and list the things you have to repent for. Dead men don't get that chance, so don't miss this opportunity."

The cell was too small for everyone to sleep on the floor, but that was a problem for later. First, Rory had to care for his hard-worked gelding and then get a bath and dinner for himself.

30

THREE DAYS LATER, RORY, SIDED BY WILEY, LED THE FOUR captured criminals into Stevensville. Their trial before Judge Anders P. Yokam had taken much of the day before. Although each of the criminals swore on the Bible that it was Desmond alone who had done the killings, the judge didn't figure that was solid enough evidence to commit a man to hanging. Every man had a vested interest in pointing toward Desmond and away from himself. There were no witnesses left alive at the stage stations, so the judge was in a quandary. He wanted full justice for the dead station operators, feeling especially that way with one of the dead being a woman. But quiet contemplation reminded him that the law doesn't distinguish between a man and a woman in a murder case. To go beyond the strict requirement for evidence might glare back at him, looking more like personal feelings of anger than the upholding of the law.

In the end, the men were all sentenced to lengthy prison terms. It was that or hang them all, and that was a step the judge couldn't take. Now it was Rory's task to get them down to the city.

As he had so often, he wrestled between using horses, a wagon, or a special stage. He opted for a stage. Tate had agreed to drive. They would leave after two nights in Stevensville. It would take that long to arrange for the special stage.

~

WHEN THE PRISONERS were safely tucked into the cell in Stevensville, Wiley peeled away and went to the school to have a visit with Hannah.

Rory rode out to the ranch. He needed a change of clothing and a night in his own bed. He thought he might switch to another horse. The gelding he had been riding had seen some tough miles.

He rode back into town the next morning, a Saturday, with a new idea swimming to the surface of his mind. He grinned as he thought it through. Silently he said, *I love it!*

Officially, Key Wardle was guarding the prisoners. But on the half-barrel chairs in front of the jailhouse, Ivan and My Way were taking their ease, each well-armed and aware of their surroundings.

Rory tied the gelding off at the rail in front of the office and swung to the ground with a big smile on his face. He looked well rested, well bathed, and well dressed. He had shone his worn boots, and he had changed horses. Ivan looked him over in detail and finally said, "Well, don't you look fit and ready. I'm thinking you're planning what might happen in the big city if you should find the Strombeck sisters in town again."

Still smiling, Rory said, "No. That can't happen this time."

"And why not?"

"Because, Ivan, my dear friend, I'm not taking these men to prison. You are. You and My Way."

Tempest Wardle had walked up behind Rory in time to hear that statement. Before Ivan could think up an objection, Tempest said, with great enthusiasm, "I'm going too. I've never seen the big city, and this is my chance."

Ivan and Rory studied her, looking for a reasonable excuse to put a stop to her foolish idea. They were still silent when Tempest burst out with, "Sonia and I. We'll both go. It will be a fine change from the dreary ranches and the dreary small town. I'll go and tell her to talk to Ma about taking a few days off."

She was halfway across the street and nearing the dining room before Ivan said, "She can't do that. Can she, Sheriff?"

But the sheriff's smile, instead of turning into a doubtful grimace, had silently turned into a conspiring grin as if he was in the plot with someone else.

Marshal Wardle had been leaning against the jail-house wall listening to it all. Ivan, starting to feel trapped, turned halfway around and said, "She's your sister, Key. You've got to talk to her, put a stop to this."

"I'm not sure if I've ever seen Tempest change her mind or give in on a discussion. It sounds to me like you've got company for the trip. And you'll remember that Sonia is your sister. I'm not sure you'll change her mind either, after Tempest works up her imagination."

If My Way had an opinion on the matter, he kept it to himself, although it was clear that he had been listening intently.

Rory and most of his family rode into town for church on Sunday. They were joined by Sonia and Ivan, who was feeling strange and uncomfortable in the unfamiliar surroundings.

Ma was keeping the dining room open only until the out-of-town visitors were fed, she was then taking the rest of the day for herself. That she was visiting banker Jesse Ambrewster was no one's business but her own.

～

Early Monday morning, Tate wheeled his stage onto the street in front of the jailhouse. Ivan inspected it thoroughly to assure himself that it was sound and could make the trip safely. He also looked under the seats and into any place a weapon might have been secreted. Food, blanket rolls, and other needs for the trip were stored in the rear boot or tied between the rails on top. Finally, he was ready to load the prisoners.

The four glum men were seated with their hands firmly tied. Their feet were secured to the metal brackets that held the seats in place. Ivan and My Way would sit facing the prisoners. Their position also controlled the two doors.

My Way stepped into the strange conveyance slowly and with great care, feeling his way along step by step. It would take some time to ease into trust. He would be far happier on a horse. But finally, he took a seat. Ivan slid in beside him, placing a carpet bag under the seat. He had secured Anders P. Yokam's written judgment for each of the men, as well as Rory's lengthy report in the carpetbag. Ivan would get the reports to Oscar Cator, with handwritten copies going to Block.

At Tate's urging, the girls would ride on top, sharing the seat with him. Rory was there to lend them a hand up.

With a wave but no final word, Rory nodded to Tate, and the stage rolled forward. They wouldn't pick up speed until they cleared the southern edge of town.

31

AFTER TWO DUSTY, BONE-RATTLING DAYS—DAYS THE GIRLS found to be exhilarating—the stage rolled into Denver. Tate directed it right to the city lockup, where the prisoners would settle down until the arrangements were made for their transfer to the state penitentiary.

It was too late in the day for the county office to be open, but Block was still at work in the federal marshal's small bureau. My Way and the girls waited on the boardwalk while Ivan entered the building. The federal marshal accepted the documents and then asked about the sheriff.

Ivan said, "I guess he's alright. Mean, though. And getting meaner. Took these four prisoners down with no one getting shot. Did it by himself. Then he cornered me into delivering the prisoners. Me and My Way. Mean. See what I'm saying?"

Block laughed, assuring Ivan that an evening in Denver wouldn't qualify as mean. But when Ivan talked about the girls tagging along, he shook his head in wonder.

Silently Block thought the sheriff knew exactly what he was doing. Getting a deputy to suffer the long, hated stage ride was the sheriff's privilege if he didn't want to do it himself. And it was a good experience for the deputy.

Changing the subject, Ivan said, "Rory's been wondering if you have a way of getting us a dozen sets of good handcuffs. We have just the one blacksmith-made set, but they're awkward and heavy. About fill a saddlebag by themselves."

Block said he'd put out an inquiry to his head office. If they couldn't supply them, they could at least provide the name of the manufacturer.

THE NEXT MORNING, Ivan and My Way walked to Oscar Cator's office. The girls were intent on wandering the sidewalks to see what wonders the city had to offer. Rory had advised that Ivan should take some little thing for Bertha, just to ease their way into the office. The deputy, not at all familiar with the niceties of what was sometimes known as politeness or little favors, came up with a plan that would be novel if nothing else.

Entering the office, Ivan and My Way were confronted immediately by the grim-faced Bertha guarding the entry door. She glanced at Ivan as he came in first and then nearly jumped out of her chair as her eyes fell on a buckskin-clad, grim-faced Indian with an eagle feather woven into the single braid hanging over his back collar. Before the poor woman could form a thought or say a word, Ivan said, "Bertha. My name is Ivan. I'm deputy to Sheriff Rory Jamison, down to deliver some prisoners. This is my friend and fellow deputy. He's known as My Way. He has a small token for you, brought directly from the Blackfoot lands."

With that, My Way reached to the back of his head and pulled the braid over his shoulder to hang in front. With a small tug, the eagle feather fell free. With great formality and a grim face, he offered it to the terrified woman, holding it reverently across both palms. When she didn't reach for it, he gently laid it on the desk in front of her. Ivan and My Way, holding back conspiratorial grins themselves, were wondering what was going to happen next.

By this time, Oscar had come from his private office to see what all the talk was about. When he saw My Way's actions and Bertha's horrified response, he stepped in and picked up the feather. Holding the Blackfoot's gift in one hand, he shook hands with Ivan while saying, "Good morning, Ivan. It's good to see you again. And this must be My Way. You've told me about him. It's good to finally meet."

With that said, he shook hands with the Indian. Taking his eyes off My Way, he glanced again to the feather, then to Bertha, holding the feather out to her.

Although he could see that the gift was at least half in jest, he looked directly at Bertha and said, "Bertha, My Way has given you a valuable token. A token his people hold in high esteem. I think a simple thank you would be in order."

Bertha managed to hold the feather pinched between two fingers while she stumbled with words of thanks. Oscar then invited the men to join him in his office.

They left for Stevensville later that day, arriving home in the normal two days. The girls were giddy with memories of the lights, the big hotel that somehow, magically, had running water and bathtubs available whenever a person felt the need, and a large and beautiful dining room. The lovely clothing the ladies wore turned the large foyer into a place of wonder. The excitement of walking the sidewalks by lamplight with the men on guard, and the gadgets found and purchased in the stores, along with the few clothing items that were new and wonderful for the ranch girls, made the long dusty miles of travel worthwhile. Ivan didn't know how much money either girl had brought with her, but he guessed they were coming home with that amount considerably reduced.

Somewhere along the way, they walked past a shop offering both new and used items for sale. The girls and Ivan continued their slow stroll, but My Way slipped off by himself and entered the shop. Among used saddles, miner's picks, a stack of tanned buckskin, and a host of other items, My Way found an eagle feather. He laid out the ten-cent piece the bewhiskered and wizened old man operating the shop asked for and then, with deft fingers, somehow wove it into the braid that was just long enough to hold over his shoulder so he could see what he was doing. When he rejoined the others, Ivan noticed the feather immediately, but thought it best to say nothing.

~

Ivan's report to Rory would have to wait for a ride to the fort. The sheriff had been there the past several days. My Way was acting as if nothing at all important had happened on the trip, but Ivan had inwardly smiled as the Indian had twisted his head this way and that, trying to take it all in.

He wasn't sure he wished to repeat the trip, but Ivan, at least, had proven that he could manage prisoners and complete the reporting side of the law business.

32

LEAVING MY WAY WITH KEY IN STEVENSVILLE, IVAN RODE up to the fort to report to Rory.

Returning to Stevensville had been a simple matter for the men, but for the girls, it was a return from an adventure. Sonia, again waiting on tables at the dining room had what seemed like an endless trail of girls and young women coming in to hear all the exciting news. Tempest had fewer admirers at the ranch supply store, but several men grinned, teasing her about never being satisfied on a ranch again. She returned small smiles, but inwardly she was thinking it would depend on who was sharing the ranch with her.

The day was cool and drizzling rain. Ivan arrived at the fort wet and cold, ready for a hot lunch and several cups of strong coffee. His need was satisfied at the small cantina, where a rotund Mexican man with a mustache that all but hid his nose and mouth served highly spiced foods that Ivan had come to favor since taking up residence in Stevensville.

When Ivan began telling the story of their gift to

Bertha, Rory wondered how the story would end. But it wasn't long before both men were laughing good-naturedly about the event. Rory said, "I think I got a small smile out of her once, but I'm not sure. It might have been a grim warning.

"Now tell me the rest."

The two lawmen were discussing the needs of the gold country when Ivan broke the news to Rory about Block's plan.

"He had nothing firm to report yet, but he hoped to have something soon. He took all the information you were able to provide after the time in MacNair's Hill and around the new gold strikes. The men we arrested up there haven't gone to trial yet, but they've been transferred to the safer holding cells down at the penitentiary. The lawyers are working over everything, hoping to find the next of kin for the murdered miners. Until they sort that out, the mining claims are on hold. Terrence Climber has gone back to see to that matter.

"Someone in Block's office thought he had heard the name MacNair before. They've wired east for information but are still waiting for an answer.

"The gold coin thing has moved on to Texas. With any success down there, we'll never be bothered by it again. Both Oscar and Block threw the uphill matter back at you. It's in your county so it's your problem to solve. They both suggested, separately, that you were going to have to return to the city quite soon to acquaint yourself on the work of the lawyers and the answers to the telegrams that were sent.

"Oscar said, too, that the county is pretty soon going to have to figure out how to raise some tax money. You've done alright up to now on impounded cash and horses and such, but as your expenses rise with deputy's wages, you'll need a firmer financial base."

Rory was quiet, enjoying his lunch as he soaked in all of that information.

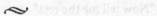

IVAN WAS FED and saddled up before full light the next morning. There was nothing to add to the discussions from the afternoon and evening before, so with a simple wave and "see ya" to Rory, he rode back to Stevensville.

There was no sign of trouble around the fort that Rory could see, so he decided to scout the countryside a bit. Just to check things out. If that ride should somehow take him in the direction of the Horace Gridley ranch, he would be doing nothing more than his sworn duty to the taxpayers. And if Julia happened to have a bit of spare time from her ranch chores and wanted to ride with him for an hour or so, where was the harm in that?

33

RORY RODE ALONE TO THE CITY. BLOCK'S LAWYERS HAD been given enough time, in his opinion, to put things together. It would soon be snowing in the high-up region, and he had no desire to battle through that kind of weather. It was time to get it done.

He had made a side trip to the I-5 Ranch to retrieve the sacked gold Ivan had left there for safekeeping. Those small sacks were now stuffed into the bottom of his saddlebag with his change of clothing folded on top.

The same hotel had a room available, so he booked for two nights. The day was about done when he arrived. He stabled his horse, checked in at the hotel, soaked in a bathtub until the water cooled, and with fresh clothing on, went for dinner. With each trip, he found he was enjoying the luxuries of the city more and more. The crush of people and the almost constant noise still over-balanced the luxuries, though.

His first stop the next morning was one of the banks he held his money in. He had placed the four gold sacks together into a tough paper bag he had brought from Browning's Mercantile. As he stepped to a wicket, he noticed a fashionably dressed lady looking intently at him. As she was simply standing off to the side, he didn't figure she was there to do business, but it was none of his affair, so he turned back to the man standing behind the brass grill.

"Good morning, sir. May I help you?"

"Good morning," answered Rory. "I have some gold I wish to have weighed out."

The clerk put a small *closed* sign in his wicket and said, "Please come with me, sir."

As Rory rounded the counter to follow the clerk, he noticed that the lady was no longer there, but a man was just coming out of a door marked *manager*. The manager said, "Wilber, when you're finished with your business with this young man, please escort him to my office."

As Rory and the clerk took their seats in the tiny private office where the gold transfers took place, Rory asked, "What was that all about?"

"I have no idea. But if you will give me your bankbook and the gold, I'll get it weighed out, and then you can find out what Mr. Tremblay wants."

The deposit was made to Rory's personal account, but when he returned to Stevensville, he would have Jesse Ambrewster transfer it to the county account in the Stevensville bank. Leaving the gold room, Wilber led Rory to the manager's office. A light tap on the door soon had Rory facing Hebert Tremblay and the lady he had seen earlier. Tremblay introduced himself and his wife, Frieda, saying, "I believe, young man, that you are the gentleman that did my wife a great kindness a few weeks ago."

Rory had to think back to understand what Tremblay was talking about. He finally thought of the incident in the alley, but he said nothing in case he was wrong. When he remained silent, Tremblay said, "I think I understand your reticence, young man, but please be assured that any concern for what our city police at first referred to as frontier justice, has been put well aside. I am not without influence in this city. When I advised, rather strongly I admit, that there was no constable anywhere around when there was need to deal with a rather unsavory matter, and that a good citizen had stepped in when he was most needed, the police chief put a damper on the entire affair. But that left Frieda and I with no one to thank personally. And Mr. Cator, who was also helpful to Frieda, was quite closemouthed as well.

"But Frieda recognized you. So please accept our heartfelt thanks. And know that the incident has caused a review at the highest levels of the administration. I shouldn't wonder that we will be hiring and training more officers in the near future."

Rory almost grinned, trying to sort through Tremblay's rambling speech, but he finally said a simple, "Glad to help," and hoped to be released to get about his day's work. Tremblay shook his hand. Frieda made a hesitant effort but finally took a reluctant grip on his fingertips, as if he might really be a wild man about to break into violence at any time.

There was nothing more to say, but they all stood uncomfortably for another few seconds. Finally, Rory said, "If there's nothing more, sir..."

"No. No. Just to say thank you. I'm sure you have a lot to do in town. I will just say it is the bank's pleasure to have a gentleman such as yourself as a client. If there is ever anything we can do for you, you have only to ask."

With more assurances of thanks behind him, Rory was finally on the street. It was only then he chuckled, recalling that neither Tremblay nor his wife had asked his name.

34

RIDING UPHILL FROM THE CITY, HE ARRIVED AT IDAHO Springs late in the day. Rather than riding back to Stevensville and beginning his tour of the high country from there, he thought to reverse the ride they had taken while bringing the prisoners down from McNair's Hill a few weeks before. There had been a snowfall, but most of it had melted, leaving a mucky mire on the city streets and a chill in the air that seemed to go right through him, even with his leather coat with a sheep hide lining. He had heard somewhere that older people felt the cold more. Perhaps the life he had been living had aged him to that point. He directed his gelding toward a sign that announced the recently built brick structure as a hotel. He stepped directly onto the boardwalk, trusting his horse to stand until he returned. He had no desire to wade through the mud and muck. Exactly how he would get from wherever he found a livery for the horse and back to the hotel was a problem yet to be faced.

The hotel was busy, but there were three rooms available. He grinned at the young lady manning the check-in counter and said, "Well, I just need the one, so I guess I'm in luck." The clerk stumbled out a couple of meaningless words but finally got him registered after dropping her pen twice on the floor. After the second time, an older woman bent and picked it up, saying, "Do you want me to take care of this?"

Without a word, the young lady grabbed the pen and completed the registration form. As he was walking away, he heard the older woman say, "They come, and they go. You can't get goggle-eyed about every handsome young man that walks through this lobby."

What Rory didn't see or hear was the young lady lifting a magazine from under the counter and laying it before her workmate. Silently the older woman glanced at it, took a slower look, leaned over to look at the name on the register, and then, reading the story title from the cover of the magazine, said out loud, "Sheriff Rory does what no other could have done."

With a matronly smile at the young woman, she passed the magazine back with the comment, "Penny dreadfuls. All trash."

The younger girl didn't hear, she was distracted, flipping pages to find just the right story, the one she had read earlier.

After carrying his saddlebags and the pannier that held his personal needs to his room, he rode the gelding to the nearest barn.

"Help ya there, young fella?"

"You can if you can put this fella up for the one night."

"Got room to spare. Step down and get him settled in."

"I have a better idea. You climb up here behind me and ride me over to the hotel. You can bring the animal back and treat him to a rubdown and a pail of corn. And my boots will remain clean, and I'll try to find an extra coin for you."

"Never before heard of such a thing. But this road is a mess, I've got to give you that. Alright, give me a stirrup."

～

THE DAYS WERE GETTING SHORTER and the nights longer. Rory left town the next morning before full light, heading along the mine-filled gulch, heading toward Hovel Hill and then MacNair's Hill. The ride took the full of a day. He rode through Hovel Hill without stopping. There was no decent place to bed down there anyway, and it was beginning to snow again. At MacNair's Hill, he would bunk in the marshal's office along with Buck Canby.

The town was in total darkness except for the well-lit dining room and a single light at the marshal's office. The temperature had been dropping during the day as the snow fell. The road, which he expected to be as mire filled as the Idaho Falls Road, was instead frozen solid. His first stop was to stable his horse. The hostler was awake and longing for business but the way his little office was situated, no light managed to stream out. The hostler was one of the few of his kind that Rory had been unable to form some kind of a bond with.

Rory led the gelding into the dark interior through the single door built for the convenience of people, not horses, not bothering to slide one of the big doors open. He hollered, "Anyone home?" as he slowly moved further into the dim interior. Within seconds the hostler came, carrying a lantern. He hung the lantern on a peg and said, "Anywhere there's room, young fella."

The quietness and loneliness of early winter must have been working on the man. For the first time, the sheriff and the hostler visited for a few minutes while Rory saw to the care of the horse. Along the way, the hostler said, "Few toughs just came in coupl'a days ago. Strange. Most folks are heading out, looking for sunshine and warmth. Not much happening up here now. Snow and cold till spring. Most of the pick-and-shovel men have gone to the outside. She's sett'n up to be a slow, quiet winter. The quiet I like, although just once in a while, I miss the sound of a human voice."

As if it was an afterthought, he added, "There's precious little profit in a peaceful, quiet day."

Rory responded, "Where did the toughs go?"

"Danged if I know. Must be settled into one of the abandoned miners' shacks. I've got their horses but haven't seen their money yet."

Rory walked out into the darkening evening. He figured it probably wasn't more than six in the afternoon, but it was already too dark for a man to see where he was going. But with his eye fixed on the marshal's office and trying to remember where things were before, he managed to get there without tripping over anything. A quick rap on the door and a twist on the handle showed him an empty room with the cell door closed on the unused space. The warmth in the room was inviting, and the crackling in the woodstove was a welcoming feature.

He closed the door and made his way across the road. The snow continued to fall. Entering the dining room, he immediately thought this must be the warmest place in town. There were a half dozen miners sitting together at the long table, three on each bench seat. They seemed to be having good fellowship. Rory decided not to disturb them. He took a seat against the wall and away from the window. Looking out, he could see nothing but black, but anyone outside would see him clearly. He was just asking Gloria what was available when Buck walked in. Rory was surprised to see the young lady shine a big smile Buck's way.

Buck made his way across the small room, sat down, and asked, "When did you get in?"

"Maybe a half-hour ago. I've been working over my horse. There's been some hard going, he deserves what little bit of care I can give him. Now, tell me, how is it up here at the Hill?"

"Do you mean other than cold and snowy?"

"I mean things I can't see for myself."

"Most of the miners are gone. Some will return in the spring. Some won't. The big operations at The Falls and places like that keep mining all year, but they're under shelter. A few of these mines will go that way next summer, I figure. That's depending on what you're going to tell me the lawyers have figured out."

Rory leaned back to allow Gloria to set a plate before him. She walked away and was soon back with the coffeepot. Rory picked up his knife and fork and waited. He could see Gloria returning with Buck's meal. When both were served, Rory said, "Buck, I normally give thanks silently when I'm with a bunch of men. Would you mind if I prayed now?"

Buck didn't mind. They were soon eating and bringing each other up-to-date at the same time. Rory ended that conversation, saying, "We'll wait till we're alone to talk about the rest. But perhaps you can tell me about MacNair's store."

"I've been keeping it locked except when I'm available to run it. Folks still need things, and I'm not so busy that

I can't do that. I'm keeping a record and setting the money aside. If MacNair returns, he'll have lost nothing. Other than that, I'm spending a bit of time at my mine. I've hit a bit of a pocket. The quartz looks like jewelry rock. It's almost a shame to break it apart. But there's no value in the quartz, so I do what has to be done. It's too cold at the mine, so I've been gathering it all up in a sack and hauling it home. I figure I must look like Santa Claus, coming with the town's gifts. But that gift is for me. I break it up on the cell floor and lock it in when I'm not there. It's going to be a long winter, but I want to be on the ground in case someone makes a try at opening one of the stolen mines.

"Of course, with MacNair gone there's nowhere to sell, but I have a bit of cash to hold me over."

It wasn't long before Rory looked at Buck's empty plate and said, "Ready if you are."

AT THE MARSHAL'S OFFICE, they pulled up chairs close to the stove. These were better chairs than the ones Rory had scrounged. He didn't bother asking where they came from.

Buck looked at Rory and said, "So tell me."

"This isn't in any special order. First, it would appear that our involvement with the tarnished coins is over. There are several folks that will be happy to hear that. You only touched the one small piece of that, but it's been a thorn in my side for a year or more. For others too. The Federals and their lawyers are now looking to Texas, and I hope that's the way it stays. It's going to leave a bunch of unanswered questions, but I can live with that if it's truly over.

"Then, the lawyers figure you have a right solid claim to the Cam One Mine. Those others couldn't prove any claim at all. It seems they were hoping to high-grade the thing and be gone before anyone caught on. So good for you on that.

"There's no sign of next of kin for Halverson. The lawyers will keep trying, but I was firm that there had to be a final answer before spring. They seemed to accept that.

"A couple of the other mines, those up at Hovel Hill, are less clear. The Gray Lady appears like it was stolen. The others, Hobbit and The Blue Bell, were sold. They found the original owners and made that clear. The trouble with that now is that I can't go arresting people on appearances. Until we get final word on the Gray Lady, I have to leave it alone.

"Terrence Climber really is working with the Federals. I had some doubts, but he doesn't need to know that. He's coming back up in the spring.

"Herc Branson, Tidy Sampson, and Montana Red proved to be nothing more than toughs. The federal marshals knew their names. That leaves us trying to sort out who the murderer is. Until we know better, the crime will rest on the shoulders of those three we arrested and hauled down. Chouse Ramble, he's dead, but Grit Price, Toby Whitelaw, Diego Ramirez—could be any of those, or maybe all of them—working together. The lawyers will have to deal with that too. Whatever evidence was up here is gone. All we have is what I overheard in the mercantile and what the men themselves said.

"Emmett Streetly swears his innocence. Says he was just using his skills as an accountant to help businessmen with their finances. There's no proof of anything else, so he was turned loose. But I still have my doubts.

"That leaves me with Simon Webb. You don't know him, and you don't want to. He was a federal marshal, but they cut him out of that job. He was causing too much trouble. He seems to have disappeared, but I'm not trusting that. He'll show up again. He's got a bone to pick with me and with the marshal down in Stevensville. I doubt if he'll show up here. If he does, leave him alone. They tell me he's lightning-fast on the draw and that he seems to enjoy killing. If he shows up, just play ignorant."

Buck had listened intently without interruption. He seemed to absorb the information and then said, "Doesn't leave much up here for me to do. Perhaps we should drop the deputy thing."

Rory reached into his shirt pocket and lifted out a folded-over envelope. He passed it to Buck and said, "No. I like that you're up here. You might keep your eyes open for someone to take the position up at Hovel Hill too. If we can hold the line on the criminals, we'll have a better chance of keeping the peace in the long run. That's your pay till spring. It'll keep you in coffee and Mila's roast beef. If MacNair shows back up, you'll have some wages to collect from him too. And if that snow keeps falling, you'll get lots of rest before spring.

"I'll be pulling out in the morning. Somehow get a message down to Stevensville or come yourself if you need help."

With a little more idle chatter, both men spread out their bedrolls.

35

I⊤ BOILED DOWN TO THREE CHOICES. S⊤EVENSVILLE COULD be reached by the better road that went back to Idaho Springs and down to Denver. But that was a three- or four-day ride in the summer. The way the snow was falling, who was to say how long it would take.

Rory's destination could also be reached by winding through some of the lower valleys that would take him to the Triple T Ranch and then down to the Denver Road and into Stevensville. That would be a two-day trip, even with the snow.

But the shortest ride, and one that Rory was comfortably familiar with, was down the hill past the workings of Badger and Rawlins, who had probably gone out already themselves. From there, it was a steep, but not too long, drop to arrive at Kiril's cabin. After that, it was easy and quick. A short three- or four-mile ride to the I-5 Ranch, across the ranch, and down the hill, arriving right on the edge of the town. A one-day ride if he started as soon as the sky lightened enough to see. Or perhaps, Rory thought, for the horse to see since the horse had better eyes than any man would have.

The choice seemed simple, and he made his decision. The trail south was covered in snow to a depth that would about reach the tops of his riding boots. But as long as Rory stayed in the saddle, there should be no problem remaining warm and reasonably dry. To fill his riding boots with snow would be another matter altogether.

Turning off the wagon road and pointing east and down, the horse balked just a bit. There was a grade, but the animal would soon get used to it. Rory steadied him with a stroke on the withers and reassuring words.

By the time they reached the cutoff to the Badger and Rawlins claim, the horse was sliding almost as much as he was walking. And the snow was still falling. Rory held a tight rein, speaking to the animal constantly, telling him what to do, although he well realized how foolish the words must sound to the horse.

From that last cutoff and down to Kiril's cabin, the trail leveled for about one mile and then turned steeper again. And narrow. And the corners seemed to never end. A group would have to ride single file, although, with Rory being alone, that caused no hardship. Unless a rider considered having snow-laden branches dropping snow onto his shoulders, under his collar, and down his back—to be a hardship.

He had come too far to go back and seek an easier path, but he had no intentions that way anyway.

He guessed the distance to the cabin at about seven or eight miles, although it could be more. Summer riding and what he was currently struggling through were two different things. His judgment could be off some.

As he rode, the trail got steeper. He remembered that

portion and knew it would end in less than one mile. From there, the trail had a grade to it, but it would be manageable. Knowing the horse was feeling fatigued from the constant battle to maintain his footing, Rory thought to dismount. Both horse and rider could use a short rest. But the horse had worked up a sweat. It would be better to keep going rather than run the risk of the animal attracting a chill.

Digging in his memory for trail signs, Rory was sure the cabin would appear out of the snow-laden forest in the next few minutes. He wasn't sure if the air had warmed, but there was no doubt there was considerably less snow. The fresh snowfall had ceased a mile or two back.

The last grade leading to the cabin yard was much easier. He remembered that much. Trusting the animal, he had been riding with his eyes closed for the past half hour, except for occasional peeks. The sky had partially cleared, and the bright sun reflecting off the snow was blinding. But when he felt the slope of the saddle make a distinct change, he knew they were nearing the cabin. It was a satisfying feeling. Now down to the I-5 and home.

HE FELT the bullet before he heard the echoing sound of the exploding powder. Knowing he was hit, he opened his eyes and lay as flat against the gelding's neck as he could. The horse took several sideways leaps as a bullet grazed his hip, almost unsaddling his rider. Rory couldn't spot the shooter, but he kicked the animal into a run, hoping his direction was right. He veered off to the south, heading toward the entry to the I-5 trail. But immediately, the horse took another shot, this time grazing the top of his neck and taking a chunk of mane hair with it as it careened off, into the forest. But that had been a handgun. The shot that hit Rory was from a rifle, he was sure of that, judging by the sound.

So, the I-5 trail was blocked and guarded, and he knew there were at least two men. The horse was feeling the fatigue of the trail and now some loss of blood. Rory was also losing blood, but he couldn't possibly worry about that at the time. He kicked more speed out of the suffering animal and headed to Kiril's barn. As he rode, shots echoed through the forest, but no more lead reached him. Then he figured it out. They weren't shooting at him. Whoever the shooters were, they wanted the horse down. That meant they wanted him alive. And he couldn't think of one single thing that would be good for him if he was taken prisoner. He could not allow that to happen. If it cost him one of the magnificent Double J geldings, that's how it would have to be.

His coat was tightly buttoned up, making the Colts nearly impossible to get at. But he had his carbine, and he knew he could manage that weapon with one hand. He often had. He lifted it from the scabbard and rode.

Foolishly, a man stepped from the shelter of the chicken coop, hoping for a clear shot. Rory tilted the carbine till his instincts told him it was right and squeezed the trigger. He had racked another bullet into the chamber almost before the first shot landed. Squinting through his sun-glazed eyes, he saw the man crumple into the snow.

The barn was now only thirty or forty yards away. If he could get that far, he would have choices. He might be able to find a point for defense. The bush, the barn itself —if no one had taken shelter there—the loft, the corral, perhaps behind the watering trough. In any case, it was all he had.

Another shooter emerged from the corral. He had been hiding behind the big gatepost, a good enough shelter if he had stayed there. He took two steps into the open, probably thinking Rory was out of it, as he lay along the horse's neck. But he would never know how wrong his judgment of the sheriff's condition was. The man's single shot struck the faithful gelding. His legs began to fold, but his momentum carried him right to the shooter. Expecting nothing like that, the man waited too long. As the horse's front legs folded completely, Rory made an awkward, hurting leap from the saddle, landing on his back and crying out in pain as the shoulder the bullet had buried itself in hit the ground. The shooter was lifted from his feet by the weight and momentum of the collapsing horse and tossed into a heap in the corral like a rag doll. He landed just a few feet from Rory, who was gathering his senses and his carbine, which he had dropped within arm's reach.

Taking no chances that the shooter would recover, and hoping the barrel hadn't been packed with wet snow, Rory laid the carbine out at arm's length, putting the muzzle less than two feet from the man. He moved the weapon just a bit and put a bullet though the man's heart. Just to be sure, he cranked the loading lever and did it again.

Knowing there were still shooters out there, Rory, struggling to a low crouch, scrambled for the barn door, hoping not to meet anyone once he got there. He made it safely, and just as he was coming to a standing position, he heard a shout, "He's made the barn."

"Well, go get him."

That last voice. Rory knew that voice. An angry and

shrill voice, sheathing with frustration and shouting orders. That could be no one else but ex-federal Marshal Simon Webb. Exactly why the man had taken on so with Rory, he had no idea. And who the men with him were, was a mystery too. But that the ex-marshal wanted him alive could not be doubted.

He had already lost two men, but the voice, loaded with a killing rage, showed no intention of giving it up and riding for safety. And now Rory was cornered in the barn by two killers. He corrected himself. At least two killers. There could be others. He needed to get out. But where? His shoulder hurt abominably, and his horse was down. He couldn't fight off both men forever. Winter darkness would be upon them before too long. The attackers would have free rein after that.

Feeling the need and taking a long chance, he shuffled a bit closer to the water trough. It hadn't been used for some time. Under the skim of ice, it was scummy on top. But it was water. He pulled his sleeve up to keep it dry and swished the surface around a bit, after breaking the ice. He then dropped his cupped hand in. He got little more than a sip but repeating the action a couple more times satisfied his immediate need.

He stood there, sheltered by the timbers lining each side of the barn door, trying to figure it out. He had lost blood. He had lost his horse and was now on foot. No matter which way the day went, that was the situation he had to deal with. It had been a long, fatiguing day, and he could think of little through the pain. He could find no way of escape. And he had to admit it, he was sorely frightened.

But suddenly, like a flash into his weary brain, he thought, *The trail. The bush trail. Of course.*

36

THE INTERIOR OF THE BARN WAS CAST MOSTLY IN DIMMING shadow as the slanting sun dropped behind the Rockies. But enough light remained for Rory to take a careful look around. Kiril had been a builder. A builder and a schemer. What had he hidden in the barn? Perhaps nothing. But perhaps there was a chance.

Rory sized up the single, small window in the back wall. He might squeeze through given enough time. But he would have to remove his heavy coat and his guns. Even then, it would be tight. And he would be fully, helplessly exposed to anyone that had snuck around the back or dared to try the big barn door. And with a bullet in his shoulder, his ability to wiggle and squirm through a small hole would be questionable.

What else was there? The mysterious trail through the woods starting at the back of the barn indicated, at least, a possibility of another access rather than around the outside of the building and through sheltering aspens and shrubs, with a gunman waiting for his opportunity.

Stepping back to gain a broader perspective, Rory's eyes fell on the timber beside the window. It seemed out of place. Rory was no builder, but even he could see that there was no need for a single supporting timber right at that place, unmatched anywhere else in the small building. He stepped closer and ran his hands down the wood. His fingers immediately fell into the space behind the upright timber. That made no structural sense either. Pushing his fingers into the depth of the space, he ran them up as far as he could reach without feeling anything. He then ran them down. Almost immediately, he felt something. A protrusion of some sort. He couldn't see what it was. He would have to figure it out by feel. Rory drifted his hand around the protrusion for another few seconds. At first, the lever felt like a simple bolt latch such as a person might use to hold a gate closed. But pulling on it accomplished nothing. Lifting had the same negative result. So did pushing it down. But by twisting it at the same time as he was pulling on it, he managed to ease it outward, causing movement. It was stiff and needed some effort, but with some work, he moved it further. Suddenly there was a click and a release. The wall beside the vertical timber moved. Just a bit, but it moved. A narrow piece of wall containing the window swung outward. It was so well disguised that he hadn't even noticed the seam in the woodwork. It was stiff, and undoubtedly, the bush had grown up around it. But he didn't need much space. Just enough to squeeze through. He pushed with all his waning strength, and slowly, the wall moved. Wondering why the old man had included this well-disguised escape hatch, Rory thought it was little less than genius. A casual eye would have never suspected it.

Caring that his shoulder didn't get bumped in the

process, Rory turned sideways and eased forward. He was soon out and in the bush. The barn was now behind him, and the trail ahead of him. He started to walk, looking back often to watch for an enemy who might be following.

As he walked, the thought crossed Rory's mind to expose the wound and pack it with snow in the hopes of slowing the bleeding. But there was little snow and less time. Not only was darkness going to be a problem, but he had no idea when one of his pursuers would find the trail he was on. He stepped up his speed, hoping to find his way along the path before darkness overtook him. There was no way to know what strength he had left in his body, but he would push until he could push no more.

He was well along the trail when he heard a faint shout, "There's a door in the back of the barn. Leads to a trail through the bush. That's where he's gone."

"Well, go get him." That had to be Webb shouting.

Rory glanced back but saw no one. But then, a chunk of bark flew from an aspen too near his head for comfort. He heard the second shot just as he had stepped around a bend and down a bit, as the trail veered off the line it had been following. The bullet missed, nearly cutting another small tree in half, but it had come close. Too close.

The shooter had a straight path to follow right up until that little bend. He could run and catch up in no time at all. Rory had to move. And move as fast as his weary and hurting body would allow.

Evasive moves were difficult on the narrow opening through the bush, and if he attempted to create a new way, he might be slowed to the point that he would be overtaken. Or he might get so lost he wouldn't find the outlet behind Tippet's barn.

Rory took a few jogging steps, hoping to make it around the next bend he could see ahead of him. The bouncing made the pain from his wounded shoulder almost unbearable. Anyway, he wasn't anywhere near fast enough. Before he reached his destination, the chaser shouted out a jubilant, "Got you. You're mine."

He should have aimed and shot instead of shouting a warning. Rory dropped to his face on the trail and then wiggled around until he faced back the way he had come. The drop did nothing at all good for his shoulder but facing the choice between pain or death, with gritted teeth, he prepared for battle.

He had the attacker in his sights when the man shot again. An experienced fighter would know to take the extra second or two to be sure. Rory's adversary shot too quickly. The flying leaves and dirt said it was a close call. But that gave Rory his chance.

Rory brushed the debris away from his eyes and caught the shooter in the *v* of his rear site. Bringing the muzzle up just slightly but quickly, the front bead took the place of the man's head. But a rushed headshot is a low-percentage shot. He dropped his aim a bit and squeezed the trigger. The two desperate men exchanged shots, each rolling and squirming, trying to change position on the narrow trail. But finally, the return shots ceased. Rory listened into the silence until he was sure. Then he slowly, cautiously, rose to his knees. He saw no movement from the shooter. Never taking his eyes or the muzzle of the carbine off his enemy, Rory walked back. There was no doubt. The man was dead. A bullet had taken him in the top of his head. His bullet-scarred hat lay beside him. His head lay resting on his bent arm as if he was simply sleeping. His carbine was under his body. Rory turned and walked away.

There had been no sign of Webb.

SIMON WEBB LISTENED to the gunfight in the bush. Knowing the hated sheriff had taken at least two bullets before he escaped to the barn, he had no doubt that his man had been victorious. He then would have no further use for the shooter. He had already been paid the few dollars he had been promised. He would be free to saddle up and ride off, leaving his two dead companions behind. Perhaps he would think to retrieve the money from their pockets. He didn't care.

Take it and be off with you. And now for that smart-mouthed town marshal. Looks as if I'll have to take care of that problem myself.

Webb rode as fast as his gelding would carry him, down the bush trail onto the I-5 and across their range, ignoring the shouts from Pavel as he rushed past the barn. He nearly upset his horse when he moved onto the downward road with its mud and remnants of snow. But with a vicious pull on the reins, he had the animal under control and moving toward Stevensville. He could feel victory over his adversaries even as he rode.

RORY WALKED until he got to the steep downward slide. He was weak and weary beyond description. He wasn't sure if this was the big slide. There had been more than one, but just the one that was larger and steeper than the others. His mind wasn't bringing up the memories as he had hoped it would. But then he saw the rope lying where he had left it on his first time through there. He bent and reached for the rope, but in his weakness and trying to favor the gunshot shoulder, he overbalanced himself, nearly dropping onto the slide face-first. Desperately he grabbed a small aspen and twisted around until he could land on his rump at the top of the slide. It was slippery. Slippery and wet, and his weight carried him forward and down, like a kid sliding a toboggan down a snow-covered hill. In his weakness, he could do nothing to stop himself. He slid downward on the snow-dampened hillside, but he had lost the rope. He was moving faster than wisdom would have dictated, but there was not much he could do about it. To dig in his heels might be to turn sideways. He had the feeling that the next bump on his shoulder would send him beyond his pain threshold and he would never see home again.

Finally, he felt himself slowing and then easing to a stop. He collected his thoughts for a moment and then got to his feet. The rest of the trail was simpler, with only a couple of smaller hills. It was probably another two miles through the bush, but he could do that. He would do it. He had to if he was to see another sunrise. *Just, please, no more falling.*

The bottom of the trail was nearly level, finally opening up where he would see the back of Tippet's barn. It was coming to full dark in the bush, but the outside world would still have some light. That bit of light glinting off Tippet's barn wall told him he had made it. He could dimly see the unpainted and weather-worn barn wall, standing there like a promise fulfilled.

He took the last step out of the bush and laid his hand on the wood. He stood there for the pace of a long breath, thankfulness and hope coursing through his mind.

With great relief, he made his way along the wall, holding his carbine in his left hand and guiding himself by running the flat of his right hand along the rough lumber, all the while being careful not to trip over some piece of junk the hostler had discarded. Before he stepped into the clear, he heard shouting. Simon Webb. Again. Would the man never stop? Not knowing what to expect, he checked the carbine, removing the bits of broken leaves and twigs that gathered there during one of his falls. And slowly, with clumsy fingers, he reloaded. He also unbuttoned his coat and pushed the sides apart to clear the Colts.

STANDING in the center of the street and shouting for all to hear, Webb hollered, "Your sheriff pal is dead, Marshal. And you're a coward, hunkered down in the jailhouse, hoping I'll go away. But that's not going to happen. Not until you and I have had a little go-around anyway. Come out and at least pretend you're a man."

The shouted taunts were aimed at Key, of course. Rory was tempted to simply step out and shoot the man. But if he did that, the townsfolk would forever wonder about Key. Was he a coward, not fit to be marshal? Not fit to call Colorado? Forever needing the sheriff's protection?

The questions were answered when Key stepped out of the dining room and said, "I'm not in the jailhouse, Webb."

Key, trembling at the thought of his first face-to-face meeting over guns, had worked himself up, expecting the

ex-federal marshal to turn, and to draw as he was turning. He had no thought that he could outdraw the man,
but he was pretty sure he could outshoot him if Webb's
first bullet didn't kill him.

It was time for Rory to make himself known.

"And I'm right over here, Webb."

Webb again twisted a half circle, focusing on where
Rory's voice had come from. A big smile crossed his face.

"You're shot through with luck, Sheriff. But your luck
ends today, right here."

With that, he drew. The fastest draw Rory had ever
seen. But it wasn't as fast as a .44-40 Winchester, already
aimed and ready.

Was it cheating when the sheriff had his weapon
cocked and ready? As Rory had told the kid up at the fort
who called himself Sky Blue, "This isn't a game. There
are no rules such as a game might have."

The truth is that when a known killer has a weapon
loaded and aimed your way, you do whatever is necessary to see the next sunrise. When you're the sheriff, that
advice always holds true.

Key was only a fraction slower. Rory didn't make a
clean hit. He was using the last of his strength just to stay
on his feet. Aiming the carbine was a maybe thing, at
best. But he did hit Webb. He hit him in the big bone
running down the length of his thigh. His collapse to the
roadbed saved Webb from Key's shot, which went over
his head.

Holding his carbine as steady as he could, Rory
stepped away from the barn. He didn't see it, but Tippet
followed him out with his double twelve shotgun at the
ready. Key stepped off the boardwalk and onto the road,
away from the business establishments. He was fearing
for anyone in the dining room or any other adjacent

store. A stray bullet could do nasty work. But he needn't have worried. There wasn't a soul in the direct line of fire. No one, that is, except Ma Gamble, who seemed to be more concerned for the glass in the big front window of her dining room than she was for her own life. She stood with her hands on her hips, casting a silent warning to Webb. All the others had moved off to safer locations, although none had left. This night would be talked about until the young folks present had turned into gray-haired grannies and grumpy old codgers. No one wanted to miss the action, although lives were at stake.

Webb wasn't finished. Lying on the road, his shot-up leg useless to him, he was shouting threats at anyone who came into view. Heedless of the fact that Rory and Key had him in their sights, he twisted on the ground until he could point his Colt at Rory. Key seemed to be a secondary enemy. First, he wanted the sheriff.

He lifted the Colt, but he never got the shot off.

The first bullet that knocked him back came from My Way. Then, as if rehearsed, Key, Rory, and Ivan all squeezed their triggers. Tippet held ready but could easily see he wasn't needed. Webb collapsed, and there was no need to check if he was breathing.

Rory turned to Ivan and My Way, who were still sitting on their horses, and asked, with slightly slurred words, "Where did you two come from?"

Before an answer could be heard, the sheriff slumped to the ground. With his last strength, he tried to rise. He got his head lifted and was trying, with the leverage of his good arm, to rise. He was almost to where he could put some weight on his elbow when strong hands grabbed him and forced him back to the road. Ivan said, "Hold still, old buddy, no one knew you'd been shot. But getting this close, I can see your shirt and coat are soaked through. Tippet's gone for his wagon. Key ran to tell the doctor to be ready for business."

TIPPET ONLY TOOK the time to harness one horse, quickly hooking the traces to one side of the doubletree. The other side could drag. They weren't going far. Thinking only of the time that was passing, he didn't bridle the animal either. Giving a quick tug, he soon had the wagon moving. He ran along the road with his finger looped through the ring in the bottom of the halter. The horse was nervous with the unbalanced pull, but Tippet kept him aimed right. As he drew near, Ivan bent and, as if Rory weighed nothing at all, picked him up and laid him in the back of the wagon. Tempest and Sonia were already seated there. They held Rory's head and upper body free of the bouncing wagon by laying him across their extended legs. Rory's eyes were closed. The girls didn't do more than hold him while Tempest stroked his forehead. She kept repeating, "Almost there. Almost there. You hold on, Sheriff."

37

THE ENTIRE FAMILY FROM THE DOUBLE J RANCH SADDLED
up and rode to town. George and Eliza were leading the
procession in the buggy. The news, delivered by Key
Wardle, was that the doctor had put Rory to sleep using
the much-dreaded ether. He wasn't expected to be
waking up for some hours. But the family wanted to be
there. There was nothing they could do. But they could
be there. Those that wished to could pray. And
many did.

At the news of the wounded sheriff, a quietness,
almost a hush, settled over the town. Even the gunfight
was a subject for future discussion. For the time at hand,
all concern was for their sheriff, a boy who had grown
into a man right there in their community.

Strangely, it was Tippet that appointed himself to
wait in the doctor's small foyer, hungry for any news
from the adjoining surgery room. As soon as they
reached town, George and Eliza joined him in their
silent vigil.

∾

KEY KEPT the lamp turned low inside the sheriff's office. He himself sat in silence on his familiar chair on the boardwalk in front of the office. Beside him sat Ivan. My Way had stalled his horse and disappeared, walking into the bush. No one knew where he went, but the man could take care of himself, so he'd never be asked any questions about the night.

∾

MA SERVED several late dinners and many cups of coffee. It was all done either in silence or through hushed whispers.

When the news finally found its way out of the doctor's office, it was Tippet who brought it. He went first to the dining room where the Jamison family, except for the parents, were drinking coffee.

"Outside of his shoulder's grazed, is all. Flesh wound. More like the top of his arm, really. Another shot glanced off a couple of ribs and buried itself in his arm just below the shoulder after running against the bone there. Doc got the bullet out and cleaned it all up. A few stiches. It will take some time to heal. Won't know for some little while if he's lost any use of the arm. Needs quiet and rest and lots of good food to make up for the blood he lost."

Smiling for the first time, he said, "Doc tells me he'll need a new shirt too."

There was no cheering from the gathering, only a great escaping of held breath and a few relieved smiles. As Tippet left the dining room to report to Key and Ivan, he could hear the level of conversation slowly building.

38

RORY WAS TAKING HIS EASE ON THE SMALL PORCH IN front of his cabin, enjoying a beautiful fall day. The sun was bright, but there was little warmth in it. There had been a filtering of snow, but it was melted away. It was a good day to be alive. Rory had confirmed the opinion he had held since his father's murder; any day was a good day to be alive.

Nancy and Hannah had taken a side each and carried the big rocking chair from the kitchen to the cabin. Rory had, at first, mocked the idea that he would enjoy the rocker.

"I'm just shot up a bit, girls, I'm a long way from old enough for a rocker."

They grinned at him and then at each other, as if there was a secret only they knew, and Rory would be some time figuring it out. As the girls had predicted, he had sat nowhere else since the rocker took up its new home on his porch.

He had received a letter from Block explaining that the lawyers had gone to the penitentiary.

There they met separately with Mike Wasson, the phony Stevensville marshal, and MacNair. They promised Wasson early parole if he would lay out all the facts on the judge's rustling activities. He was only too happy to have the hope of freedom in his near future. We now know the trail the stolen gold took to finally be used as a tool in the rustling of cattle. Wasson told us, "The way I heard it, although I wasn't there myself, was that a few gold coins were saved out of the trunks of contraband before the big deposit was made in that Texas bank. Saved just for a novelty. No one dreamt that they would be the focus of any investigation."

MacNair also welcomed the news that he wouldn't be hung if he laid all the mining thefts out, naming names. He wouldn't escape prison, but he would be alive. He seemed to understand that there was a significant difference between the two options.

His information led to the same source of stolen wealth as the marshals. So now the investigation moves on to Texas. You might find you would enjoy a trip down that way. We have a rich cattleman to talk to. And a heavy hitter in Washington to make happy.

Terrence Climber will be riding back up to MacNair Hill in the spring. He has all the details on the legal ownership of the mines and will be putting things to rights as much as possible.

Get well, my young friend, and God bless.

Rory was sitting on the rocker with a warm blanket draped over his shoulders when Ivan and My Way rode up. They were leading another horse. The first thing Ivan said was, "We cleaned up that mess you left behind up on the hill. Put a lock on Kiril's cabin door. Brought your saddle and packs down on this horse. If you can get it back to Tippet, he'll keep it until Sonia makes another trip home. She can take it along with her to the I-5."

They then moved on to the usual greetings. Rory said, "You both look as if you're packed for the trail."

"Going to be gone for a few days, boss. My Way has worked up a hankering to go home. He can see that Tempest no longer needs his care. Probably never did, the way she can ride and use a gun. Turns out he has a wife and son living in the village up in the Blackfoot lands. It's time he went home."

Rory directed his comment at My Way.

"That's a long ride, My Way, and it's late in the year. You could run into some bad weather."

"I go. Not too far. Many villages. Friends. I stay if snow deep. Go home when snow gone."

Rory struggled to his feet. It was no longer a struggle to rise or walk, but he still found it a struggle to get out of the rocker. He held out his hand to the Indian and said, "My friend, it has been good to ride with you. You are a man to know. You have many stories I would like to hear. Maybe we will meet again and tell stories."

My Way just nodded and, with a small smile, said, "When we old."

"Yes. That would be good. When we old."

Rory asked the two to sit for a moment. He went into the cabin and was out in just a few moments with a small canvas sack of coins. He held it up to My Way and said, "For you to buy what you need along the way. Maybe buy a present for your wife and another for your son."

Again, My Way just showed a small smile as the sack disappeared into the folds of his buckskins.

Ivan said, "I plan to ride with him as far as Laramie. Might go on to the Mirrored W. We'll have to see how things look. There's still enough, and more, fools that would be only too happy to cause problems for an Indian. Not everyone is yet civilized. Perhaps I can see My Way through some of that if it shows itself. From Laramie, My Way says he will ride into the hills. There are trails he knows that will avoid the white man's towns. I'll study on the situation before I decide what to do. I shouldn't be gone more than a week, maybe two."

With a firm handshake, a practice My Way still found strange, the men parted. As Rory stood watching them ride away, two other riders turned onto the Double J Ranch driveway. He stood watching as they came nearer. He didn't recognize them. He turned to look back at the small table he had placed there. A table that held his coffee cup and his books. And one of his Colt .44s. He needed to confirm what he already knew. The weapon was there and loaded, with the muzzle safely facing the log wall.

But as the riders got closer, a broad smile brightened his face. He wouldn't be needing the gun.

Horace Gridley and his daughter, Julia, entered the yard and immediately spotted Rory standing and waiting. Both visitors were smiling, but perhaps Julia's was the broader of the two expressions. She waved a small greeting well before she was within talking range. Nancy was watching from the kitchen window.

The news of his wounding must have reached the fort and beyond. Rory could think of no other reason Gridley would leave his ranch to escort his daughter over the miles.

George watched the visitors from the barn door. Not knowing who it was, he sauntered that way. Rory was pretty much up to speed, but if it turned out he needed help, George intended to be close by.

George could see there was no need for fear, but he

still wanted to know who the visitors were. As he neared the cabin, Rory called him closer.

"George. I wish you would say hello to good friends."

With the introductions complete, George had figured out that Gridley was a third party to a conversation for two.

"If you're not tired from riding, Horace, come, I'll saddle up and show you the ranch."

THE SHERIFF WASN'T SO WOUNDED that he couldn't enjoy a bit of company. He would have to get back to work soon, but he hoped the bad guys would do their evil deeds somewhere else. For a while, at least. As quickly as thoughts can flit through a man's mind, he considered Wiley, up at the fort; Key, closer by in Stevensville; and Buck, holding down the law up in gold country at MacNair's hill. They were all good men. Capable. Reliable. And that was a good thing. He had no illusions about enjoying a totally peaceful winter, but those young men could handle most things.

"Here, Julia. Take the rocker. I'll get another chair from the cabin."

Her smile was broad as Rory reached for the reins of her gelding. A nice visit might be just the thing.

Rory would have to be back in the saddle soon, but for right now, the sheriff had a visitor.

DREARY DAY IN TEXAS

A SNEAK PEEK AT BOOK FOUR

Action-packed and full of history, award-winning author Reg Quist delivers book four in a series that details the turbulent adventures of a young lawman.

Sheriff Rory Jamison wants nothing more than to protect and serve his county—and start over after the last few years. But when the federal government intervenes, he is forced to embark on a dangerous mission with a brand-new federal marshal straight out of Washington, D.C.—who has no idea just how deadly the west can be.

Stolen cattle lead them to Texas, where they battle ruthless rustlers and harsh weather conditions on the hunt for the truth. And just when they think they've solved the case, they discover that stolen cattle are the least of their worries.

Uncovering a level of crime that goes deeper than a county sheriff should go, Rory is convinced that his responsibilities lie with his own county and is determined to head home. Too bad the feds feel otherwise.

Full of heart-pumping action and moments of reflection, Rory is on a steadfast mission to protect the county he was elected to serve...but he might have to solve a federal crime before he's able to make the trek home.

AVAILABLE MAY 2023

SHERIFF RORY JAMISON WAS ASTRIDE HIS BIG GELDING, staring at the dust cloud boiling up in the north and blowing toward the fort. Although it was deep into the fall season, easing into winter, the skies had been clear and sunny, if not particularly warm. The single skiff of snow that had dropped weeks ago was gone without a trace. The couple of showers had also soaked in and disappeared. The road was dry, but still, that was a lot of dust.

As the cloud neared the stage company's horse barns, with perhaps a half-mile to go, Tate drove his stage into town. Coming in from the north, he would drop his passengers at the hotel and then return to the stage corrals to be rigged out for the next run. He pulled to a halt beside the sheriff.

Curious, and sensing that the dust cloud might somehow involve him, Rory hollered over to the stage whip, "What's going on out there, Tate?"

Tate's response reflected his normal approach to the

difficulties of life: anger, frustration, and assurance of his own rightness.

"'What's going on out there' the man asks. I'll tell you what's going on. Some fool is driving his herd along the road. With all those empty miles off to the east there for his using. Wouldn't give me the right of way neither. I had to take this rig off into the grassland by more than a mile and hump the whole kit and caboodle over hill and hollow to pass them. There's maybe two thousand head and a cavvy of horses. Longhorns. Mixed stuff. Cows and calves. Steers. Scrubs such as we ain't seen in this area for years. Should all be shot, cattle and drovers alike."

Rory, familiar with his friend's ways, thanked the man and said, "Maybe I'll just ride up there and take a look."

HE RODE ALMOST to the horse barns, and by then, he could clearly see the truth of what the stage whip had told him. Knowing it was too late for talk and having no choice but to stop the herd from entering the town, he stepped to the ground and lifted his Big Fifty from its scabbard. He untied the leather pouch he had drawn tight around the workings of the big gun to keep the dust out and checked the load. The weapon was ready. Fishing two more loads from his jacket pocket, holding them in the fingers of his left hand, he dropped to one knee. The plodding herd was now almost upon the big barn and corrals.

His left shoulder still wasn't completely healed from the bullet that had taken flesh and bone a few weeks earlier, but he could use it if he was careful. Holding the weight of the rifle in his right hand, he propped his left elbow on his left knee and cradled the forestock of the fifty in his left hand.

A herd that large would normally be wider at the front, but it seemed clear that the riders had slimmed it down to seven or eight beeves, narrow enough to be pushed through town. As sheriff, carrying the burden of the county and town's safety on his shoulders, Rory couldn't let that happen.

Taking careful sight on the big lead steer, Rory squeezed the trigger. In perfect timing, with a boom to waken the dead and gain the full attention of the drovers, the steer folded his front legs and dropped in front of the next animal. As quickly as the sheriff could lever and reload the fifty, two more steers dropped to the ground, one of them kicking up a dust cloud of his own before taking his final breath. The startled animals directly beside and behind the dead steers turned in fright, a couple to the side, pushing against the point riders, the remainder, back into the herd. The repeated boom and roar of the fifty had folks running into the street, slamming store doors open and emptying out of saloons to see what was happening.

The point riders, leaving the herd to itself, kicked their animals into a run, heading directly toward the shooter.

The point rider on Rory's right pulled a rifle of some sort and, even though his horse was moving too fast and too erratically for accurate shooting, took a careless one-handed aim and, regardless of the risk to the residents, fired toward the town. The other point rider was coming on also, but he hadn't yet reached for a weapon. Seeing the risk was from the right, Rory took aim again and dropped the rider's animal. As the horse's front legs folded, its nose went into the dirt of the road, and its hind end rose into the air, resulting in a complete flip. The rider flew over the animal's head, took a solid fall onto the road, rolled and twisted a couple of times, and lay flat, unmoving.

Rory swung his reloaded fifty to the other point rider, but that man, perhaps being wiser, left his rifle in the scabbard and took evasive action, turning sharply back toward the herd.

The cattle, just recently driven from their hidden mountain valleys and canyons of Wyoming, were completely out of control. When the lead steer went down, the drag riders were too far back to see what was going on. They kept pushing the herd forward, while the front animals were forcing themselves back, creating a melee. Finally, the herd burst into the open grassland to the east with the riders chasing, hoping to turn them into a mill, but that wouldn't be happening for a mile or two. The swing and flank riders from the east side were riding for their lives, hoping to stay ahead of the stampeding herd.

One more man rode forward and, after a few words together, he and the point man came slowly toward Rory, cautious of the fifty and the damage it could do. Both men held their empty hands well out away from their holsters.

Rory, somewhat satisfied, mounted again, slid the fifty into its scabbard, and swung the sides of his coat apart to give him easy access to his Colt .44s. Someone from town, Rory didn't know who, was kneeling beside the downed rider.

He sat still, allowing the two cattlemen to approach him. As they closed the distance, he recognized the riders. With a burst of shock and anger, he hollered,

"Micah? Junior? What has your fool father got you doing now?"

Without waiting for an answer, he said, "You're under arrest. Both of you. And when your father wakes up, he'll be under arrest too. What kind of fool would drive a herd of longhorns right through a town? No one but Boon Wardle and his equally foolish sons. Ride ahead of me to the jailhouse. I'm sure you know that if you touch a weapon, you'll be dead the next moment."

Micah opened his mouth as if to say something in rebuttal. The sheriff ignored the effort, simply pointing his finger toward town and the small jail.

ABOUT THE AUTHOR

Reg Quist's pioneer heritage includes sod shacks, prairie fires, home births, and children's graves under the prairie sod, all working together in the lives of people creating their own space in a new land.

Out of that early generation came farmers, ranchers, business men and women, builders, military graves in faraway lands, Sunday Schools that grew to become churches, plus story tellers, musicians, and much more.

Hard work and self-reliance were the hallmark of those previous great generations, attributes that were absorbed by the following generation.

Quist's career choice took him into the construction world. From heavy industrial work, to construction camps in the remote northern bush, the author emulated his grandfathers, who were both builders, as well as pioneer farmers and ranchers.

It is with deep thankfulness that Quist says, "I am a part of the first generation to truly enjoy the benefits of the labors of the pioneers. My parents and their parents worked incredibly hard, and it is well for us to remember".